First paperback edition: July 2025

Book cover by DreamStudio AI

ISBN   978-1-9680273-9-1 (5x8 paperback)

The Survivor's Compound

Part IV
Junior's Regiment

M.P. Hendy

Table of Contents

Chapter 40:

Orientation to David's World

David, leaning back in his favorite leather armchair, observing the newcomers with a calm, almost unsettlingly gentle gaze. "Alright," David began. "I imagine you all have quite a few questions. But before we get to those, let's establish a few ground rules. Consider this…orientation." He offered a small, almost apologetic smile. "It's a little unorthodox, I admit."

The newcomers, awestruck by the sheer physical presence of these women, shifted nervously. Marvin, clutching Sara's hand, cleared his throat. "Ground rules, sir?" David nodded. "Firstly, respect. Respect for each other, for the existing community here, and most importantly, for the women in this house." He paused. "They're…integral to the smooth running of things. And I'm rather fond of them." A wave of knowing chuckles rippled through the room.

Jennifer, ever the playful minx, leaned forward. "He adores us, actually. Don't let him fool you." She winked at the newcomers, then fixed her gaze on David, her eyes sparkling with mischief. "Isn't that right, Master?" David sighed dramatically. "Jennifer, please. We have guests." He ignored her playful pout and continued. "Secondly, contribute. Everyone has skills, talents. We'll find a place for you to use them. Whether it's tending the garden with Brian, assisting Andrea at the clinic, or lending Aidan a hand in the garage, everyone pulls their weight."

He glanced at Little David, who nodded in agreement. "And thirdly… safety. The world outside these walls is dangerous. We've established defenses, procedures. Listen to Junior, listen to Kyle, listen to any of my children. They know what they're doing. And for God's sake, don't wander off alone." He paused, letting his words sink in. "Any questions so far?"

Olivia, the young woman who seemed to be perpetually glancing at Junior, tentatively raised her hand. "What…what exactly is this place? It's…incredible." David chuckled. "The long and short of it is… this is our home. We are not an organization. We are not a government agency. We are a family. My family, specifically." He emphasized the word "my" with a subtle gravity. "My focus is to ensure the propagation of my family, a safety net to rebuild the future through our bloodlines and philosophy. To set a new path in the future, not to reestablish a broken one."

He saw the confusion etched on some faces, the dawning understanding on others. Marvin, Sara's boyfriend, shifted nervously. "So… you're not trying to, like, rebuild society?" Summer stepped forward, her voice gentle. "We're not trying to recreate what was, Marvin. What was… failed. We're focused on building something new, something better, starting with a strong foundation of family, community, and self-sufficiency."

"Let me clarify," he said, his voice firm but reassuring. "I am not interested in brainwashing you. I am interested in enabling you. We offer training, resources, a safe environment to grow and become stronger, both physically and mentally. We offer knowledge, skills, and the opportunity to contribute to something meaningful."

He saw a spark of interest flicker in some eyes. Kathy, who had been quietly observing, spoke up. "So, you're saying... we can learn to defend ourselves? Learn to build things? To... survive?" "Exactly," David said, a smile playing on his lips. "Survival is the baseline. But we aim for more than mere survival. We aim for prosperity, for innovation, for a life of purpose. We offer you the tools to create that life, but the choice of how to use them is yours."

Tiffany, ever the pragmatist, cleared her throat. "Honey, they're probably wondering where they're going to sleep." "Right, right," David chuckled. "Alright then, let's address practicalities," he announced, clapping his hands together. "Living arrangements. The couples amongst you will be assigned an apartment. Private, comfortable, and hopefully far better than what you've been dealing with thus far. The singles," he nodded towards Olivia, Kathy, Noah, Darrel, Riley, Sophia and Caleb," will be given individual rooms in the garage. Also comfortable, but with a communal kitchen and bathroom. We'll try to separate the males from the females so you guys can leave the toilet seat up."

A ripple of nervous laughter went through the group. Even Junior, standing silently in the background, cracked a small smile. David saw the confusion swirling in their eyes. "Now, I see the question marks hovering over your heads like little cartoon balloons," David said, his lips twitching. "Don't worry about the 'where' and 'how' of it all just yet. Think of it as… magic. Or extremely efficient planning. Let's just say your accommodations are being prepared as we speak."

He leaned back, steepling his fingers. "Now, before you start picturing me as some sort of Willy Wonka of the apocalypse, let me reassure you, there's a method to my madness. And a lot of hard work." He straightened up again. "Speaking of which... it's time you met the folks who'll be helping you get settled in. They're the backbone of this… shall we call it, 'community.'"

With a sweeping gesture, he gestured towards the women flanking him. "First, you'll be getting to know my lovely wives. Each of them brings a unique skillset and perspective to the table." He winked. "And, of course, they keep me in line. A feat I assure you, is no small accomplishment." Behind him, David's wives stood in order from his right to his left, something he would certainly thank them for later.

"First, this stunning woman to my far right, is Tiffany, my first wife, and the Matriarch of this Ranch. She runs the ranch operations and has a degree in agriculture, animal husbandry, and veterinary medicine. Her son Aidan is our engineer and mechanic." Tiffany offered a warm, reassuring smile.

"Next to her is Jennifer, my second wife. She keeps our garden growing and our air and water clean, literally. She has several degrees in horticulture, botany, and farming agriculture." Jennifer, radiating earthy energy, nodded. "Her oldest son Brian, is her right-hand man. While her youngest son is my junior." David added, a touch of pride in his voice.

He turned back to the group. "Then we have Summer, my third wife. Six years in the Army reserves, and a pharmacist. She and Jennifer collaborate with herbal medicines and keep track of everyone's dietary needs. She is also in charge of the main house, so you'll usually find her here. Her daughter Lily is my lead security officer." Summer, with her gentle smile and knowing eyes, projected an aura of calm competence.

"Next, we have the lovely Elena. Ten years in the Army, very intelligent. She is my auditor. She makes sure I don't let anything slip through the cracks and always opposes me. Which, honestly, we all need sometimes." Elena raised an eyebrow, a playful smirk dancing on her lips.

"Beside her, we have Taylor. Taylor is our nanny, but I expect you to treat her with the same respect you treat the rest. She makes sure the younger generation is well-rounded and not overburdened." Taylor, despite her youthfulness, possessed a calm maturity, a steady hand guiding the children through these turbulent times.

"Then there is Nicole, whom you've all met. Nicole was also in the Army, and she's a good shot. She is one of our maintainers, ensuring everyone is looked after equally. Her twins are my intelligence team." Nicole, with her kind face and sharp eyes, nodded.

"Behind, to my left, is Jessica. She is my bloodhound. She can smell bullshit under a pile of potpourri, but don't let her small size fool you. She's ruthless when it comes to protecting her family." Jessica, perched like a tiny warrior, gave a small, almost imperceptible nod, her eyes glinting with steely resolve.

"Next to her is Kayla, she's my logistician and our resident mixologist. Nothing on this ranch gets eaten, flushed, or used without her knowing about it. She's also quite the chemist." Kayla, waved shyly.

"Finally, on my far left, is Tanya. She's the chief esthetician. Her and her sister Seo-Yeon keep everyone in tip-top shape. So let her know if you need anything skincare related." Tanya, radiating exotic beauty, offered a warm smile.

He paused and cleared his throat, shifting gears slightly. "Now, about tomorrow," he continued, his voice a calm, steady baritone. "We need to get a few things squared away." He focused his gaze, calculating and kind, on the group. "First thing, Andrea will be conducting a basic health check on everyone. Just a quick once-over, make sure you're all healthy and have any immediate needs addressed. She's a fantastic nurse, and she knows what she's doing, so please cooperate fully."

David then turned his attention towards Sara, who looked understandably nervous. "Sara, you will also get a prenatal check as well. It's important that we ensure you and your baby are healthy throughout your pregnancy."

David continued, "After Andrea's done, you'll be meeting with Kyle in the work shed. He's our resident gunsmith and he'll be assigning you your weapons based on your experience and preferences. He'll also be conducting a weapon-handling and safety course. We have a shooting range on the property, and we take safety very seriously. Junior here is often the lead instructor."

He paused and a faint smile played on his lips. "Now, here's the part you might find…interesting. Before dinner tomorrow, either Tanya, Seo-Yeon, or Taylor will be stopping by your rooms. Don't be alarmed." He chuckled softly, watching the confusion bloom on their faces. "They're not going there to interrogate you or anything. They're going to offer you haircuts and grooming. We don't exactly have a centralized barber shop, so that's how we do things around here. Consider it a little taste of our life."

A wave of murmurs rippled through the group. Olivia, her eyes wide, whispered something to Riley, who giggled nervously. Marvin looked at Sara, a mixture of disbelief and amusement on his face.

Junior stepped forward. "Just to clarify," he interjected, his gaze sweeping across the group, "all three of those women are married. Admiring them is fine, but inappropriate behavior will be seen as disrespect, plain and simple. They are beautiful women, but they are taken." He paused, letting his words sink in before adding, "You're free to admire them, but as someone else's property."

David nodded in approval. "Thank you, Junior. Well said." Then, Tanya chimed in. "It's also a practical matter. We can assess your hygiene and health. Notice any potential concerns early on. Then we can personalize your diet, soaps and shampoos." She smiled sweetly. "Infection, lice, poisoning, allergies, they can also be detected by a close, physical examination," she annunciated.

"As Junior mentioned, he'll be your primary point of contact for any immediate concerns. I trust him implicitly, and you should too," David stated, his voice calm. He rose to his feet, his movements fluid and surprisingly graceful. He inclined his head towards the group. "Now, shall we get you settled in? It's been a long day, and I imagine you all could use a good night's rest. Alright, follow me," David announced, turning and heading toward the hallway. He kept his pace deliberate, allowing the group to keep up.

As he turned into the back hallway, he stopped in front of the door. "This is the only door that leads to the garage, and the kitchen is back that way," he said, pointing in the opposite direction. As David waited for everyone to catch up, one of the newcomers, Sophia, pointed to the window. "That glass… it's awfully thick, isn't it?" she observed, a hint of curiosity in her voice, "Like bulletproof." David paused. "Sharp observation," he complimented. "Indeed it is. Photochromatic too. Darkens when it's sunny, clear when it's not. Practical considerations, given the circumstances." He left the rest unsaid.

He opened the door, revealing a set of concrete stairs leading down. The temperature immediately dropped a few degrees. "Careful on the stairs," David cautioned, beginning his descent. "It's a bit of a change of scenery, I assure you." The newcomers hesitated for a moment, exchanging glances. The contrast between the luxurious interior of the house and the utilitarian concrete staircase was jarring.

David waited patiently as the group descended the concrete stairs, their faces a mixture of apprehension and curiosity. The sheer size of the garage seemed to surprise them, even though only the Ford Transit was parked within its vast expanse. The walls were spotless, the floor meticulously clean, and an almost sterile order reigned.

"So," David said, his voice echoing slightly in the large space, "Welcome to subterranean living. A bit less scenic, admittedly, but considerably safer. We're only partially underground, but if you noticed, the walls, to include the ceiling are two feet thick."

He gestured to the two doors on the right-hand side of the garage. "The gentlemen will be in there. There are three empty rooms for Darrel, Noah and Caleb. Basic but functional. Plenty of privacy, and hopefully a decent night's sleep." He gave a small, knowing smile. "Also, there are no windows, but ask Junior about the window features later."

He then turned and pointed to the door straight ahead. "The ladies will be in there. Four empty rooms, same treatment. Each section has a shared bathroom, kitchen and dining area. And beyond that, to the left, you'll find the classroom and the infirmary. That's where you'll get your medical checkup done. Janet will bring y'all up to speed on the homeschooling. Though, I suspect some of you will be helping her soon enough." He chuckled.

"Alright, why don't you folks head on in, drop off your things, and get a feel for your new room? We'll reconvene back here in a few minutes. Then, we can take you guys to meet Kyle." A murmur of agreement rippled through the group, and they started dispersing towards their designated doors. David leaned back against a reinforced post, crossing his arms over his chest. Junior, standing beside him, mirrored his stance, a smirk playing on his lips. "Fun stuff, huh?" Junior murmured, his eyes twinkling mischievously. "You gonna tell them about the rest?" David chuckled. "Not yet, Junior. Let's ease them in."

A few minutes later, the newcomers trickled back into the garage, their whispers and wide-eyed glances betraying their surprise. Kathy stopped short, her mouth hanging open. "Did you...did you see the windows?" she stammered, looking at Olivia. "They're like...TV screens! But they show the outside!" Noah nodded, equally flabbergasted. "Yeah, it's...crazy. And the beds are like...top of the line." Darrel, chimed in, "And the kitchen! Did you see it?"

Sophia looked around the garage with a newfound sense of wonder. "I was expecting…concrete and bare walls. But it was…nice. Much better than the barracks." Susan, her eyes still wide, approached Junior. "Excuse me, Junior? They said something about the windows…what were those guys talking about?" Little David smiled. "Don't worry, they're pretty standard here, you'll have some in your apartment."

"Alright," David announced, clapping his hands together to gather their attention. "Everyone ready to meet Kyle?" He let the anticipatory silence hang in the air for a moment, then with a flourish, pressed a button on the wall. The low hum of the double winch system filled the air as the massive garage door began to slowly rise.

The effect was immediate and visceral. The oppressive blast of Texas heat washed over them, a stark reminder of the harsh reality outside their temporary oasis. The newcomers visibly flinched, their faces contorting in discomfort as they gradually reacclimated to the apocalyptic world outside. "Right," David said dryly, his voice laced with amusement. "Welcome back to the apocalypse. Don't worry, you get used to it. Sort of." He gestured towards a path leading around the house and toward the barn. "Kyle's in the work shed. He's eager to meet you all."

The little group followed David, their initial awe slowly morphing into a mixture of curiosity and apprehension. Sophia hung back, still marveling at the unexpected comfort of the garage. "Standard?" she muttered to herself, picturing the oversized pizza ovens she'd called home for the past few months. "If this is standard, I can only imagine…"

Susan, her face still flushed from the burst of heat, kept pace with Junior. "So, these apartments…" she began hesitantly, "Are they…safe? From the…you know…" She trailed off, gesturing vaguely towards the outside world. Junior chuckled, a low, reassuring sound. "Safer than anything you've seen, Susan, you'll see." He winked.

As they rounded the corner of the house, the imposing structure of the barn loomed into view. The contrast between its rustic shape and the high-tech equipment visible through the open door was jarring. As they approached the work shed, the sound of metallic clinking grew louder, punctuated by snippets of easy conversation. David approached the shed, "Kyle, we're here!"

Inside, the air wafted with the smell of gunpowder and lubricant. Kyle glanced up, his face breaking into a grin as he spotted the newcomers. Grace, perched beside him on a stool, paused her meticulous work and offered a shy wave. "Welcome, everyone!" Kyle boomed, his voice hearty and welcoming. He wiped his hands on a rag and stepped forward, extending a hand to the nearest member of the group. "Kyle's the name. Glad to have you all here."

Noah cautiously shook Kyle's hand, his eyes darting between the gunsmith and the ethereal girl beside him. Grace, ever the observant one, subtly evaluated the newcomers, her gaze missing nothing. She nudged Kyle, a playfully comfortable gesture. "Kyle, aren't you forgetting something?" she prompted. Kyle rolled his eyes playfully. "How could I forget?" He gestured to Grace with both hands, turning to the group with a flourish. "Everybody, this is Grace, David and Nicole's daughter."

The newcomers exchanged glances, a subtle recognition flickering in their eyes. They remembered Little David mentioning Grace, describing her as a master of stealth, her silvery hair a striking resemblance to Nicole. Grace leaned forward over the table, her voice clear and surprisingly assertive for someone her age. "And Kyle," she declared, her gaze sweeping over the group with a territorial air, "is going to be my husband."

The statement hung in the air like a dropped anvil. Kyle chuckled nervously, ruffling Grace's hair. "Grace, we've talked about this. Maybe when you're a little older..." "Nope," Grace replied, popping the 'p'. "I'm staking my claim now. So, any of you hoes start having thoughts about my man, lose them," her gaze softening as she sat back down.

"Well, that's... direct," David chuckled, leaning against the workbench. He watched the newcomers' bewildered faces with a knowing amusement. "Grace, honey. Let's not embarrass Kyle in front of the newcomers. Remember, you still look like a child." Grace lowered her head slightly. "Yes Daddy." She turned to Kyle. "I'm sorry if I embarrassed you, Darling," she said, patting his arm.

Kathy tentatively raised her hand. She couldn't shake the feeling that something was off. "Um, Mr. David?" she began, her voice hesitant. "With all due respect, isn't... isn't this a little inappropriate? A teenager... declaring she's going to marry a man probably twice her age? Are you just... allowing this to happen? It sounds like an unhealthy crush, at best."

David straightened up. "An astute observation, Kathy," he said, his voice calm and measured. "And a valid concern, given societal norms as they were before. But let me assure you, here, in this place, things are not always as they seem." He glanced at Kyle, then back at Kathy, a hint of a smile playing on his lips.

"I trust my children implicitly," David said, his gaze unwavering. "All of them. They are… different. They possess abilities and maturity far beyond their chronological ages." He paused, letting the weight of his words sink in. "Grace doesn't have a crush on Kyle, but she is certain about what she wants." Grace piped up. "Kyle doesn't treat me like a child, and we work really well together. I think we would make a very good married couple."

Meanwhile, Kyle was trying to hide the blush on his face. "I know I'm only fourteen, but mentally, I'm... well, I'm not. I have my father's knowledge, his experiences. I know what it is like to be an adult and do things that adults do." She paused, taking a deep breath. "Look, I know it sounds crazy, but I feel like I have been waiting for my body to catch up for so long. It's frustrating,

I understand everything that makes an adult relationship work. I just need a body that will obey my will."

Grace's voice took on a steely edge, surprising the newcomers, especially Kathy and Sara. "And when my body grows up... well, Kyle is in for a treat. When I'm physically mature, I'm going to marry Kyle, and then I'm going to fuck him well and often, just like a good wife should." The silence that followed was thick enough to cut with a knife. Kathy choked on a nervous laugh. Sara opened her mouth, then closed it, clearly at a loss for words. The faces of the male recruits ranged from horrified fascination to thinly-veiled envy.

David, apparently unfazed by his daughter's pronouncements, noticed Kyle's almost imperceptible smile beneath his embarrassment. Then gave him a reassuring pat on the shoulder. "Don't worry, son," he said with a sly wink. "You'll be alright. Besides, it's not like you have a choice." Kyle, despite the blush still burning on his cheeks, managed a weak smile back.

Finally, Marvin, looking thoroughly bewildered, broke the silence. "Um... Mr. David? This is all... well, nice and all. But, if you don't mind me asking, where does everyone live? I mean, we didn't see any other buildings around." David chuckled. "Excellent question, Marvin! Follow me." He gestured towards a set of seemingly ordinary concrete stairs at the back of the shed. "Junior, why don't you lead the way?

He started down the concrete stairs, the sound of his boots echoing in the confined space. The others followed warily, their initial awe replaced by a growing sense of anticipation. The temperature subtly dropped as they descended. The generator room was a sensory overload. Eight massive generators hummed with barely contained power, a symphony of mechanical aggression that vibrated through the air and into their bones. The newcomers instinctively recoiled, their eyes darting nervously between the monstrous machines and the array of weaponry lining the walls.

Andrew's eyes widened at the sight of the armory. "Holy shit!" he breathed, his gaze sweeping over the rows of rifles and pistols. David beamed, enjoying the newcomers' reactions. "Impressive, isn't it? Junior and Kyle keep this place in tip-top shape. Consider it our last line of defense, but also our community pantry, for uninvited guests."

Junior, already halfway down the next flight of stairs, paused and looked back. "Don't get any ideas, Andrew. These babies are for protection, not decoration. Though, I gotta admit, they do look damn good, don't they?" He grinned, then disappeared down the stairs. David chuckled. "Indeed. Function and aesthetics, a winning combination. Now, come on, don't want to keep everyone waiting. The tour continues." He gestured for them to follow Junior.

The hum of the generators faded slightly as David led the group down the next set of stairs. As they stepped onto the first apartment level, a collective gasp rippled through the group. Gone was the stark concrete of the generator room. Instead, they found themselves in a brightly lit hallway, the walls adorned with clean, textured plaster. Warm, inviting colors replaced the utilitarian gray they expected. Mock windows at the end of the hall displayed a realistic view of a city bustling below, the sun setting in the background.

"What in the..." Andrew stammered, his eyes wide with disbelief. He reached out a hand, hesitantly touching the wall. "This can't be real. Where are we?" "Welcome to the apartment bunker," David announced with a flourish, a hint of pride in his voice. "Home away from home, for now at least."

Riley turned to little David. "Bunker? You mean, underground? This is all...underground?" David chuckled. "Is it so hard to believe? I mean, we did descend two flights of stairs to get here." "A touch of normalcy is vital for morale, wouldn't you say? Especially after the...unpleasantness of the last few months." David said, gesturing down the hallway. "Now, if you'll follow me..."

As they walked, the group couldn't help but notice the pallets of food stacked neatly in pockets between each of the doors. Enough shelf stable, dried goods, and even some vacuum-sealed delights to last them for years. "Is that... food?" Sophia asked, pointing at a stack of what appeared to be freeze-dried strawberries.

"Indeed," David confirmed. "A comprehensive supply for sustained independent living. We planned for a long haul." He winked. "There's enough here to last us a long while, but we subsidize it with fresh produce, dairy and some fresh meat as well. So, ration properly. As long as you live here, this is what you get. If you want more, you contribute more."

The newcomers exchanged glances, a mixture of awe and confusion on their faces. The attention to detail was astonishing. The constant hum of the air circulation system was almost hypnotic, but it was completely drowned out near the "windows," replaced by the sounds of traffic. Marvin was speechless, staring at the faux cityscape outside the "window." "But... the sounds? The traffic? It's like we're actually there." He wrapped his arm around Sara, pulling her closer to him. "It's...amazing." Sara, her hand resting on her stomach, leaned into Marvin, a small smile gracing her lips. "I think I'm going to cry," she whispered.

David stopped before one of the doors. "Marvin, Sara, this one's yours." He swiped a keycard, and pushed the door open, revealing the interior of their fully furnished apartment. Marvin and Sara stepped inside, their eyes wide with wonder. Sara ran her hand over the plush fabric of the sofa. "It's...it's beautiful," she said, on the verge of tears.

David gave them a moment to take it in before continuing down the hallway. "Andrew, Susan," he said, stopping before the last apartment on the left, "this one's yours. Make yourselves at home. Junior, why don't you show them the ropes? Explain the security protocols, the common areas, the laundry facilities. All that fun stuff." David gave Junior a knowing look. "And try not to scare them too much with the self-defense demonstrations."

The fresh recruits chuckled nervously. Olivia stepped forward, her gaze sweeping over the perfectly organized hallway. "Um, Junior, sir? This is… incredible. But how many people actually live down here?" Little David thought a moment before answering. "Eleven apartments are occupied, twenty-three people total, including these four lovebirds," he said, gesturing to Marvin and Sara, and Andrew and Susan.

Olivia nodded slowly, processing the information. "Do you … do you live down here too, Sir?" Junior shook his head. "Nah, I'm up in the garage. Got one of those sweet guest rooms all to myself. Easier to keep an eye on things from up there, you know? Plus," he leaned in conspiratorially, "the amenities are better." Olivia nodded, biting her lip subtly. Junior, however, didn't notice.

Chapter 41:

Dividing the Day

The faint pre-dawn light filtered through the screen window of the room, painting soft rectangles on the wall. Junior cracked an eye open, the digital display in the corner showing November 12th, 6:00 AM. A slender arm draped across his chest, a cascade of dark hair tickling his nose. He carefully disentangled himself from her embrace. The woman stirred slightly, murmuring something unintelligible before settling back into sleep. He watched her for a moment, before he pulled on the clothes he'd discarded the previous night. He had to be at the main house for the Friday family meeting in an hour.

As he laced up his boots, she sat up, pulling the sheets to cover her chest. "Morning," she mumbled, her voice still thick with sleep. "Morning Liv," he replied, turning to face her. She stretched, a graceful, feline movement. "I'm going to take a shower before I go." Junior nodded. "Sounds good." He paused, shifting his weight. "David wants to discuss the weather again. Said it's only going to get colder, so we might be stuck inside a while."

He crossed the small room and sat on the edge of the bed. "I should head up. He gets twitchy if everyone isn't present and accounted for by seven." Olivia reached up and touched his shoulder. "Will you give me a few minutes?" she asked, batting her eyelashes playfully. Little David nodded. He had plenty of time after all.

Olivia ran a brush through her hair, studying him in the reflection of the small mirror. "Junior," she said, her voice taking on a more serious tone. "You know, you could move into one of the apartments. There's plenty of room there." He knew what she meant. The apartments were designed for couples, families. It was the next logical step, wasn't it? But he hesitated. "I like being here," he said, gesturing around the small room. "Close to the house, close to the main bunker. It's… convenient." "Convenient?" Olivia raised an eyebrow, a playful smirk tugging at her lips. "Or are you just afraid of commitment?"

He laughed, swatting her playfully on the arm. "Don't start, Liv. You know it's not that." "Then what is it?" she pressed, her eyes searching his. "We're not pressuring you, but it would be nice to all be together. A real home, you know?" Little David sighed, running a hand through his hair. "It's…complicated," he admitted, finally. He hated the word, hated how much his life seemed to revolve around things that were, well, complicated. "You know I care about you. You know that, right?" Olivia softened, stepping closer and taking his hands. "Of course, we do, Junior. We wouldn't be having this conversation if we didn't."

She paused, choosing her words carefully. "Is it… your dad?" He blinked, surprised. "Dad? What does Dad have to do with this?" "Well," she said, shrugging slightly, "he's kind of a big deal around here. And you… you want to live up to him, right? Maybe you think moving into an apartment, settling down, would make you… less available? Less like him?" He hadn't thought about it that way, but Olivia's words struck a chord. "I… I don't know," he confessed. "Maybe you're right. He saved everyone, and I'm trying to do the same. I don't want people to need me and I'm not there for them." "He would want you to be happy, Junior," Olivia said gently. "And we want you to be happy too. We just want to understand."

He squeezed her hands. "Okay. Okay, I'll think about it. Seriously." He glanced at the small digital clock on the wall. 6:52 AM. "Damn, I gotta run. He'll have my ass if I'm late for the Friday Follies." He grinned, trying to lighten the mood. "Besides, breakfast duty calls. You're on with Jennifer and Kayla. That's gotta be a special kind of hell." Olivia laughed, the tension easing from her face. "Tell me about it." She leaned in and kissed him quickly. "Go on, get out of here. And think about what we talked about."

The aroma of coffee, bacon, and fruit hung heavy in the air as Junior practically teleported into the main house kitchen. Kayla, clad in one of David's old t-shirts and a pair of fuzzy socks, was indeed being flirted with by the man himself. "Morning, Junior," David greeted, not missing a beat in his suggestive banter directed at Kayla. "Sleeping in again, I see? Someone's got to keep this place safe while we old folks are still blinking the sleep out of our eyes."

Junior rolled his eyes. "Yeah, yeah. Keeping the dream alive, Dad. Just making sure the monsters under the bed are behaving." He swiped a piece of bacon from a nearby platter, earning a playful swat from Kayla. "Hands off, you gremlin," she said, laughing. "Jennifer's already threatening to withhold my share of the bacon if we run out."

Olivia entered the kitchen with a forced casualness, her cheeks flushed a delicate pink that had nothing to do with the chilly morning air. "Morning, everyone," she chirped, her voice a touch too high-pitched. "Ready to set the table." Jennifer raised an eyebrow in Olivia's direction, then glanced at Junior with a knowing smirk. She was already stacking waffles on the plate beside her, a stack of golden deliciousness growing steadily. "Someone's bright and chipper this morning," she commented. "Must have had a good night's sleep."

Olivia's blush deepened, and she busied herself with cutting fruit, silently cursing Jennifer's teasing. Junior, on the other hand, seemed perfectly at ease, leaning against the counter and watching Olivia with an amused expression. "Speaking of good nights," David boomed, effectively diverting everyone's attention. "With the temperature dropping, we can expect more wildlife seeking shelter closer to the ranch. Junior, I want you to make sure the new guys know what to look out for."

"Already on it, Dad," Junior replied, pushing himself off the counter. "I was planning to check the property later, then log the locations. Caleb and Darrel are eager to lend a hand; they're getting restless." "Excellent," David said, nodding approvingly. "See if the dens we set up are being used. People aren't the only things suffering because of the weather out there." Parker, who was pouring himself a cup of coffee, frowned. "Dens? For… animals? Why are we so concerned about the wild animals, David? We've got enough on our plates keeping ourselves alive."

David fixed Parker with a patient look. "The wildlife keeps the environment going, Parker. It's all interconnected. The animals keep the insects down, they help with seed dispersal, they even help with keeping the land from overgrowing. As long as they have a place to settle, they won't come to the house. Besides," he added with a wink, "it's not like we don't have the resources to spare. A few dug-out burrows and some strategically placed hay bales? It's a small price to pay for a healthy ecosystem and not having deer trying to get into the barn."

Jennifer, lounging on the arm of David's chair, piped up. "Master, the schedule is getting a bit… crowded. Now that the tunnel's finished, getting around the property underground is much easier, but we are just running out of time and space. It's like everyone's on top of each other"

"I agree," David said, stroking her head. "Especially with the weather limiting outdoor activities, the useable spaces are packed. It's time to delegate some responsibility. We need someone to take over operations at night; training, security checks, the whole nine yards, and another to manage the daytime schedule. I want to relinquish some command and control."

A murmur rippled through the room. Everyone was accustomed to David's leadership, his meticulous planning, his unwavering presence. The thought of him stepping back, even a little, was unsettling to some. Jessica, cradling Poppy in her arms, raised an eyebrow. "Are you sure about this, Daddy? You know everyone trusts you."

David smiled reassuringly at Jessica. "I'm not stepping down, Jess. I'm just… diversifying. Think of it as expanding the leadership team. I'll still be here, making the big decisions, ensuring everything runs smoothly. But I want to give others a chance to lead, to learn, to grow. It will free me up to focus on other critical issues. And frankly, I need the help." He chuckled, running a hand through his hair. "I'm not getting any younger, I even feel like I've lived three lifetimes already." Tiffany, ever practical, leaned forward. "So, what qualities are you looking for in these… managers?"

"Qualities?" David echoed Tiffany's question. "Leadership, obviously. The ability to make tough decisions, to think strategically, to inspire confidence. But also… practicality. Common sense. A willingness to listen and learn. And perhaps most importantly, a deep commitment to the well-being of this community."

He paused, looking across the faces in the room. "I've already thought long and hard about who would be best suited for these roles," he continued, his voice steady. "And I've decided to start with two individuals. For now, at least." Aidan, leaning against the wall beside Alissa, straightened up, his eyes widening slightly. Across the room, Junior, who'd been quietly observing, shifted his weight. David could practically feel the anticipation humming in the air.

"Aidan," David said, his gaze locking with his. "You're in charge of managing the ranch during the day. You have my wisdom, and if you need help with anything, don't be afraid to ask." He then turned his gaze to little David. "Junior, you're in charge at night. You have your team and anyone else who wants to join you."

David stood, adjusting his stance. "Remember, this isn't an outpost, this is a home. But with so many of us running around, we shouldn't be competing for hot water or gym equipment. This is a timely division of available space and amenities, not a night watch." He gestured around the room. "We're all in this together. We'll be staying inside and as comfortable as possible, especially with the cold weather."

Elena, perched on the arm of David's chair, cleared her throat. "David's laid the groundwork, but let's be clear: this isn't just about dividing up day and night like some kind of weird shift work. Plenty of jobs aren't bound by the sun." She gestured towards Brian and Seo-Yeon. "The hydroponics needs constant attention, regardless of the hour, generator repair is a twenty-four-hour gig, and self-improvement is important at any time." She winked. "Plus, those training dummies won't beat themselves up, will they?"

Darrel raised his hand. "So, with half of us taking the night shift, are we talking tiptoeing zone at night? I don't want to accidently wake someone up, and last thing I need is someone doing parkour above my head while I'm sleeping." Tiffany chuckled. "Honey, the only place you need to worry about is the main floor of the house. And even then, those walls are thick, the doors too. I doubt you'll hear more than a muffled thud."

Clarence, bless his grumpy old soul, chimed in from the corner, "He's right, kid. I haven't been woken up by Junior's morning wake-up calls since he started doing them. And those things sound like a herd of buffalo stampeding through a tin can factory." Junior, lounging casually against the wall, offered a sheepish grin. "We try to be... considerate. But yeah, training is gonna happen. The rooms and bunkers are pretty soundproof, though. Thick concrete and all that." "Considerate by Junior's standards," Riley muttered, earning an elbow nudge from Olivia. "Hey!" Junior protested, feigning offense. "We wear socks now!"

David chuckled, appreciating the banter. "I designed and built this place with everyone's... eccentricities in mind," he said, his eyes twinkling. "Which means someone can practice their guitar at night without waking up someone in the adjoining room." He paused, taking a sip of his coffee. "Plus, at night, while me and my wives sleep, traffic in the main house will be limited. Anything that needs to be done can happen elsewhere."

"So," David gestured toward Junior. "You and your crew, whoever wants to stay up all night. I recommend getting as much sleep as you can. Your clock is officially flipped." Jill raised her hand, a concerned look on her face. "Are they just going to cook for themselves?" Little David spoke up before David could answer. "Those of us that don't cook for ourselves will be eating breakfast while the rest eat dinner. Which means, our dinner meal will mostly be breakfast food. Cooking duty is officially divided."

The conversation lulled for a moment, the silence only broken by the scraping of forks and murmured conversations. Caleb suddenly piped up. "So, uh, what are we supposed to do for the rest of the day?" He looked around, a hopeful glint in his eyes. "Anything fun planned?" Before anyone could answer, Darrel stood up abruptly. He strode over to Caleb and, with a theatrical flourish, delivered a light slap to the back of his head. "Go to sleep, dumbass!" Darrel announced, his voice dripping with mock exasperation. "You're on night shift now. Night shift people sleep during the day! It's, like, the whole point."

Caleb rubbed the back of his head, looking bewildered. "But... but I'm not tired! And I wanted to hang out!" "Too bad," Darrel retorted, clapping Caleb on the shoulder. "We're on vampire hours now. Embrace the darkness. Think of all the cool stuff you can do while everyone else is snoozing. Like... sharpen knives! Or...

clean guns! Or… stare intensely at the wall until you hallucinate!"

Junior chuckled, shaking his head at Darrel's antics. "He's got a point, Caleb. Look, this isn't a suggestion, it's an order. We're flipping our schedules to cover the graveyard shift. That means being functional and alert when everyone else is asleep. And the only way to do that is to actually sleep during the day. It might take a few days to adjust, but we're staying up all night, whether we get a head start on sleep or not."

He looked around the room, meeting the eyes of his team, Caleb, Noah, Kathy, Susan, Andrew, Darrel, Sophia, Olivia, and Riley. "Alright guys, we're officially the night crew. Tonight, we start with hand to hand combat in the Rec bunker. We'll rotate for patrols, Caleb and Kathy, you get first watch." Little David looked at Jennifer and his father. "Riley, Olivia and I will have breakfast ready at 7 o'clock, so we'll see you for dinner tonight." And with that, they all dispersed, going back to their rooms.

Junior sighed, running a hand through his already disheveled hair. The weight of the responsibility was starting to settle in, heavier than usual. He glanced around his small room, a space that suddenly felt incredibly cramped and… temporary. Olivia's words from earlier echoed in his mind: "You should move to the Apartments, so we could live together." The image of a small, cozy apartment, flashed through his mind, a welcome change of scenery from the spartan room he currently occupied. He imagined the possibilities: movie nights, cooking together, and the simple comfort of waking up next to them every morning.

But then, the rational part of his brain kicked in. Moving to the Apartments meant officially acknowledging, at least publicly, the unusual arrangement he had. While no one in their close-knit community seemed to judge, it was still, not like him. Coffee, that would fix it, coffee can fix anything. Junior left his room and walked toward the kitchen. As he entered, he found Brian, already making a pot with Seo-Yeon watching him as she leaned on the counter. "Oh, hey guys. Didn't expect to see you in here," Junior mumbled, reaching for a mug. He'd always been more of a "doer" than a "talker," and mornings like this only amplified that tendency.

Brian, ever the observant one, furrowed his eyebrows. "I thought you'd be cool with working nights. Why do you look like someone pissed on your legos?" he asked, starting the urn. Junior sighed, spinning the cup on the table. "I am, it's not that," he sighed. Unconvinced by his answer, Brian and Seo-Yeon joined him at the table. "You know, Seo-Yeon and I were thinking about joining you. I mean, mom has the garden during the day, and with Tanya here, Seo-Yeon can do her part for the vampire crew."

Junior chuckled. "Thanks guys, that'll help out a lot." He said, thankfully. "I just… have a couple of things on my mind right now, but the graveyard shift isn't one of them." Brian stood, his tall figure casting a shadow over the table. "Think about it bro, with dad asleep, we'll own this shit." He grinned, a mischievous glint in his eyes. As Seo-Yeon stood to join Brian, she leaned over and kissed Junior on the temple. "You and Brian are every bit the leader your father is. That's why he chose you." She said, returning to Brian's side.

As Junior waited for the coffee to finish, Riley bounded into the dining room, her eyes locked on David. Oblivious to Brian and Seo-Yeon's presence, she approached Junior excitedly, kissing him soundly as she wrapped her arms around him. "Sir, did you think about Olivia's offer?" she asked, batting her eyelashes playfully.

Brian and Seo-Yeon shared a look, a silent conversation passing between them. Brian raised a questioning eyebrow, a silent "huh?" hanging in the air. Seo-Yeon gave a small, almost imperceptible shrug. This was… unexpected. Little David, their stoic, gun-loving brother, who probably rehearsed battle drills on the toilet, was getting peppered with kisses by a pretty redhead. And talking about moving in? This was a plot twist worthy of David himself.

Junior, caught mid-sigh, went rigid for a split second before relaxing into Riley's embrace. A faint blush crept up the back of his neck, a sight practically unheard of. The man could take on a hostile militia without breaking a sweat, but a little affection from Riley seemed to throw him for a loop. Brian and Seo-Yeon exchanged another glance, this one laced with amusement. This was better than any reality show.

"Hey, Riley," Junior mumbled, his voice a touch deeper than usual. He disentangled himself gently, running a hand through his hair, a gesture that suddenly seemed more nervous than his usual combat-ready adjustment. "Yeah, I... I'm thinking about it." Riley beamed, her enthusiasm practically radiating off her. "Really? Oh, that's great! We'd have so much fun together! We could... We could decorate! And... and we could have movie nights! And... and..." She trailed off, her eyes sparkling with a vision of domestic bliss.

Brian cleared his throat, a loud, theatrical sound. Riley jumped, finally noticing the other occupants of the dining room. Her cheeks flushed a charming shade of pink. "Oh! Brian! Seo-Yeon! I... I didn't see you there," she stammered, taking a step back from Junior. Brian grinned, all teeth. "No worries, Riley. Just enjoying the... show." He waggled his eyebrows suggestively. Seo-Yeon elbowed him lightly in the ribs.

Brian leaned back in his stool, folding his arms across his chest, a mischievous look in his eyes. "So, Junior," he drawled, stretching the word out, "apartment hunting, huh? Since when did you go domestic on us? I didn't even know you liked anyone, let alone enough to cohabitate. And Olivia apparently had a say in it this morning?"

Seo-Yeon stifled a giggle, covering her mouth with her hand. This was gold. Pure, unadulterated gold. Junior, the embodiment of control and tactical prowess, being flustered by the prospect of picking out curtains? She never thought she'd see the day. Junior's blush deepened, spreading down his neck and threatening to engulf his entire face. He turned to Brian, a flicker of irritation in his eyes. "Just because I spend most of my time cleaning guns and shooting targets doesn't mean I'm a robot, Brian," he retorted, his voice a low grumble. "And Olivia mentioned it to me this morning, yes."

"Hey, I'm not judging," Brian said, holding up his hands in mock surrender. "Just surprised. Pleasantly surprised. It's nice to see you're capable of... you know... feelings." He wiggled his fingers in the air, adding emphasis to the word. Riley, recovering from her initial embarrassment, stepped forward, placing a hand on Junior's arm. "It's not a big deal, really. Olivia just thought it would be nice if we all lived closer together. More community and all that." She smiled brightly, effectively turning the charm offensive back on.

Seo-Yeon, intrigued by the mention of Olivia, raised an eyebrow. "All? As in, Olivia would be moving in too?" she asked, her voice carefully neutral. This was getting increasingly interesting. A love triangle, or perhaps something more geometric, was apparently brewing right under their noses. And her brother-in-law was right in the thick of it.

Junior shifted uncomfortably, avoiding eye contact. "Well, yeah," he mumbled. "There would be more space with the two extra rooms." Brian burst out laughing, the sound echoing through the dining room. "Three people sharing a three bedroom apartment? So, it's going to be a party pad?" He clapped Junior on the back, nearly sending him stumbling. "Man, you were holding out on us! This is fantastic!"

Riley, as if a dawning realization slapped her in the face, suddenly exclaimed. "That's right, there's three bedrooms! We could use one for Junior's tactical stuff and the other for whatever we want!" "Tactical stuff?" Brian echoed, his laughter dying down to a low chuckle. He looked from Junior, who was now actively trying to melt into the floor, to Riley, whose enthusiasm was practically radiating off her. Then, his eyes widened in sudden understanding. A slow, knowing grin spread across his face.

"Wait a minute," he began, his voice laced with amusement. "So, you're saying... you guys weren't planning on using separate bedrooms?" He raised an eyebrow, a silent question hanging in the air. "Because, and correct me if I'm wrong, that implies a certain level of... intimacy. Three-way intimacy, to be precise." Junior lowered his head. He wanted the floor to open up and swallow him whole. He risked a furtive glance at Riley, who was now giggling, a perfectly unrepentant expression on her face. Seo-Yeon, who had been quietly observing, placed a hand on Brian's arm, a silent message to dial it back a notch. But Brian, fueled by the pure comedic gold that had just been presented to him, was beyond restraint.

"Seriously, David," Brian continued, his voice a conspiratorial whisper, "you're a chip off the old block! I mean, Dad would be proud. Following in his footsteps in more ways than one, huh?" He punctuated the statement with a playful wink. "Brian!" Seo-Yeon hissed, smacking his arm playfully. "Leave him alone. It's their business." "Hey, I'm just congratulating the guy!" Brian protested, rubbing his arm theatrically. "He's embracing the family tradition!" He turned back to Junior, his grin widening. "So, tactical stuff in one room, and... tactical maneuvers in the other?"

Junior groaned, burying his face in his hands. "This is why I didn't want to tell anyone!" Riley reached across the table and squeezed Junior's hand. "Don't worry, Junior. He's just being Brian." Seo-Yeon added, "He's just jealous. I won't let him have any more wives." She winked. Brian sputtered indignantly.

Junior finally managed to lift his head, his cheeks still a shade of embarrassed red. "It's not like that. Not exactly. Olivia brought it up. I'm still thinking about it. It's all... complicated." Brian, surprisingly, seemed to take the hint and reeled himself in. He cleared his throat, his expression shifting to something resembling seriousness. "Alright, alright. I get it. It's a big step. And... well, it's you we're talking about. The guy who treats his weapons like they're Faberge eggs." "Hey!" Junior protested.

Brian ignored him. "Seriously though, Junior," he continued, "you're a good guy. Honest. And you're crazy capable. I mean, you practically single-handedly rescued half the people in this place. If Olivia and Riley are happy with the arrangement, then who are we to judge? Besides," he added with a sly grin, "Dad's got nine wives. If anyone can handle a harem, it's someone who learned at his knee." Seo-Yeon smacked him again. "Brian! Seriously!"

Brian grabbed her hand and kissed it. "Okay, okay, I'm done. No more jokes. Promise." He looked at Junior, his eyes sincere. "Look, man, what I'm trying to say is, you've got my back, I've got yours. Whatever you decide, I'm here for you. Just... remember what dad says. Leverage them. Don't be afraid to be yourself around them. And if I know you, it wasn't your charming personality that caught them."

Junior managed a weak smile. "Thanks, Brian. I appreciate that. It's just... I don't want things to change. I don't want people to think I'm... I don't know... getting a big head or something." "Change is inevitable, Junior," Seo-Yeon said softly. "The world changed in February. We all changed. But that doesn't mean you have to lose yourself in the process. Just be yourself, be honest with Olivia and Riley, and everything will work out."

"Leverage them?" Riley asked, raising an eyebrow. She sat across from Junior, her arms crossed, a playful smirk dancing on her lips. "Is that really the advice you're taking, Junior? You're going to 'leverage' us?" Brian choked back a laugh, earning another swat from Seo-Yeon. "It means, don't be afraid to enjoy each other. Companionship, love, and sex, they create the best memories. Plus, with all the bullshit we have to deal with now, good memories are just as important as food and water."

Riley's smirk widened. "Oh, I intend to enjoy Junior. Very much." She winked, making Junior blush furiously. Just then, the communal dining room door swung open, and Olivia walked in, her dark hair was pulled back in a messy bun. She scanned the room, her eyes lighting up when she saw Junior. "There you are!" she exclaimed, a relieved smile spreading across her face. "I've been looking all over for you. I wanted to talk about…" She trailed off, noticing the atmosphere in the room. "…something," she finished lamely.

Without another word, she walked over to Junior and promptly crawled into his lap, straddling him in the chair. She wrapped her arms around his neck and nuzzled her face into his shoulder. "Found him," she mumbled into his shirt, as if announcing a successful completion of a very important mission. Junior, already flustered by Riley's earlier comment, turned an even deeper shade of red. He awkwardly patted Olivia's back, unsure of how to react. "Hey, Liv," he managed to choke out. "What's up?"

Olivia lifted her head, her dark eyes gleaming with mischief. "Night shift," she whispered conspiratorially, her breath warm against his ear. "We're all on it tonight. And… well, I was thinking… maybe we could, um…" She trailed off again, feigning shyness, though the knowing glint in her eyes betrayed her act. "Maybe we could, you know, go back to bed, together."

Riley's eyes widened, and she dramatically gasped. "Olivia!" she exclaimed, placing a hand over her heart in mock offense. "You hussy! Didn't you sleep with him last night?" She turned to Junior with an exaggerated pout. "Besides, I haven't had my turn yet!" Junior groaned internally. This was it. The day his life officially turned into a sitcom. He was pretty sure canned laughter would start any second now. He looked pleadingly at Brian, hoping for some kind of intervention. But Brian just gave him a thumbs-up and a knowing grin. Traitor.

Seo-Yeon chimed in. "Actually, Junior, Olivia has a point. The generators are working overtime to keep the whole bunker warm. A little extra body heat could actually help conserve fuel. Think of it as... sustainable energy." She nodded sagely. Junior gaped at her. "Sustainable... you're actually using 'sustainable energy' as an argument to justify... this?" He gestured between Olivia and Riley, feeling utterly bewildered. As Brian and Seo-Yeon stood to leave, he clapped little David on the shoulder. "Give 'em hell buddy, otherwise, they'll never leave you alone." With that, Junior stood up, Olivia still latched onto him. "Alright ladies, off to bed," he said, heading toward the door.

Chapter 42:

The Night Shift

Little David, momentarily disoriented, blinked against the dim light filtering through the screen in his room. Olivia was curled against his left side, her dark hair splayed across the pillow like spilled ink. Riley nestled on his right, a wisp of red hair tickling his nose. Both were deeply asleep, radiating a peaceful warmth that almost tempted him to stay put. Almost. He needed a shower, a strong cup of something, and a mental reset before his evening training session.

Carefully, he extracted himself from the bed, mindful not to disturb either woman. He tiptoed across the cool floor, grabbing a towel and clean clothes from the small chest of drawers in the corner. He slipped out of the room and into the hallway, closing the door softly behind him. "Sneaking around, are we, little David?"

The voice, laced with amusement, made him jump. He turned to see Aidan leaning against the wall opposite his door, arms crossed, a smirk playing on his lips. "Jesus, Aidan, you scared me!" Little David said, clutching his towel a little tighter. "And it's David, or Junior, if you have to," he mumbled his usual complaint to anyone that referred to him as Little David. "What are you doing lurking around here?"

Aidan chuckled, pushing himself off the wall. "Just waiting for Alissa. She's having a check-up with Andrea. You know, making sure the little gremlin is still kicking." He patted his stomach theatrically. "Sympathy pains are a real thing, man." Junior rolled his eyes. "Yeah, I'm sure. Listen, I gotta grab a shower. You didn't see me. I didn't see you. Cool?" he said, turning towards the bathroom.

Aidan raised an eyebrow, his smirk widening. "Oh, I saw you. Emerging from the love nest. You looked like a disheveled teddy bear who'd just won the lottery." He paused, a playful glint in his eyes. "You know, Olivia was telling me about how you should move into the Apartments... say hi to the girls for me, will ya?" He nudged Little David with his elbow.

Junior's face flushed slightly. He hated that his siblings always seemed to know exactly what was going on in his life, even when he tried to be discreet. "Shut up, Aidan. It's not like that and how's that your business anyways?" He grumbled. "And I don't know what Olivia's been saying, everyone always sticks their noses in my business it's infuriating."

Aidan just laughed. "Hey, no judgment here. Just sibling concern. Besides, happy people are more effective at defending the ranch. And you know David wants everyone relaxed... especially Alissa and Taylor." He nodded towards the bathroom. "Go on, get cleaned up. Tell Olivia and Riley I said hi. And maybe bring them some of that herbal tea Jill made? They seemed to enjoy that."

Junior grumbled under his breath as he stepped into the shower. The hot water pounded against his skin, doing little to soothe his frazzled nerves. He couldn't deny there was some truth to what Aidan was saying, but the blatant teasing still stung. He wasn't sure about moving in with Olivia and Riley. It was a big step, and he wasn't entirely sure he was ready for everyone to know the details of his… unconventional relationship.

He finished his shower, scrubbing away the last remnants of sleep and the lingering scent of Olivia's lotion. He wrapped a towel around his waist and stepped back into his room, only to find it completely empty. Olivia and Riley were gone. A wave of unexpected disappointment washed over him. Where had they gone? He briefly considered tracking them down using his… heightened senses, a perk of being David's son, but quickly dismissed the idea. That felt too much like stalking, and he wanted to respect their space.

Sighing, he pulled on a pair of worn jeans and a t-shirt. He decided to head upstairs and talk to his mother, Jennifer. Maybe she could offer some sage advice, or at least a distraction from his swirling thoughts. He found Jennifer in the main living room, sprawled on one of the plush sofas with Poppy nestled asleep on her chest. Jessica was perched on the armrest, petting Luci, who seemed to be judging everyone with feline disdain. David was standing by the window, surveying the grounds with that ever-watchful gaze of his.

"Hey, Mom," Junior said, trying to keep his voice casual. Jennifer looked up, her eyes softening as she saw him. "Junior, dear. Sleep well?" He hesitated, then decided to plunge right in. "It was… eventful. Listen, can I talk to you for a sec?" Jennifer patted the sofa beside her. "Of course, sweetie. What's on your mind?"

Junior cleared his throat, feeling a little awkward under the combined gazes of his mother, Jessica, and even Luci, who seemed to have paused her grooming to listen intently. David, as always, remained a stoic presence by the window, though Junior knew he was listening. "Well," he began, "it's about Olivia and Riley. And… me, I guess."

Jennifer's eyes twinkled. She gently shifted Poppy on her chest. "Oh, sweetie, spit it out. Are you lost in the wilderness of womanly wiles? Because, honey, that's a very crowded wilderness with this family." She gestured around with a flourish, careful not to wake the baby. Jessica snorted, petting Luci with deliberate strokes. "He's discovered the joys (and terrors) of multiple girlfriends. Welcome to the club, Junior. You're a chip off the old block."

Junior winced. "It's not like that! Dad didn't really date anyone before marrying them. It was almost, definite, from the beginning." "Details, details," Jennifer waved a dismissive hand. "Love is love, Junior. Besides, with who your father is, what do you expect?" David finally turned from the window, a slight smile playing on his lips. "Are there complications, son?"

"Well, yeah," Junior admitted. "It's... new. And Olivia suggested I moved to the apartments. Which... I don't know. It feels fast. And I don't want to mess things up between them. Or me." "Is their understanding of their... place, or your authority, being undermined because of these... feelings?" David asked, his gaze sharp and assessing.

Junior shook his head, a genuine look of surprised confusion on his face. "No, Dad. Not at all. If anything, they seem more motivated now than before. Which... surprised even me. I thought maybe... maybe there'd be some jealousy, or resentment, maybe even a little entitlement. But they're working harder, training more... it's like they're trying to prove themselves."

Jennifer chuckled softly. "Honey, that's women for you. We thrive on competition... especially when it involves a handsome young man." She winked at Junior. "They probably see each other as allies, pushing each other to be the best version of themselves for you." Jessica considered thoughtfully. "Junior, it makes sense that they would be attracted to you, especially since you and Nicole brought them back here. But, did anything happen? Anything that might... accelerate their attraction?"

"Well," Junior began, rubbing the back of his neck, "There was the, uh... car flipping incident. And the..." he trailed off, feeling a flush creep up his neck. "The...?" David prompted, his eyebrow raised in anticipation. "The... headshots," Junior mumbled, barely audible. Jessica burst out laughing, Luci jumping down from her lap in surprise. "Headshots? Oh, Honey, you're killing me! You flipped a car and pulled off a John Wick impression? No wonder they're practically tripping over themselves for you. Good men are hard to find, especially ones who can do what you did."

A beat of silence followed his confession. Then, Jennifer burst out laughing. "Oh, Junior! You sweet, oblivious boy!" She wiped a tear from her eye. "You know what that does to women, right? A little bit of raw, untamed power? Irresistible!" Jessica, reaching for a bowl of popcorn, added, "Yeah, honey, you basically took them to the primal movie. The whole 'strong protector' thing? It's baked into our DNA. Add in a sweet face, a genuine heart, and a willingness to share... Junior, you're screwed."

Jennifer patted Junior's hand, her eyes crinkling at the corners. "Honey, it's like when I was in high school. David was all quiet confidence and raw strength, and... well, let's just say the mall became a lot less interesting." She winked, her playful smile hinting at the whirlwind romance that followed. "Seeing him handle himself, knowing he could protect me, and yes," she added with a mischievous glint, "knowing he was incredibly capable... it was an instant connection." David, observing the scene with a mixture of amusement and paternal pride, chuckled softly. "It's a powerful instinct, Junior. When the world goes to hell, people gravitate toward strength and security. You provided both, in spades."

Jessica, sprawled on the couch next to Jennifer, popped a piece of popcorn into her mouth. "Yeah, but see, here's the thing, Junior. Back then, Daddy had competition. Hot guys who could also protect her and drive cool cars. Now? There's no competition. The dating pool is now a kiddie pool, filled with the same handful of people. And you didn't just stick up for them, you saved their lives, not once, but twice, and with a level of competence and skill that borders on the super heroic. You flipped a car, for Christ's sake. That's not something you see every Tuesday."

Jennifer nodded in agreement. "Exactly! It's not just the strength, Junior. It's how you used it. You instinctively protected them, put yourself at risk. That kind of selflessness is rare, especially these days." Junior shifted uncomfortably, running a hand through his close-cropped hair. "I just... did what needed to be done. They were in trouble."

"And you handled it like a damn pro," Jessica retorted, pointing a popcorn-filled fist at him. "Don't be so modest. You think Olivia and Riley are blind? They saw what you did. They felt it. Now they're throwing their panties at you... so why are you so dumb?" Before Junior could stammer out a reply, Jennifer smacked him lightly on the back of the head. "Don't be dense, honey. You're smart, capable, and you know you are. Olivia and Riley know. They're practically throwing themselves at your feet. What's the problem?"

Junior sighed, the weight of their expectations settling heavily on his shoulders. He knew they were right, logically. Intellectually, he understood the situation. But...

"It's one thing watching it happen, you know? Watching David with all of you." He gestured around the living room. "It's a whole different thing being in the middle of it."

David nodded, his gaze softening with understanding. He knew that fear, that hesitation all too well. "That means you care, plain and simple. Fear of messing things up is understandable, it's that you care about these girls." He paused, taking a sip of his iced tea. "It's not a bad thing, Junior, it just means you want to do your best for them."

Suddenly, as if cued by the gods of irony, Olivia and Riley entered the living room from downstairs. "David, darling, everyone is getting ready, but Kathy is over at Marvin and Sara's place. She's watching little Jake while they make dinner," Olivia reported. Junior nodded before standing. "Will she be back before first watch?" he asked, looking at Riley. "Yes sir, just wanted to let you know," Riley answered, a faint blush spreading across her ears.

As junior turned to go downstairs, he looked back. Staring back at him, were four sets of eyes, and four, very purposeful, thumbs up. The image was almost comical, the absurdity of it all threatened to overwhelm him. He could practically hear the collective "Good luck!" echoing after him as he descended the stairs to the maintenance bunker.

Olivia and Riley followed close behind, their presence a strange mix of comforting and nerve-wracking. He had to admit, having them trailing him like… well, like affectionate puppies, definitely made him feel better. "So," Olivia began, her voice a soft murmur in the echoing concrete bunker. "What are you going to do?" Junior rubbed the back of his neck. "I... I don't know exactly. Just going to check on them, make sure everything's alright. Kathy's been helping out a lot with Jake, especially since he's been... fussy. Thought I'd see if they need anything."

"It's sweet of you to check on them," Riley said, her voice laced with genuine fondness. "Being a new parent is gotta be tough, especially with everything going on." Olivia nodded in agreement. "Yeah, Sara and Marvin seem pretty overwhelmed sometimes. And it's sweet of Kathy to help out." Junior sighed. "Yeah, Lily, Seth, and Grace were always... different. Even Poppy. Jake's... Jake's a regular baby." He emphasized the word "regular" like it was a foreign concept, something he'd read about in a dusty textbook. "And that throws you for a loop?" Olivia teased, bumping his shoulder with hers.

He chuckled, a short, breathy sound. "Maybe a little. I mean, I'm used to babies who practically come out of the womb knowing how to shoot, move and communicate. Jake mostly just cries and spits up." Olivia frowned, a delicate furrow appearing between her eyebrows. "Wait a minute. What do you mean, 'come out of the womb knowing how to shoot'?" She tilted her head, her eyes searching his face. "Is that... a saying? Because I'm pretty sure babies don't actually know how to shoot."

Riley, ever observant, mirrored Olivia's confusion. "Yeah, Junior. That sounds… a little out there, even for you." Junior froze, his mental gears grinding to a halt. He'd slipped up. He hadn't meant to say that, hadn't meant to reveal even a sliver of the strangeness that permeated his family. He cursed his own loose tongue. He was so used to being around his family, that he sometimes forgot other people didn't know about David's previous life.

He stopped walking, forcing Olivia and Riley to stop as well. He looked at each of them in the eyes, looking for any signs of judgement. "Look, can I… can I ask you both something?" He paused, taking a deep breath. The air felt heavier now, charged with his anxiety. "Can you… can you keep something between us? Something I'm not… ready to share with the others yet?"

Olivia's expression softened. "Of course, Junior. You know you can trust us." Riley nodded firmly, her hand reaching out to squeeze his arm reassuringly. "Always." Junior led Olivia and Riley further away from the hydroponics greenhouse toward the generators in the Maintenance bunker. Attempting to use the hum of the generators as cover for their clandestine discussion.

He cleared his throat, the sound echoing slightly in the confined space. "Okay, so… what I said before about babies… It's… complicated." Where to even begin? How could he explain the inexplicable without sounding completely insane? Olivia rested a hand on his arm, her touch grounding him. "Just… start somewhere, Junior. We're listening." He took another deep breath. "Okay, so… my dad… David… He's… different. He's lived through this life before. He remembers everything."

Riley's eyebrows shot up. "He… what? You're saying he has like… deja vu? Intense deja vu?" "No," Junior said, shaking his head. "Not deja vu. He remembers everything. His whole life. He's… reliving it." He watched their faces, searching for disbelief, or worse, pity. Olivia's brow furrowed again, her lips pursed in thought. "And… you're saying that… that affects you? And Aidan and Brian and Lily and Seth and Grace?"

He nodded, relief washing over him that they weren't laughing or calling him delusional. "Yeah. It's… hard to explain. It's like… when he came back, that experience became part of his DNA, we… kinda inherited it. His knowledge, his skills, his experiences… We get a watered down version, a temporal enhancement." Riley's eyes widened. "So, you're saying… you're basically born with… memories that aren't yours?" Junior shook his head. "Not exactly memories. We can't picture anything, we just know it."

Riley's eyes lit up with a mix of astonishment and dawning understanding. "So… is that why you're, like, so strong? Is that how you were able to flip that car in San Angelo when we were getting shot at? I mean, most people can't just flip a freakin' car! Olivia squeezed his arm again. "So, you're saying… this 'temporal enhancement'… it's why you're so good at everything?"

"Pretty much," Junior admitted, feeling a wave of self-consciousness. He wasn't trying to brag, but explaining his existence felt like showing off a superpower he didn't even ask for. "We're all born with the same knowledge, the same experiences. The same baseline. The difference is, Dad started late, when he was thirteen. Plus, his focus was all about preparing for the collapse and protecting his family."

He continued, resting against the concrete wall. "My brothers and sisters and I all followed our own path. I mean, I can rebuild a car, but I couldn't fix a generator like Aidan could, and I don't speak Latin like the twins." Olivia's gaze was fixed on Junior, her eyes filled with admiration. "It's amazing, really," she said, her voice filled with awe. "I can't even imagine what it must be like to have all that knowledge and skill at your fingertips."

Junior shrugged, feeling a little embarrassed by the attention. "It's just how we were born," he replied modestly. "I don't really think about it too much." Riley, who had been quiet for a moment, suddenly spoke up. "But what about your relationships?" she asked, her brow furrowed in thought. "I mean, you're all so close in age, and you all have these... these superpowers, for lack of a better word. Doesn't that make things complicated?" Junior shook his head. "Not really," he said. "We're all different people, with our own personalities and interests. Sure, we have a lot in common, but we're not just defined by what we can do. And as for relationships, well, that's a whole other story."

He started walking again, gesturing towards the faint green glow emanating from the hydroponics greenhouse. "And then there's the homeschooling. Dad said regular school was useless, which it is. But can you imagine trying to explain to some poor, unsuspecting teacher how to use the ground when shooting into a crowd of people, as your desk mate eats another crayon? Or why you already knew about WWI when you were eight. We were homeschooled more to protect the other students and teachers. Can you imagine the parent-teacher conferences?"

"Protect the other students," Olivia repeated, a chuckle escaping her lips. "Okay, yeah, I can see that." She fell into step beside him, her curiosity piqued. "But seriously, how did you guys even meet anyone? I mean, you're all so… capable, and you were homeschooled. It's not like you were hanging out at the local coffee shop." Riley nodded, mirroring Olivia's inquisitiveness. "Yeah, how did Aidan even meet Alissa? And Brian and Seo-Yeon? It's not like David put out a matrimonial ad for super-powered spouses." She winked.

Junior smiled, at least his relationship was more normal. "Well, we all understood the implications of adult relationships. Some of us more than others. Aidan picked Alissa, Lily picked Josh, Seo-Yeon picked Brian, but that's a different story. Then we have Seth, who has his eyes set on Bonnie, and you remember Grace's proclamation?" Olivia and Riley exchanged a knowing glance, a fresh wave of giggles threatening to erupt. "Oh, that proclamation?" Olivia said, her voice dripping with mock innocence. "The one about her… future nuptial plans with Kyle? And what she intended to do with her 'grown-up body'?" Riley snorted, suppressing another giggle. "I think Junior's implying there's a pattern of 'David's kids have slightly… unconventional… views on relationships' going on here." She grinned, nudging Junior playfully.

As they approached Marvin's door, Junior waved his hand. "Alright, ladies, let's keep it down," Junior murmured, tapping lightly on the door. "Just checking in on the tiny human and his caregivers." A muffled, "Coming!" preceded the door swinging open, revealing Marvin, his hair slightly disheveled as he grinned sheepishly. "Hey Junior! What's up? Everything alright?"

Behind Marvin, Sara peeked out, a wooden spoon clutched in her hand. Her brow was furrowed with concern. "Is something wrong? We heard you guys talking..." Junior offered a reassuring smile. "Just a routine check, making sure everyone's staying warm and, you know, sane. How's little Jake doing?"

Sara visibly relaxed, stepping aside to reveal a glimpse of their small apartment. Kathy was perched on the edge of the sofa, bouncing a cooing Jake on her knee. The aroma of the simmering… something… intensified. "He's been a handful today, but Kathy's been a lifesaver," Sara said, gesturing towards Kathy with a grateful smile.

Kathy looked up, her eyes a little tired but bright. "He's a sweetheart. Though his lungs are definitely developing." "You heading to training later, Kathy?" Junior asked. Kathy's face fell slightly. She glanced at Jake, then back at Junior. "I… I don't know, Junior. I promised

Sara and Marvin I'd help out tonight. They need a break. And, well…" she trailed off, her gaze softening as she looked back at the baby. "I like helping."

Junior held up a hand, silencing Kathy. "Don't worry about patrols tonight, Kathy. I can cover you. You're doing good work here. Just let me know if you need a break. Got it?" He gave her a reassuring nod. He knew Kathy had a soft spot, and seeing her with Jake, it was pretty clear where her priorities were right now. The apocalypse had a funny way of rearranging things.

Marvin and Sara exchanged relieved glances. "Seriously, Junior, thanks," Marvin said, running a hand through his already messy hair. "We were starting to feel like we were failing at this whole parenting thing." Sara nodded vigorously. "Sleep deprivation is a weapon of mass destruction. I think I've aged ten years in the last week." She shuddered dramatically. "And the smell… oh, the smell. I swear it's permanently embedded in my nostrils."

"Alright, lovebirds, me and my heavy heart will leave you to it," Junior said with a slight smile. "Kathy, you're a star. Don't let them work you too hard. I'll swing by later if you need anything." He turned to leave, then paused, remembering his father's constant reminders about community and support. "Hey, Sara, Marvin? You know, we got, like, a house full of mothers back in the main house. And plenty of others who would probably kill for some baby snuggles. Don't be afraid to ask for help. Seriously. It takes a village, and all that."

Sara and Marvin exchanged a look that screamed "Understatement of the Century." "Yeah, we know, Junior. It's just... hard," Sara admitted, sighing. "Feeling like we gotta prove we can do it ourselves." "Forget about proving anything," Junior countered, his voice firmer. "This isn't some reality TV show. It's freaking survival. Use the resources we have. That's what Dad always says, right?"

He made his way further down the hallway, stopping outside Apartment eight, then took a deep breath, and knocked firmly. A moment later, the door cracked open and Andrew peered out, his eyes wide and a little nervous. Susan stood behind him, her expression a mix of apprehension and gratitude. "Hey, Junior," Andrew said, his voice low. "We... we're ready. Just, uh, a little behind schedule. Sorry."

Junior waved a hand dismissively. "No sweat. Just wanted to make sure you guys were still up for it. First shift can be a little rough, especially when you're not used to it." He leaned against the doorframe, studying their faces. They both looked... well, like they expected the world to end all over again. "Alright, listen up, you two," Junior started, his tone shifting to a more serious, yet still reassuring, one. "I know night shift sounds all 'zombie apocalypse' in your head, but trust me, it's mostly just... organizing the chaos." He chuckled, earning a weak smile from Susan. "Mostly traffic control, right?" Andrew asked, his eyes darting around nervously. "Your dad mentioned something about that."

Junior nodded. "Exactly. Picture this: we got, what, forty-seven people crammed into this little valley. Everyone's got their own schedule, their own needs. And everyone's trying to escape the heat, or the cold, or whatever else Mother Nature throws at us." He gestured vaguely. "If everyone decided to hit the gym at the same time, or go for a late-night swim, it'd be a free-for-all. Someone would end up drowning or get bonked in the head with a dumbbell."

He paused, letting the image sink in. "So, night shift is all about keeping things flowing smoothly. Staggering activities, making sure people aren't tripping over each other in the dark. Plus, you gotta keep an eye on the generators, make sure they don't decide to spontaneously combust. Little stuff like that." Susan frowned. "Generators? I don't know anything about generators."

"Relax, Susan," Junior said, a reassuring smile spreading across his face. "Tonight, it's all about training. David's got a whole checklist of things he wants everyone to know. And trust me, it's not rocket science. Even I can handle it." He winked, earning a genuine smile from Andrew this time.

"Think of it like this," Junior continued, gesturing with his hands, "with everyone awake at the same time, it's like Black Friday at Walmart. People are fighting over the last can of peaches, the gym equipment is all hogged, and the damn pool looks like a jacuzzi from all the bodies crammed in there." He shuddered dramatically causing

Susan and Andrew to crack smiles. "But with shifts," he pressed on, "it's like a timeshare. You get your designated hours for the pool, the gym, even the hydroponics lab if you want to grow your own prize-winning zucchini. It keeps things civilized, and everyone gets a fair shot at the amenities."

Andrew finally spoke, his brow furrowed in understanding. "So, if half the ranch is asleep, it's like… there are only half as many people here?" "Exactly!" Junior exclaimed, snapping his fingers. "You got it. Less competition for everything. Plus, it's quieter. Some people, like Brian and Seo-Yeon, have already decided to switch as well." Andrew looked at Susan, a look of relief washing over them. "I thought we were going to be working all night.

David shook his head. "No, we already have everything we need, but some things still have to be maintained. You know, more people now causing wear and tear. But There's still training, we're just going to do everything at night. So, get dressed, and meet me by the pool by 8 o'clock. After that, I don't care what you do, just find something that interests you." Susan nodded, a wave of understanding filling her eyes.

Junior, relieved to finally be done explaining the sleep schedule rationale to Andrew and Susan, turned to Olivia and Riley, a slightly nervous smile playing on his lips. "Hey," he greeted them, trying to sound casual, "Sorry about that, got a little carried away with the timeshare analogy, huh?" He chuckled, hoping they didn't think he was a complete idiot. "Apartments," he remembered, snapping his fingers again. "Yeah, I was thinking about it. Actually, I think it's a good idea. You guys wanna pick one out?"

Suddenly, Olivia and Riley launched themselves at Junior, enveloping him in a squealing, giggling hug. "Yes! Yes, we do!" Olivia chirped, squeezing him tight. Riley, equally enthusiastic, added, "We were hoping you'd say that!" The force of their combined hug nearly knocked Junior off balance, but he managed to steady himself, a wide, genuine smile spreading across his face. "Alright, alright, easy there," he chuckled, gently disentangling himself. "Didn't want to get trampled by enthusiasm. We have a few hours before training. Let's go see what's available. I think some of the rooms downstairs would be best."

As the trio headed towards the stairwell, Susan and Andrew exchanged bewildered glances. "Did... did you know about that?" Andrew asked, gesturing subtly towards Junior, Olivia, and Riley. Susan shook her head, her mouth still open. "No way! I thought Junior was just... I don't know what I thought. I had no idea he was… dating two of them!" She paused, thinking. "Actually, it kind of makes sense. They have been eyeballing him since they got here."

Chapter 43:

Operation Apocalyptaclause

The rhythmic thud of weights and the squeak of sneakers on the rubberized track filled the Recreational Bunker. Junior, pausing from his sparring with Caleb and Sophia, surveyed his team. Darrel, ever the comedian, was attempting to bench press Noah, who, despite being nearly the same size, was feigning terror. Olivia, focused as always, was running laps, her ponytail a dark whip against her back. Riley and Kathy were engaged in a surprisingly intense game of one-on-one basketball, fueled by more trash talk than actual skill.

"Alright, settle down, chuckleheads," Junior boomed, clapping his hands. "It's December 11th. Two weeks 'til Christmas." A confused murmur rippled through the group. The apocalypse had blurred the lines of time; holidays felt like distant memories from another life. "Christmas?" Darrel asked, pausing his questionable bench press. "You mean, like, the thing with the fat dude in the red suit who breaks into your house?" "That's the one," Junior replied, a grin playing on his lips "So, anyone got any feelings about it? Good, bad, indifferent? This is your safe space, people. Lay it on me."

Darrel was the first to speak. "Honestly? Seems kinda pointless. I mean, who are we gonna buy presents for? Each other? Besides, where are we gonna find a tree?"

"I kinda miss it," Susan chimed in, wiping sweat from her brow. "My mom always went all out. We'd have a huge dinner and open presents all morning. It was…normal." "Normal," Andrew echoed, his voice tinged with a longing that resonated with many in the room. "Yeah, I miss normal."

"It's just gonna be another day," Riley declared, dribbling the basketball with unnecessary force. She was trying to sound indifferent, tough, but Junior saw the flicker of something else in her eyes. "We got enough to worry about without some made-up holiday." Olivia stopped running and walked towards the group, her expression thoughtful. "Christmas was always about family for me. And… well, we're kind of a family now, aren't we? Maybe we could do something, even if it's small."

Caleb, emboldened by Olivia's words, spoke up. "I always liked the lights. Made everything feel…brighter." "Brighter, huh?" Junior mused, stroking his chin. "I think we can manage 'brighter'. David actually has a whole pallet of holiday lights and decorations in the storage area, to include a few Christmas trees," he added, looking at Darrel." Kathy added, "What about the kids? Beth and Lori and all the little ones? They need some Christmas magic."

Junior pushed himself off the wall where he'd been leaning, a glint in his eye. "Okay, listen up. I get it. This whole Christmas thing feels…weird. We're not exactly living in a Hallmark movie here." He paused, letting his words hang. "But Olivia's right. We are a family now, and families do Christmas, even if it's a little…apocalyptic."

He clapped his hands together. "Here's the deal. We're gonna do Christmas. For the kids, for Susan's 'normal,' and yeah, even for Riley, who's trying way too hard to be the Grinch." He smirked, earning a playful glare from her. "First things first," Junior continued, his voice gaining momentum. "Tomorrow night, after our shift, we are hitting the storage bunker. We are gonna grab all the lights, tinsel, and decorations David hoarded. I'm sure the man has it all, knowing him." He gestured around the bunker. "We'll start by decorating the main house.

"Second, the tree. We have a few, so those of you that want one, we got you covered, thankfully. Otherwise, we'd have to run around looking for a real tree. Brian, can you ask Seo-Yeon if she has some tricks to make it smell real? Think pine scent, strategically placed air fresheners, the works." Brian, who was on the stationary bike, grinned. "Consider it done.

Junior nodded approvingly. "Third, presents. Now, I know we're not exactly able to run down to the toy store, but we can try." He turned to Caleb. "See if you can fabricate some kind of mailbox for the children. I want to give them something to look forward to." Olivia, standing at the edge of the running track, her brow furrowed in thought, finally spoke up. "Presents… what are we even supposed to get? I mean, it's not like they can ask for the latest video game or anything."

Junior walked over, squeezed her shoulder reassuringly. "That's a fair point. Which is why," his eyes sparkled with a hint of mischief, "we're going to have to plan a field trip." "A field trip?" Susan asked, perking up from her stretches. "Where? To the ruins of Walmart?" "Not exactly," Junior chuckled, waving a dismissive hand. "First, we need intel. We need those Christmas lists. Then... we hit town. We go scavenging for the stuff they actually want. It'll be a real treasure hunt."

A ripple of excitement went through the group. Darrel, surprisingly enthusiastic now, clapped his hands together. "Alright, now you're talking! Stealth mission: Santa's Workshop. I'm in!" "Hold your horses, Darrel," Junior cautioned, grinning. "It's not just about grabbing whatever shiny thing catches your eye. We need to be smart. Safe. And, most importantly, we need to make sure we don't raise any unwanted attention."

He glanced around the group, his gaze settling on Sophia, who had been quietly observing the proceedings. "Sophia, you've got the best handwriting, I need you to do me a favor." Sophia, caught off guard by the attention, blushed slightly. "What is it, Junior?" "I need you to make some Christmas stationery. Nice paper, festive borders. I want three lines on each for three gifts and then matching envelopes as well. This will be our intel." Her eyes widened slightly. "For... presents? I can do that." Junior nodded. "I want enough for everyone, this isn't just about the kids, I want everyone to get in the spirit. Can you do that?"

"Yeah," Sophia replied, a small smile gracing her lips. "Yeah, I can do that."

Susan piped up. "Okay, so we've got the tree, the presents, the intel… but what about the snow? It's freezing outside, but no snow. It's just not really Christmas without snow!" Junior stroked his chin thoughtfully. "Snow, huh? Well, that's a tough one. We could try rigging up a snow machine somehow. Or…" he paused, a mischievous glint returning to his eyes, "We could add a woodchipper or a snow thrasher to the Christmas list. We'd have to find one, but the kids could make snow all day!" The group erupted in laughter. "Alright, alright," Junior said, chuckling. "Seriously, though, we'll figure something out. Maybe we can collect some ice and crush it or something. We'll brainstorm."

Riley, finally finding her Christmas spirit suggested. "We could leave buckets of water outside and just save up blocks of ice?" Junior smiled, pulling her close for a kiss. "That's a good idea, my little pop tart." He winked at Susan. "See? Teamwork makes the dream work."

Noah, usually quiet, spoke up, a glimmer of excitement in his eyes. "Speaking of dreams… you think any of the old video game consoles survived the EMP? I mean, imagine playing some classic Mario Kart on Christmas!" A wave of nostalgia washed over the group. Darrel, the resident wit, chimed in. "Dude, if we find a working console, I'm calling dibs on the first round of Goldeneye. Slappers only, of course."

Brian raised an eyebrow. "The EMP... it fried most electronics. But... it's possible some shielded ones survived. I could take a look, fix 'em up maybe. Just bring plenty of spares." Junior slapped his leg dramatically. "That's right, Brian here can fix anything. So, get everything you can, games, consoles, controllers, just no game passes." He paced a bit, mentally organizing the new objectives. "Okay, so here's the updated Christmas plan. Operation Mad Maxiclause is a go!"

He stopped and looked at the group. "First, mission 'Ice Bucket Challenge' is initiated. Patrols will carry out buckets of water and leave them at the edge of the property tonight. Once they freeze solid, they'll bring the buckets back. Susan, you're in charge of coordinating the patrol drops. Make sure it's spaced out enough that we don't create a slip-and-slide hazard."

He turned to Sophia, who was quietly sketching in a notebook. "Sophia, you got the stationery covered, right? Christmas cards, letters to Santa... the works?" Sophia nodded, a small smile gracing her lips. "Already on it, Junior. We can even set up a little writing station for the kids." Junior grinned. "Perfect! And Caleb," he said, singling out the young man, "work with her. You're both going to collaborate on intelligence collection. I want secret wishes, details on childhood memories, all of it." Caleb straightened up, eager to impress. "Got it, Junior! We'll get right on it."

Finally, Junior addressed Marvin and Noah. "You two are on console duty. Work with Brian. Get a list of potential spare parts. You're going to find every scrap of electronics you can get your hands on. Spare parts, consoles, controllers, cartridges… anything that might resurrect some classic gaming. Brian, you're the resident tech wizard. See what you can salvage."

Later that morning, the biting Texas wind whipped at Darrel and Noah as they trudged towards the work shed, their breath misting in the pre-dawn gloom. "Twenty-nine degrees is an insult," Darrel grumbled, pulling his scarf higher. "This is Texas, not fucking Siberia!"

Noah simply shrugged. "David did say the weather's gonna be all messed up now. Hotter summers, colder winters. He said something about the lakes and rivers going bad too, once all the plants and fish start dying off." Darrel stopped dead in his tracks, a perplexed frown etched on his face. "That's what I don't get, man. How does David know all this stuff? It's like he's got some kinda freaky precognition or something. It's kinda creeping me out."

Noah chuckled, pushing open the heavy door to the work shed. "Come on, Darrel, don't get all conspiracy theorist on me. He's just... smart. Really, really smart. And he reads a lot. Plus, he's probably seen this kind of thing in some movie or documentary before. Remember that one about the Yellowstone supervolcano we watched? Gave me nightmares for weeks."

Darrel remained unconvinced. "Yeah, but that was after he built the bunkers! He knew about the EMP way before anyone even thought it was possible. And he always seems to be one step ahead. It's unsettling."

"So," Darrel drawled, leaning against a workbench cluttered with reloading supplies, "serious question. With, like, zero judgment. Which one's your favorite?" He gestured vaguely towards the main house with a jerk of his head. "Of David's wives, I mean. Gotta be one you think is, like, the coolest, right?"

Noah choked on his spit. His eyes widened, darting around the generator room as if the walls had ears. "Dude! What the hell? Are you trying to get us killed? Or worse?" He lowered his voice to a near whisper, even though the thick concrete walls muffled sound effectively. "You don't just talk about picking favorites among David's wives. That's... that's sacrilege!"

Darrel just grinned, unrepentant. "Relax, man. It's just a hypothetical. We're guys, right? We appreciate beauty. There's nothing wrong with admiring from afar. Besides, it's not like they're going to suddenly ditch David and flirt with us. We're just… admiring the architecture, so to speak." He winked.

Noah continued to glare at Darrel, his face a mixture of disbelief and apprehension. "Admiring architecture? Seriously? That's your cover story if one of them overhears you?" He shook his head. "Look, man, I get it. They're all...amazing. But you need to keep those thoughts to yourself. Trust me on this."

Darrel held up his hands in mock surrender. "Alright, alright. I'll dial it back on the architectural appreciation. But you gotta admit, it's a valid question. I mean, if you had to pick, hypothetically speaking, which one would it be?" He nudged Noah with his elbow.

Noah sighed, running a hand through his hair. He knew he shouldn't engage. He knew it was a bad idea. But Darrel's persistence, combined with the early hour and the lingering chill from their patrol, chipped away at his resolve. "Fine," he relented, lowering his voice even further. "But this stays between us. Got it?" Darrel zipped his lips and mimed throwing away the key. "Jessica," he mumbled, almost ashamed of admitting it.

Darrel raised an eyebrow. "Jessica? The one with the cat? Interesting choice. What about her?" Noah sighed. "Just… she's got this way about her," he stammered, feeling his cheeks flush despite the cool air of the generator room. "She's… adorably cute, you know? And that sass! It's kind of endearing. Plus," he hesitated, glancing around as if someone might be listening, "she's a total daddy's girl. And there's just something about that…" He trailed off, unable to articulate the potent combination of qualities that made him pick her.

Darrel whistled softly. "Okay, I see where you're coming from. The whole 'daddy's girl' thing can be… appealing. But Jessica? Really? I mean, all of them are stunning, in their own way." "It's just an observation. I honestly prefer curvy Latinas anyway. But what about you, Darrel?" Noah asked, trying to steer the conversation away from his own embarrassing confession.

Darrel stroked his chin thoughtfully. "Hmm, decisions, decisions… Kayla. It's gotta be Kayla. She's just got this… vibe, you know? Like she's too precious to be alone, but she's got her shit together. Plus, she kind of reminds me of my mom." He laughed, a touch nervously. "Don't judge me, man. It's a comfort thing." Noah frowned, his eyes narrowing into slits. "Dude, she has like, no tits. What about her has you so caught up?"

Darrel thought a moment. "I really didn't notice the tits, but every time I see her ass, I have to bite my hand. Plus, her eyes are just… so… pretty." Noah shook his head slowly, then chuckled. "Alright, alright, I get it. The heart wants what the heart wants. Or, in this case, the eyes want what the ass shows." He clapped Darrel on the shoulder. "Just don't let David catch you staring too intensely, alright? He might think you're trying to steal his wife or something."

They reached the bottom of the stairs and started walking towards the tunnel entrance to the Maintenance bunker, the hum of the generators growing quieter with each step. As they approached the Apartment bunker entrance, they both froze. Junior stood there, arms crossed, leaning against the doorway like a post-apocalyptic bouncer. He had that 'caught you doing something you shouldn't' look on his face. Darrel and Noah exchanged terrified glances, a silent prayer escaping each of their lips.

Darrel cleared his throat, trying to sound nonchalant. "Hey, Junior! What's up, man? Just… uh… finished up the patrols. You know, taking the scenic route, figured we check the hydroponics on the way back up." Noah nodded vigorously, his eyes wide. "Yeah! Apocalypse preparedness! That's our motto! We're, uh… preparedness professionals!" He winced internally. Smooth, Noah, real smooth.

Darrel's forced, casual tone hung in the air like a bad joke. Noah's "preparedness professionals" comment only made the situation worse. Junior remained unmoving, an unreadable expression on his face. The silence stretched, punctuated only by the distant thrum of the generators and the frantic beat of Darrel's heart.

Finally, Junior pushed himself off the doorway, the movement exaggeratedly casual. "Hydroponics, huh? Good thinking. Can't hurt to check up on the… lettuce." He raised an eyebrow, a hint of a smirk playing on his lips. "Say, I was planning on helping Susan and Kathy with breakfast before the masses descend. Figured I could pick up a few fresh veggies. Mind if I tag along? Two heads are good, three are better, and all that."

Darrel and Noah traded another frantic glance. Was he being serious? Did he actually believe their flimsy excuse? Or was this some kind of elaborate punishment for their… appreciation of David's wives? "Alright then, lead the way, preparedness professionals. I'm particularly interested in hearing about your day."

He fell into step beside them as they started towards the tunnel entrance. The air crackled with unspoken tension. Darrel and Noah struggled to maintain their composure, aware of Junior's presence like a hawk watching its prey. As they walked, Junior spoke up, his voice surprisingly even. "So, patrol go alright? Anything interesting going on out there?"

Darrel swallowed hard, his witty nature momentarily deserting him. "Uh, yeah, patrol went fine, Junior. Real fine. Just cold, you know? Real cold." He punctuated his statement with a nervous chuckle that echoed awkwardly in the concrete corridor.

Noah, ever the "preparedness professional," chimed in, trying to sound nonchalant. "Yeah, standard perimeter check. Just confirming the integrity of our defensive positions. Everything's secure, as always. Bit icy on the grass, though. Slippery stuff." He gave a knowing nod, as if this was some profound observation.

Junior listened to their stilted explanations with an unnerving intensity, his gaze flickering between them as they stumbled over their words. He didn't seem convinced, but he didn't interrupt either. The silence stretched again, broken only by the rhythmic thump-thump-thump of the generators and the sound of their boots on the concrete floor. Darrel could practically feel the sweat beading on his forehead.

Finally, they reached the entrance to the hydroponics greenhouse. The warm, humid air hit them like a wall, a stark contrast to the chill of the tunnels. The gentle hum of the hydrothermal pumps filled the space, a soothing sound that did little to ease Darrel's anxiety. Rows upon rows of leafy greens stretched before them, bathed in the artificial UVB light.

Darrel stared at the rows of verdant lettuce, desperately trying to look interested. He plucked a leaf, chewed it thoughtfully, and declared, "Robust flavor profile! Excellent work with the… uh… nutrient solution." He looked at Noah for support. Noah, not to be outdone in awkwardness, examined a tomato plant with the seriousness of a botanist. "Fascinating trichome density. Clearly, optimal light exposure." He cleared his throat, feeling like a complete idiot.

Junior remained silent for a long, excruciating moment, his expression unreadable. The only movement was his eyes, scanning their faces with unnerving precision. Finally, he gave a slow, deliberate nod. Then, the hammer dropped. "So," Junior said, his voice surprisingly casual, "Let's say… hypothetically… David wasn't in the picture. And you had your pick of the… ahem… older wives. Which one would be your top choice, and why?"

Darrel choked on his lettuce. Noah nearly backed into a row of pepper plants. The artificial sunlight suddenly felt a lot hotter. "Dude," Darrel finally managed, his voice a strangled whisper. "Seriously? We were just… you know… joking around." "Hypothetically," Junior repeated, his eyes glinting in the artificial light. "Humor me. Besides, you already picked Jessica for her adorableness and Daddy's girl dynamic, and Kayla for her pretty eyes and splendid ass. Perfectly valid assessments, by the way. But that leaves a few more… shall we say mature… options. Let's assess the first batch; Tiffany, Jennifer, Summer, and Elena."

Darrel swallowed hard, trying to formulate a response that wouldn't get him killed. "Okay, okay," Darrel said, trying to sound nonchalant. "But just so we're clear, this is purely hypothetical, right? Like, if... suddenly David disappeared, and we had to take care of his... women?" Junior chuckled, a low, rumbling sound. "Hypothetical in the extreme. Now, let's begin with Tiffany. What's your take?"

Darrel swallowed hard. Tiffany was David's first wife. She was kind, strong, and had a no-nonsense aura that both intimidated and reassured him. "Tiffany... she's... solid. A rock. You know? She's got that rancher vibe, totally self-sufficient. Plus, she's got a great personality and she's a good listener." "Good listener," Junior repeated, his expression unchanging. "Elaborate. In a post-apocalyptic relationship dynamic, why is being a 'good listener' a desirable trait?"

Noah jumped in, seizing the opportunity to take the heat off Darrel. "Well, she's like... a safe space. You can go to her with anything. Stress, worries, problems... she'd probably have some practical advice." "Practical advice," Junior echoed again, tapping his chin thoughtfully. "And her physical attributes? Are we disregarding those entirely? Or does 'practical advice' outweigh... other considerations?"

Darrel flushed. He hadn't dared to think about Tiffany in that way, but now that Junior had brought it up... she was attractive. In a mature, powerful way. "She's... um... she's fit. And she carries herself with confidence.

That Southern drawl is kinda cute, too, and she's tall so she's easy to spot in a crowd." Junior nodded slowly. "Fair enough. Now, Summer."

Darrel groaned inwardly. Summer was David's third wife, a pharmacist with a sharp mind and a perpetually empathetic expression. "Summer is super smart. Super empathetic. Like, scary levels of intuitive. If you're having a bad day, she'd know before you did." "And that's a positive attribute because...?" "Because," Noah said, "she'd actually care. She'd listen without judgment and make you feel good. Plus, she's a pharmacist. Super useful in the apocalypse." Darrel added, "And, I mean, she's kinda hot. That platinum blonde hair, those captivating eyes...she's surprisingly... alluring." "Alluring," Junior repeated, a hint of amusement in his voice. "Eloquent. Now, onto Jennifer."

Darrel and Noah froze. Jennifer was... complicated. David's second wife was playful, overtly sexual, and had a tattoo collection that could rival a biker chick. She was also Junior's mom. "Look, man," Darrel said, his voice suddenly subdued, "I don't think that's a good idea. She's your mom." "Precisely," Junior said, his eyes narrowing. "I want an unbiased opinion. No holding back. What are her... assets?"

Noah cleared his throat nervously. "She's... vibrant. Full of energy. And she's got this... confidence that's really infectious. She's also really smart." Darrel shifted uncomfortably. "She's... unapologetically herself. Which is... admirable. She's also kind of a MILF." He immediately regretted the word. Junior raised an eyebrow. "MILF," he said slowly. "Explain the appeal."

Darrel felt like he was walking on eggshells. "Well, she's... experienced? She knows what she wants. And she's not afraid to get it." Junior was silent for a moment, his gaze fixed on Darrel. "And is that something you find... attractive?" Darrel blanched. "Hypothetically? Maybe. But seriously, this is getting weird." Junior finally cracked a smile. "Relax, boys. I'm just messing with you. Though, I am impressed with your assessment of my mother and my aunts... assets." Darrel chuckled. "Almost time for breakfast, right?"

As the three men walked into the main house. The aroma of frying bacon and brewing coffee wafted down the hallway. As they entered the large kitchen, Kathy and Susan were indeed cooking up a storm, their movements a well-practiced dance around the long kitchen.

But it wasn't the breakfast preparations that caught Darrel and Noah's attention. It was the sight of Tiffany, Jennifer, and Summer sitting at the dining room table, a scene of domestic tranquility that seemed impossibly... normal, given the absurdity of their reality. They were laughing, their heads tilted together as they shared some inside joke. Tiffany, ever the maternal figure, poured coffee into Jennifer's mug, while Summer sketched something on a napkin, occasionally gesturing animatedly.

Darrel nudged Noah, whispering, "Look at them. They look like... best friends." Noah nodded slowly, his brow furrowed. "I know, right? It's...weirdly wholesome."

He had always seen them as David's wives, a collection of distinct personalities orbiting a central figure. He hadn't considered the bonds they might have formed with each other, independent of their shared husband.

Junior noticed their stunned expressions and chuckled, a low rumble in his chest. "See? Told ya. They're a surprisingly tight-knit bunch. All of them. That's how Dad keeps the peace, I guess." Jennifer, ever perceptive, caught the stares. "Well, good morning, boys! Don't just stand there gawking. Come join us. Kathy and Susan have made enough for an army, haven't you, ladies?"

Kathy chirped, "More the merrier! Grab some plates and dig in." Susan, equally efficient, added, "Coffee's fresh. And there's orange juice." A little self-consciously, Noah and Darrel grabbed plates and joined them at the table. The rich smell of bacon filled the air, and Kathy piled crispy strips high on their plates, next to fluffy scrambled eggs. Noah felt decidedly out of place, a deer caught in the headlights of this domestic tableau. Darrel, ever the witty observer, just looked amused.

"So," Darrel began, his voice a little too loud, "what are we all chatting about this fine morning? Planning Dad's birthday? Strategizing world domination?" Jennifer snorted, reaching for a piece of bacon herself. "Much more scandalous than that, Darrel. We were just reminiscing about Christmases past." "Ah, Christmases," Noah chimed in, remembering what Junior told him. "I bet those are… interesting, around here."

"They are unique, that's for sure," Tiffany said, breaking the brief silence. A fond look flickered across her face. "This Christmas will be our twenty-third Christmas since we've been together as a family." Darrel perked up, his eyes gleaming with mischievous curiosity. "Twenty-three years! Wow, that's... dedication. So, what's the most memorable Christmas you've all had? Spill the beans!"

Summer chuckled, a warm, comforting sound. "Oh, there are so many. But I think our very first Christmas together maybe takes the cake." She glanced at Tiffany and Jennifer, a shared smile passing between them. "Remember we were living in California?" Summer had finished her reserve contract and just finished college. She drove all the way from Texas and moved in immediately.

Jennifer took a sip of her coffee, a playful glint in her eyes. "Oh, California... that was a trip. We just met Elena too." Darrel leaned forward, practically vibrating with anticipation. "Okay, okay, you're burying the lede! What happened in California? Was there mistletoe-related drama? Did someone try to deep-fry the Christmas tree?"

"Nothing quite that dramatic," Tiffany said, chuckling. "But it was definitely... unexpected. Summer decided to gift us something rather...meaningful." Noah shifted uncomfortably. He remembered the rumors of David's past, the unconventional beginnings, the... everything. He glanced towards the hallway, hoping David wouldn't walk in right then. He wasn't sure he was ready for a full explanation of Dad's romantic history.

"I had just moved in. It was a whirlwind, getting settled and trying to figure out where I fit," Summer began, her voice softening. "I didn't have a lot of money, and I felt like I needed to give them both something. Something... personal." Jennifer grinned, her eyes sparkling with amusement. "And she did. She really, really did."

Summer sighed dramatically. "I decided to paint portraits. Of all of us. As a family. I know, I know, it sounds... quaint now. But back then, it felt like the best way to capture us." Darrel's eyes widened. "Wait, you painted everyone? Like, Renaissance-style?" Jennifer laughed. "Not quite Renaissance. More like... early-2000s-slightly-awkward-art-school-project."

"Oh, they were definitely awkward," Summer admitted, blushing slightly. "I was still learning! But I poured my heart into them. There was individual portraits, of course. And then... the group one." "The group one?" Noah squeaked, his voice cracking slightly. He could only imagine what that looked like.

Tiffany chuckled. "Oh, the group one was special. Summer, bless her heart, decided to immortalize a specific moment in our... relationship. A moment that perfectly encapsulated the era, and our collective fashion choices."

Darrel, piecing things together, snapped his fingers. "Wait a minute! Junior mentioned something about a prom portrait! Is that...?" He trailed off, his eyes darting back and forth between the three women.

Darrel, on the edge of his seat, clasped his hands together. "Please, please, please tell me that's it! The legendary prom portrait! I've heard whispers, rumors... Junior says it's famous!" He practically vibrated with anticipation. Noah, equally intrigued, leaned in, nudging Darrel for a better view. Summer giggled, covering her mouth with her hand. "Oh, it's definitely... a statement piece." Tiffany just smiled knowingly. "Let's just say, it perfectly captures who we were back then."

Before anyone could fully elaborate, Jennifer, propelled by a mischievous grin, sprang from her chair. "Alright, alright, enough teasing! Let's give the boys what they want! Tiffany, where's the infamous artwork residing these days?" Tiffany pointed towards the hallway. "Last I checked, it was still hanging in our room. Right above the... uh... well, never mind. Just go get it, Jen." A faint blush crept up her neck.

Jennifer positively bounced out of the room, her laughter echoing in the hallway. "Don't worry, boys, you're in for a treat! Prepare to be amazed... or horrified!" Seconds stretched into an eternity as Darrel and Noah waited, their eyes glued to the entrance. Finally, Jennifer reappeared, struggling slightly to hold a large object. And there it was.

Darrel's jaw dropped. "Oh... my... God." He stared at the painting, eyes wide with disbelief and amusement. Noah was equally speechless, his mouth agape. "This... this is... unbelievable." "We told you!" Summer said, still giggling. Jennifer, beaming with pride, propped the painting against the wall so everyone could get a good look. "See? We weren't kidding. It's a masterpiece of teenage angst and questionable fashion choices!" She winked.

Tiffany, despite her initial embarrassment, seemed to be enjoying the boys' reactions. She strolled closer to the painting, studying it with a nostalgic fondness. "It's funny, looking back. We thought we were so sophisticated." She pointed to her red dress. "I remember spending weeks trying to find the perfect shade of crimson."

Summer chuckled. "And I thought silver was the epitome of elegance. I nearly blinded myself with glitter that night." She playfully swatted at the painting. "David, on the other hand, looked like he was being held hostage." Darrel burst out laughing. "He does! He looks like he's calculating the optimal escape route!" He scrutinized David's stoic expression. "Seriously, what was going through his head?"

Summer stopped chuckling, her eyes suddenly clouding over with a film of unshed tears. She walked closer to the painting, her fingers tracing the outline of David's face. "He… he wasn't happy that night," she said, her voice catching in her throat. "He wasn't unhappy either, but he was… preoccupied. Distant." Jennifer, noticing Summer's sudden shift in mood, gently placed a hand on her arm. "Summer, honey, what's wrong?"

Summer shook her head, trying to blink back the tears. "It's just… I think I know what he was thinking that night. I didn't understand it then, not really. But now…" She trailed off, her gaze fixed on David's younger self. He looked like a completely different person, yet the core of him, the intensity in his blue eyes, was unmistakable. "He was thinking about this," Summer finally whispered. "He was thinking about protecting us. All of us. From… from this. An apocalypse that wouldn't happen for another twenty-nine years."

Chapter 44:

Project Baby Boom

The gradual illumination of a seemingly warm Texas countryside displayed on the window as Junior jolted awake. Not from the sun, though, and definitely not from the gentle caress of the late afternoon. Olivia was riding him, her dark hair a curtain around his face, and her lips were very, very busy. "Morning, sleepyhead," she purred, pulling back just enough for him to catch his breath. Her eyes sparkled, hinting at the playful storm brewing within.

Junior groaned, a sound that was equal parts protest and pure, unadulterated appreciation. "Liv, it's... early-ish. And Riley's still asleep." Olivia, unfazed, simply grinned wider, pressing herself closer. "Riley's in the shower. Plenty of time to make you forget all about our secret Christmas operation." She lowered her voice, a sultry whisper that sent shivers down his spine. "Suck on my tits," she breathed, a playful command that needed no further explanation.

Any further protest died in his throat, replaced by a pleased moan as he eagerly complied. The rhythmic sounds of the shower provided a surprisingly effective sound barrier, though Junior couldn't help but feel a little guilty. Christmas spirit definitely took a backseat as Olivia expertly steered him, her playful mood infectious. "Oh, Junior," she gasped, her grip tightening on his shoulders.

"You know I cum harder when you suck on my tits like that." He grunted in response, wholly focused on the task at hand.

A few minutes later, Riley emerged from the bathroom, a towel wrapped around her fiery hair. The apartment suddenly felt much smaller. She raised a curious eyebrow at the scene before her. "Well, good morning to me," she drawled, a hint of amusement coloring her voice. "You two starting the day off with a bang, I see." Olivia, still straddling Junior, just giggled. "Riley! Perfect timing. Come join the fun." She wriggled suggestively, her eyes dancing with mischief. Junior, still slightly dazed and thoroughly enjoying himself, could only manage a weak, "Morning, Ri."

Riley strolled over, casually dropping her towel to the floor. Her body was lean and tone, honed by the same demanding training regimen as Olivia and the rest of their crew. She perched on the edge of the bed, close enough to reach out and run a hand through Junior's hair. "So, Junior," she began, her voice deceptively casual, "now that you're… occupied… I've been thinking. Strategic planning is kinda your thing, right?" She leaned in closer, her breath warm against his ear. "What strategic plans do you have for us? For us three?"

Junior groaned again, this time a mix of pleasure and exasperation. He glanced up at Riley, trying to decipher her expression. Was this a serious conversation he was about to have while being shamelessly ridden by Olivia? Only in the apocalypse. And only with Riley. "Strategic…

plans?" he stammered, his brain struggling to shift gears. "Well, I haven't exactly written up a five-year plan for our love life, Ri. We're just... living, surviving, having fun."

Olivia let out a playful smack on his chest. "He's got a point, Ri. We're all alive, we're together, and he's really good with his mouth. What more could a girl want?" Riley wasn't deterred. She crossed her arms, her emerald eyes narrowed. "Alright, alright, I get the living-in-the-moment thing. But come on, Junior. You're always ten steps ahead with everything else. You're orchestrating a Christmas operation so secret, Santa doesn't see it coming, but you don't have any grand design for us?" She paused for effect, then dropped the bomb. "Are we talking lieutenants? Housewives? Breeders? What's the long game here, Commander?"

Junior groaned, a genuine sound of overwhelmed bewilderment. He loved these women, he truly did. But sometimes, their tenacity was... a lot to handle, especially mid-afternoon delight. He closed his eyes for a moment, trying to gather his thoughts. The Christmas surprise for everyone had consumed his thoughts, everything had been going smoothly until this moment. "Okay, okay, hold on," he said, finally finding his voice. He gently disengaged from Olivia, sitting up and pulling her tight into his lap. He reached out and took Riley's hand, pulling her closer as well. "First of all, you're both amazing. I love spending time with you, and I can't imagine my life without you. But... this is a little intense. I mean, do you really expect me to have a strategic plan for us?"

He looked at each of them in turn, searching for any sign of sarcasm or hidden agenda. Riley's expression was unreadable, Olivia's was playful but with a hint of genuine curiosity. He took a deep breath. "Because if I'm being honest, my brain does work that way. I strategize everything. Survival, security, resource management… relationships. It's just how I'm wired." He paused, a nervous flutter in his stomach. "Would you… be offended if I actually did have something of a plan? Even if it was just in the back of my head?"

Riley's lips quirked into a small smile. "Offended? Junior, honey, we'd be disappointed if you didn't have a plan. You're you. David's blood runs heavy in your veins. The man plans what everyone is going to be eating for the next ten years." Olivia nodded in agreement, nuzzling into his neck. "Yeah, seriously. We'd think you were sick or something if you weren't plotting world domination… or at least, our little corner of it."

Junior stared at them, genuinely surprised. He had braced himself for accusations of being controlling or unromantic. He never expected this. "Okay… well, in that case," he began, a slow smile spreading across his face. "This could take hours, girls." Riley grinned. "We have time. Besides, knowing the plan means we get to tweak it, right? Because I have some ideas." Olivia purred, wrapping her arms around Junior's waist and resting her chin on his chest. "Yeah, consider this a collaborative project. Junior's initial framework, and then the Riley and Olivia Amendments."

Junior laughed, shaking his head. "Alright, alright. First, the core principle: happiness. For all three of us. If anyone's unhappy, the plan gets scrapped and redesigned. No compromises there." He paused, gathering his thoughts. "Secondly, sustainability. This isn't a fling. We're building something lasting, something… well, something apocalypse-proof." He winked. "Which means we need to think about the long game. Resources, shared responsibilities, personal growth, and… yeah, kids. Logistics are huge. We're talking about raising children in a world without doctors, schools, or, like, diapers. Not to mention… the gene." He gestured vaguely. "David's little… gift. We don't know how it'll manifest, or when, or even if it will manifest.

Take Alissa for example." He looked pensive. "She's due next month. I want to see how Baby Tyler is affected before we even think about adding to the population… on my end, anyway." He sighed. "Which, brings me to my secret agenda." Riley perked up. "Ooh, a secret agenda! Spill." "Let's call it… Project Baby Boom," Junior smirked, a glint in his eye. "Okay, hear me out. We have resources, we have manpower, and we have… unique genetic potential. If Baby Tyler shows signs of inheriting David's… aptitude… well, let's just say I think you two would be excellent candidates for motherhood. Especially at this point in life, with the resources that we have available."

Riley stared at him, speechless for a moment. "You… you want to manufacture super-babies? Like, genetically engineered apocalypse warriors?" "Not engineer," Junior corrected. "More like… strategically cultivate. Think of it as… selective breeding. But with love and consent!" He winced. "That sounded terrible, didn't it? Look, the point is, we have a chance to give our children an edge, a fighting chance in this messed-up world. And if we can do that, shouldn't we?"

Riley stared at Junior, her jaw slightly ajar. "Strategically cultivate? Junior, you're talking about us like we're prize-winning cattle! With love and consent, of course!" She rolled her eyes playfully, but a thoughtful frown quickly replaced the amusement. "Okay, putting the slightly terrifying implications aside… Are you saying that if Alissa's kid suddenly starts speaking fluent Spanish at six months, we're officially on the baby-making schedule?"

Olivia giggled, nestling closer to Junior. "Fluent Spanish and can point to any country on a map. Then we know he's truly one of David's." She looked at Junior, her expression softening. "I get what you're saying, though. This world is a crapshoot. If we can give our kids any kind of advantage… it's worth considering."

Junior sighed, relieved they weren't completely horrified. "Look, it's not just about superpowers and foreign languages. It's about resilience, adaptability, the ability to think strategically. These are the traits we need to survive, to rebuild. And if David's… gift… passes those on, then yeah, I think we have a responsibility to see what happens. But," he added quickly, "it's a huge decision. And I wouldn't dream of pressuring either of you." He kissed

Olivia's forehead and then Riley's temple. "This only works if we're all in, and it has to be because we want to."

Riley chewed on her lip. "It's a lot to think about. I mean, I always imagined having kids someday, but… someday was a hazy notion involving electricity, online shopping, and play dates." She glanced at Olivia, a mixture of apprehension and excitement in her eyes. Olivia nodded, her gaze meeting Riley's. "Things are a little different now, huh? Still… the idea of raising a little badass with you two… I wouldn't hate it. But, Junior," she turned back to him, her voice serious. "This isn't just about making mini-soldiers. If we do this, we do it for the right reasons. We do it because we want to give a child love, guidance, and the best possible chance in this crazy world."

Junior's heart swelled. He gently took both of their faces in his hands, looked deep into their eyes, and kissed them deeply. "Of course. It's about love. It's about building a future, together." He paused, thinking of his larger, unspoken concerns. He continued, "And it's not just about building a family. In the long run… well, let's just say, we can't stay here forever. We might eventually have to leave the ranch. The ranch is a great starting point, but it's dependent on David, dependent on this valley. What happens when it's not enough anymore? When resources dwindle? When we outgrow it?"

Riley frowned. "Leave? Where would we even go? We're relatively safe here." "Exactly," Junior said, "we're safe now. But we can't be complacent. I want us to be prepared for anything. Think of Jacob returning to Canaan.

He left for a while, built strength and resources, and then went back, ready to face whatever challenges lay ahead. That's what we're doing now. Soon, we'll have to return to the world."

Olivia nodded slowly, understanding dawning in her eyes. "So, the 'Project Baby Boom' isn't just about creating super-babies. It's about creating a self-sufficient, adaptable family unit that can thrive anywhere." "Precisely," Junior confirmed, a relieved smile spreading across his face. "And that's why I need you both by my side, always. Not just as lovers, but as partners. I need you to anticipate my orders, to understand my strategies, to be able to step up and lead when necessary. We need to be a well-oiled machine, a force to be reckoned with." He squeezed their hands. "This isn't a request, it's an observation. You're both already so perfect for the role."

Junior's words hung in the air, a mixture of ambition and genuine affection. He watched as Riley's expression shifted, a mischievous glint replacing her frown. Olivia, ever the strategist, simply nodded, her eyes already calculating the implications of Junior's vision. He knew he had chosen well. "I have an idea," Riley announced, a playful smirk dancing on her lips. "We've heard all about these…enhanced babies. But we haven't actually seen anything, have we? I mean, Poppy's been quiet as a mouse. Let's see what this whole 'genetically superior infant' thing is all about."

Olivia raised an eyebrow. "You want to…test Poppy? What exactly did you have in mind?" "Not test, observe! David's babies are all unusually strong, intelligent, tactically skilled, proficient with weapons, disciplined, friendly, proficient in hand to hand combat, multilingual, and possess his regressive experience." Riley was already bouncing on the balls of her feet with excitement. "So, you know, we gotta' see what that looks like on a baby."

Junior chuckled. "I think Jessica might object to us conducting experiments on her newborn daughter. Especially if those experiments involve weaponry." "Who said anything about weapons?" Riley protested, feigning innocence. "Maybe we just…see how quickly she learns a new language. Or how well she can stack blocks!"

"Hold that thought, Riley," Olivia purred, her gaze locking onto Junior's. She shifted, straddling him once again, her hands tracing the contours of his chest. "Business later, pleasure first. We weren't exactly finished, were we?" Junior, caught between Riley's mischievous energy and Olivia's undeniable magnetism, grinned. "Definitely not finished," he agreed, his hands moving to cup Olivia's hips.

He glanced at Riley, who was now leaning against the doorframe, a picture of amused impatience. "You gonna join us, Ri? Or are you just gonna watch us test my endurance?" Riley let out a throaty laugh. "Don't mind if I do," she drawled, pushing herself off the doorframe and sauntering towards the bed. "But don't think this delays the Poppy Project. We're observing that baby one way or another."

A few steamy, satisfying minutes later, with Riley and Olivia thoroughly sated and Junior feeling thoroughly appreciated, the trio finally disentangled themselves from the sheets. "Okay, Poppy Project it is," Junior conceded, wiping a bead of sweat from his forehead. "But we're doing this subtly. No scaring Jessica, and absolutely no giving a newborn a loaded firearm."

Olivia chimed in, her voice a low purr. "Imagine, Ri! A baby genius already plotting world domination... or at least dismantling the family toaster." She nipped at Junior's neck, making him shudder slightly. "Think of the possibilities, Junior. The data." He chuckled, running a hand through her hair. "Okay, okay, I get it. You're fascinated by the... quirks of my family." He sighed. "But you have to understand, Poppy's only three months old. Human babies, gifted or not, are basically useless for the first few months. She probably can't even hold her head up straight yet. You're picturing some kind of miniature, weapon-wielding prodigy. It doesn't work like that."

Riley frowned. "So, what? She's just... a normal baby?" "Not normal," Junior corrected, defensively. "She's...potentially advanced. But it's more subtle at this age. Increased awareness, maybe. Faster reflexes. A quicker learning curve. Basically, think of it as starting with a slightly higher base stat in... well, everything. But at three months, she is still a baby." Olivia slid off Junior, grabbing a stray shirt from the floor and pulling it over her head. "So, how do we 'observe' this subtle advancement? Are we timing her drool production?"

With a final check in the mirror, Junior led Olivia and Riley out of their apartment and into the somewhat labyrinthine corridors of the underground bunkers. "Christmas light hanging is still on, right?" Olivia asked, linking her arm through Junior's. "Absolutely," Junior confirmed. "Caleb and Sophia are already working on the invitations. I just hope we can pull this off without the kids suspecting anything. As they passed the entrance to the recreational bunker, a rhythmic thwacking sound caught their attention. Junior stopped, tilting his head. "What's that?"

He peered inside, and his eyebrows shot up. Seth was standing, facing one wall, a focused expression on his face. He was throwing three rubber balls at the wall, one after another, at an almost impossible speed. Each ball bounced back, and he caught it effortlessly before immediately launching it back at the wall. It was like watching some kind of miniature juggling machine.

"Whoa," Riley breathed, impressed. "Talk about hand-eye coordination. He's like a mini-ninja." Olivia nodded. "Definitely David's brain in kid form. Makes you wonder what Poppy's superpower will be." Junior watched Seth for a moment longer, a thoughtful expression on his face. "You know, I remember dad making up games for us that would test our strength and hand-eye coordination. Fun times."

Olivia, ever the instigator, seized the opportunity. "Ooh, tell us more! And more importantly," she leaned closer, her voice dropping to a suggestive whisper, "show us. I bet you're still pretty good at those… 'exercises'." She punctuated her words with a playful nudge. Riley snorted, but her eyes sparkled with amusement. "Yeah, Junior, show us what you've got. You can't just brag about your childhood training and leave us hanging."

Junior playfully rolled his eyes, trying to maintain a semblance of seriousness. "Come on, guys, we have things to do. And besides, I don't know, Seth is right there. I don't want to interrupt him." But before he could fully protest, a voice piped up. "I don't mind," Seth said, holding all three rubber balls in his right hand, his face a mask of calm concentration. "It never hurts to see if you still got it?"

Riley blinked, surprised. "You heard all that?" Seth shrugged. "Sound travels in enclosed spaces. Besides," a hint of a smile flickered across his lips, "I was concentrating on catching the balls so fast, I had to focus on the sounds nearby, to know when to expect the bounce." Olivia and Riley exchanged impressed glances. This kid was sharp.

"Alright, alright," Junior relented, a grin returning to his face. "I guess a quick demonstration wouldn't hurt, would it? Besides, it's a good way to gauge Seth's… progress." He winked at Olivia and Riley. "Okay Seth, stand back a bit and watch. I'll show you what your old man taught me."

Junior grinned, retrieving two steel batons from the wall-mounted rack. They were training batons, replicas of the ones used by his father, David, during his rigorous training regime. He handed one to Olivia, then another to

Riley. Both women gasped, their eyes widening as they struggled to maintain their grip. "Whoa!" Olivia exclaimed, staggering slightly. "These things are heavy! What are they made of, lead?"

Riley grunted, adjusting her stance. "Seriously. I thought you said these were for kids!" Junior chuckled, taking back each baton. "They're steel. We build our children strong around here. That includes training them to handle this kind of weight. It's all about building strength and control. And by the way, these are for kids."

Junior grinned, the batons a comfortable weight in his hands. He felt the familiar surge of focus, the world narrowing to the point of the batons and the wall. "Alright, ladies, watch closely. This is all about rhythm and anticipation." He took the three rubber balls, each a vibrant red, contrasting against the black padded tile floor of the rec bunker. He placed them carefully in a line, a few feet away from him.

Olivia watched with a mixture of amusement and genuine interest, however, Riley, still seemed skeptical. "So, you're gonna... juggle these with those things?" "Something like that," Junior replied, his eyes already fixed on the task at hand. He took a deep breath, centering himself. He bent slightly at the knees, his posture relaxed but alert, like a coiled spring ready to unleash.

Then, with a swift, almost casual motion, he kicked the first ball towards the wall. Thwack! The ball bounced back, and in a fluid motion, Junior intercepted it with the baton. The impact resonated up his arm, a satisfying thud.

He didn't stop there. He immediately kicked the second ball, then the third, each one rebounding off the wall with increasing speed.

Within seconds, a chaotic ballet of red balls and steel was in motion. Junior, a blur of coordinated movement, was intercepting, redirecting, and controlling all three balls simultaneously. The batons flashed, a rhythmic tap-tap-tap accompanying the thwack-thwack-thwack of the balls against the concrete.

Olivia gasped, her initial amusement replaced with genuine awe. "Holy crap, Junior! You're like a machine!" Riley, equally impressed, simply stared, her jaw slightly agape. "I... I don't even understand how that's possible." Seth, however, was glued to the performance, his eyes focused. He tracked each ball's trajectory, his brow furrowed in concentration. He seemed to be dissecting the entire process, absorbing every nuance of Junior's technique.

The speed was mesmerizing. The balls, mere blurs, zipped back and forth, a testament to Junior's reflexes and precision. The sound was a constant, rhythmic percussion that filled the void like a rubber machine gun sounding off. For Junior, it was like slipping into a familiar groove. The world faded away, leaving only the dance between himself, the batons, and the balls. He felt the satisfying burn in his muscles, the heightened awareness, the almost meditative state that came with mastering a complex physical skill. It was a connection to his father, to the rigorous training that had shaped him into the man he was today.

He couldn't resist adding a touch of flair, a signature flourish just for his own amusement. He bounced one of the balls off a nearby pillar before intercepting it back towards the wall, then spun the baton in his hand between catches. The whole performance was a controlled explosion of energy and precision, a display of skill honed over years of dedication.

Finally, with a final flourish, he stopped the balls with his feet, bringing the rhythmic percussion to an abrupt halt. He lowered the batons, a grin plastered across his face. "Alright, alright," Junior said, breathing a little heavier from the exertion. He bent down, scooped up the rubber balls, tossed them in the air, and caught them all in one swift motion. "Just a little something to keep the reflexes sharp. Pop quiz, Seth." He tossed a ball to the boy. "What was the critical element that allowed me to control the chaos?"

Seth caught the ball with ease, his eyes still focused on the afterimage of the performance. "Prediction. You weren't reacting, you were anticipating. You knew where the balls were going before they even got there, adjusting your movements to intercept them." Junior snapped his fingers, pointing at Seth with the baton. "Bingo! That, and a whole lotta practice." He clapped his hands together. "Alright, enough showboating. Olivia, Riley, we gotta roll." He glanced at his watch. "Poppy's genetic evaluation awaits."

Olivia, who had been leaning against one of the exercise machines, watching Junior's display with rapt attention, straightened up. "Right, right. Poppy. The tiny, super-powered overlord in training." She pushed off the machine and walked towards Riley, who had been standing stock still the whole time, seemingly hypnotized.

Riley, still slightly flushed, blinked rapidly. "Huh? Oh, yeah. The…baby." She cleared her throat, her voice a little higher than usual. "So, genetic…stuff. Very important." As they walked towards the stairs, Riley leaned into Olivia, whispering conspiratorially, "Oh god, I am so wet right now."

The upper living room was currently occupied by Jessica and the object of their scrutiny: Poppy. Jessica was sprawled on a plush rug, radiating a relaxed ease, while Poppy, a tiny bundle of humanity, was lying on her stomach, gurgling happily as she batted at Lucipurr's tail. The cat, seemingly unfazed by the miniature assault, flicked its tail back and forth with an air of bored amusement.

Junior surveyed the scene, a fond smile growing on his lips. "Looks like everything's…normal." He glanced at Olivia and Riley, his smile faltering slightly at their less-than-enthusiastic expressions. He could practically see the internal struggle playing out on their faces. "Alright, Jessica," Junior began, carefully phrasing his request. "Olivia and Riley here have been… uh… particularly interested in Poppy's development. They were hoping they could… observe her for a bit? Play with her, maybe?" He shot them a pleading look, hoping they understood the silent message: For the love of all that is holy, act normal!

Jessica, who was easily the most perceptive of David's wives when it came to emotional undercurrents, raised an eyebrow. Her gaze flicked between the three of them, lingering a moment on Riley's slightly manic grin. "Observe, huh? Like a tiny, adorable science experiment?" "Something like that!" Olivia chirped, perhaps a bit too enthusiastically. "Just, you know, seeing how she interacts with things. Standard baby stuff!" She gave a thumbs-up that could be described as anywhere from earnest to mildly terrifying.

Riley, clearly struggling to maintain composure, simply nodded, her eyes fixated on Poppy. "Yes. Interactions. Very important. For…science." Jessica chuckled, the sound light and melodic. "Alright, alright, you two crackpots. Just... be gentle. And try not to break her. I'm going to grab a drink from the kitchen. Shout if she levitates or starts speaking ancient Sumerian." She rose gracefully and sashayed towards the kitchen, leaving Junior, Olivia, and Riley alone with their tiny subject.

As soon as Jessica was out of earshot, Junior dropped to his knees beside Poppy. He quickly scanned the room, ensuring they were truly alone. Then, with a swift, practiced motion, he sat Poppy upright, supporting her with his large hands. Leaning down, he lowered his voice, and spoke clearly, "Poppy, your momma's in the kitchen. It's just us now," he murmured, his deep voice a stark contrast to the high-pitched baby babble that usually filled the room.

Poppy, perched precariously but seemingly unfazed, blinked her wide, innocent eyes. Then, slowly, she turned her head and looked directly at Junior, her gaze unwavering. Olivia, who had been bustling around fetching a colorful rattle, froze mid-shake, her movements suspended in mid-air. Riley, who was meticulously arranging a collection of soft toys, stopped her inspection, her carefully constructed tableau abandoned. "Did… did she just?" Olivia whispered, her chirpy demeanor instantly deflating. "She just heard me talking, not a big deal," Junior said, dismissively, though a flicker of surprise danced in his own eyes. "Poppy, do you want anything?" He watched her carefully, his senses on high alert.

Poppy's eyes, wide and impossibly blue, roamed the room. They drifted over the colorful toys, the plush blankets, and finally settled… on the floor. Olivia gasped, hand flying to her mouth. "She wants... the rug?" Riley burst out laughing, the tension momentarily broken. "Oh my god, she's got expensive taste already! Just like her daddy." Junior, however, wasn't laughing. He scowled at Riley. "Shut up you two, she doesn't want the rug. She wants something she can't see, but she can't say it yet." He leaned closer to Poppy again, lowering his voice. "Poppy, do you want something to drink?"

Poppy looked directly at Junior, her eyes unwavering, seemingly focused and knowing. He paused, contemplating her intent gaze, searching for any clue, any hint of understanding. Then, a flicker of recognition crossed his face. He reached behind him, grabbing her bottle and offered it to her.

With a surprising level of coordination for a three-month-old, Poppy grasped the bottle with one hand, tilting it expertly as she began to drink contentedly, her tiny hands gripping the plastic with surprising strength. He glanced at Olivia and Riley, who were staring with rapt attention, their mouths slightly agape. "Formula or breastmilk?" he asked, almost as an afterthought.

Poppy, mid-suckle, suddenly started giggling, a sound like tiny bells chiming. Olivia and Riley responded simultaneously, a chorus of slightly awestruck voices: "Breastmilk." "Right, breastmilk it is," Junior muttered, a hint of amusement creeping into his voice. Just then, Jessica walked back into the room, a glass of water in her hand. "What's all the commotion? Is my little angel okay?"

Junior nodded, trying to project an air of nonchalance. "She's fine, we were just talking." He then looked at Olivia, then Riley, silently willing them to play along. "We were just… admiring how smart she is! At three months! Look at how she holds her bottle," Olivia said, excitedly, her earlier trepidation seemingly forgotten. Riley eagerly added, "Yeah, it's amazing! And we were wondering whose breastmilk she was on." Jessica, however, wasn't convinced. Her eyes narrowed slightly, a hint of suspicion in her gaze. "Whose breastmilk? What does that even mean? She gets my milk, of course. Why would you ask such a weird question?"

Junior coughed, suddenly finding the intricate patterns on the wall fascinating. "Alright you little munchkin, I'm going to get back to work, but I'll be back later to find out what you want for Christmas, okay?" He offered a playful, if slightly desperate, smile. Poppy, perched precariously but seemingly unfazed, simply lifted her arm toward Junior, then dropped it, unceremoniously. Junior took that as his cue to escape. "Alright you two, let's head out. We have a lot of work to do tonight, and not a big window to get it done." He ushered Olivia and Riley toward the stairs, shooting them a pointed look as they passed.

Chapter 45:

Junior's Christmas Elves

The pre-dawn chill nipped at Tiffany's feet as she padded out of her bedroom. 35 degrees was practically arctic for Central Texas, even in December. She tugged her thick, hand-knitted robe tighter, despite the toasty temperature of their home. As a habit she peeked in on David, who was still asleep, balled up in the fetal position. She silently continued to the kitchen, hoping for a quick cup of coffee.

What greeted her wasn't the familiar quiet of a pre-dawn kitchen, but a scene straight out of a Hallmark movie, albeit one that had been run through a tactical assault course. The house, usually meticulously organized, was now draped in garlands, twinkling lights, and enough tinsel to blind a reindeer. In the lower living room, she could see a fully stocked letter-writing station, complete with quills, ink, and enough parchment to declare war on a small forest.

And in the middle of the kitchen, Noah, looking impossibly young in an apron that read "This guy rubs his own meat," was stacking French toast in a long pan, while Sophia quietly arranged a plate of perfectly cooked sausage. "Good morning, Tiffany!" Noah chirped, his voice surprisingly cheerful for six in the morning. "Merry

Christmas! Or, almost Christmas. We thought we'd, uh, get a head start."

Tiffany blinked, trying to process the sudden onslaught of holiday cheer. "Merry...almost Christmas? What in the Sam Hill is going on?" Before Noah could stammer out an explanation, Nicole wandered into the kitchen, rubbing sleep from her eyes. Her jaw dropped as she took in the scene. "Did...did the elves come?" she mumbled, clearly still half-asleep.

Jessica, ever the sassy one, strolled in next. She took one look at the Christmas explosion and raised a skeptical eyebrow. "Okay, who raided the storage bunker for decorations? And more importantly, who's cleaning this up?" "It was Junior's idea, and we thought it would be good for the kids! Please don't tell them, he has a whole plan. Plus, we thought it would be a nice surprise!"

Tiffany, momentarily stunned by the festive ambush, felt a warmth spread through her chest. Despite the apocalypse raging outside, despite the constant vigilance needed to maintain their sanctuary, here, inside these decorated walls, was a spark of normalcy, a defiant refusal to let the darkness consume them. Junior, that resourceful, endlessly surprising young man, had orchestrated this. And for the kids? It was perfect.

"Don't you dare tell them to stop!" Tiffany declared, her voice a low, almost conspiratorial whisper. "This is...this is wonderful. Absolutely bonkers, but wonderful. Come on, we need to get everyone up. David needs to see this." A mischievous glint entered her eyes.

"And the rest of the wives need to experience the full force of Junior's Christmas cheer."

She practically bounced out of the kitchen, leaving a bewildered Noah and Sophia in her wake. Nicole, still blinking owlishly, managed a small smile. "Well," she murmured, "at least it's...bright." Jessica, however, remained unconvinced. "I still want to know who's cleaning up the glitter." Tiffany moved with a swiftness, heading straight for the master bedroom. "David," she whispered, gently shaking his shoulder. "Wake up, my love. You won't believe what's happening."

David stirred, his eyes fluttering open. He glanced at Tiffany, his gaze filled with affection, and then his eyes looked up at the window, which was reflecting the Christmas lights from outside. "What is…" He paused, his mind still struggling to catch up. Then he sat up, looking at Tiffany with a raised eyebrow. "Why does our house look like Santa threw up on it?" "The house, David! The whole house!" Tiffany exclaimed, unable to contain her excitement. "Junior and his little band of merry elves have gone full Christmas. You have to see it to believe it."

Tiffany's enthusiasm was infectious, and soon, a sleepy but curious David was being led out of the master bedroom, his arm draped around her shoulders. As they stepped into the hallway, the full impact of Junior's festive rampage hit him. Garlands draped from the ceiling, lights blinked merrily, and a massive Christmas tree stood proudly in the center of the main living room, adorned with an eclectic mix of ornaments. David stopped dead in his tracks, his mouth stuck. "Good Lord," he murmured, a mixture of bewilderment and amusement swirling in his eyes. "Did we accidentally stumble into a Hallmark movie?"

The rest of the wives were already congregating in the living room, their faces mirroring David's, a blend of stunned disbelief and grudging affection. "I told you!" Tiffany exclaimed, beaming. "Bonkers, right?" Jennifer, recovering quickly, approached David. "Master," she purred, a playful smile dancing on her lips, "our son did this, with his little helpers."

Just then, Sophia, her cheeks flushed from cooking, scurried over to Jessica, the scent of sausage and eggs wafting behind her. "Mrs. Jessica," she said quietly, "we were told strictly not to use glitter. Tinsel was our limit." Jessica's eyebrows shot up. "Tinsel, huh? Well, that's... marginally better." She glanced around again, a glint of mischief in her eyes. "But, still, someone is going to tell me how they managed to get all of this up without waking a single soul." She paused, then pointed at David who looked as though a herd of reindeer had trampled his brain. "Including him." She smirked. "And who gave Junior the okay for this level of...festive explosion?"

David, finally finding his voice, chuckled. "Festive explosion is putting it mildly, Jessica. It's... audacious. But I have to admit, it's also... surprisingly heartwarming." He squeezed Tiffany's shoulder. "I honestly had no idea Junior was planning something this... severe." Taylor waddled over to the letter-writing station set up in the lower living room. She pointed to it with a questioning look. "Tiffany? Do you think... we could write letters too? It looks so... inviting."

Tiffany's face softened. "Of course, Taylor! It wouldn't hurt. Plus, I'd like to see what kind of schemes the boy has planned." She wrapped an arm around Taylor's shoulder and led her toward the letter station, her eyes sparkling with curiosity. As they approached the table, Tiffany noticed the little mail drop box beside it, adorned with a crudely drawn picture of Santa Claus. She chuckled. "Oh, he's good. This is too good." Taylor clapped her hands together, her face alight with excitement. "Oh, this is wonderful! We should get all the children involved, and even little Poppy! Everyone should write a letter! This is the most fun I've had in ages!" She began to turn towards the hallway, ready to round up the children.

Meanwhile, Noah and Sophia were smiling from the kitchen, listening as the others gushed over their holiday setup. Noah nudged Sophia playfully with his elbow. "Think they like it?" he whispered. Sophia blushed, her eyes shining. "Admittedly, even with the apocalypse… well, this is the most exciting thing I've ever done." The quiet girl, usually content to blend into the background, was practically radiating joy. Noah grinned, the early morning light catching the mischievous glint in his eyes. "Just wait 'til they see what else we got planned. They don't even know about the snow, the presents, or the rest of it. Everything here is just a set-up for the real Christmas."

Jessica pursed her lips, watching Taylor bounce with enthusiasm. "Okay, okay, calm down, preggo! We don't need you going into labor over a Santa letter. Good idea, though. But let's find out how this happened first. This level of… coordinated cheer requires answers." She pointed a warning finger at the kitchen. "And I have a feeling our breakfast chefs know more than they're letting on."

Jessica, still unconvinced that her beloved hot chocolate was safe from festive tampering, cautiously sipped her mug. "So," she began, her voice laced with suspicion, "are we just going to pretend that this didn't happen? That a bunch of twenty-somethings didn't turn our fortress into Santa's workshop while we were sleeping?" She gestured dramatically with her mug, nearly sloshing hot chocolate onto the meticulously decorated tree.

David, sensing Jessica's determination, wrapped his arms around her. "Don't try to expose their plans just yet, Baby girl. Any confrontation may actually backfire. We don't want to defuse their motivations." He whispered softly. Jessica huffed, relenting slightly. "Fine, fine. Appreciate the effort. But if I find out someone put eggnog in my hot chocolate, there will be consequences." She shot a playful glare towards the kitchen. "Big consequences." She helped herself to a plate of scrambled eggs and sausage, carefully inspecting them for any rogue sprinkles or candy canes.

David chuckled again, patting her arm. "You're safe, sweetheart. They know better than to mess with your food." He turned to Summer, who was standing beside him, her eyes sparkling with delight. "What do you think, Summer? Is this up to your…standards?" Summer smiled warmly, stirring her coffee with a candy cane. "It's…unexpected, David. But wonderfully so. It's exactly the kind of joy we needed, I think." She squeezed his hand, her voice laced with gratitude. "We have to thank Junior and the others, for reminding us what we're fighting for."

As the wives and David continued to marvel at the decorations and discuss the surprise, Grace, side by side with Seth, entered the living room, their eyes wide with wonder. Grace spoke with a hint of bewilderment. "This is…a lot. Did we sleep through Christmas morning?" Seth, on the other hand, was beaming. His eyes darted around the room, taking in every detail of the festive display. "Whoa! This is awesome! I knew Junior and them were up to something, but I didn't think it would be this cool!" He eagerly pointed to the mistletoe in the doorway. "Look, Grace! Look!" Grace rolled her eyes playfully but blushed nonetheless, a subtle smile tugging at her lips. "Yes, Seth, I see the mistletoe. Very subtle." She glanced at the adults, a mischievous glint in her eyes. "Maybe I should… test it out later, for authenticity purposes?"

Meanwhile, Taylor, ever the efficient organizer, was already on the phone, sending messages to Janet, Eric, Andrea and Sara, telling them to bring their children to the main house. "We need to get everyone together to appreciate this," she said, ending the call. Just then, the door swung open, and Aidan and Alissa strolled in, hand in hand. Alissa, six months pregnant, moved a little slower these days. Aidan's eyes widened as he took in the scene. "What in the name of…did Santa have a stroke?" He asked, a grin spreading across his face. "This is insane! In a good way, of course." Alissa chuckled, leaning against Aidan for support. "It's…definitely something. I think the baby likes it though, keeps kicking." She patted her belly affectionately. "It's been a while since we've had any holiday cheer around here."

Just then, Junior wandered into the living room, his brow furrowed in what he hoped was a convincing expression of surprise. "Whoa! What happened here? Did we get visited by Buddy the Elf?" He gestured wildly around the room, a genuine grin threatening to break through his act. "Did…did we get raided by a Christmas elf convention? This is… intense." He glanced over at David, carefully gauging his reaction. "Sir, did you…did you know about this?"

David chuckled, a deep, resonant sound that filled the already festive living room. He leaned back in his armchair, his eyes twinkling with amusement. "Buddy the Elf? I like that, Junior. A very apt description." He surveyed the scene with a contented smile, taking in the sheer exuberance of the decorations. "No, Junior, I had absolutely no idea. This was… quite the unexpected surprise." He paused, letting the silence amplify his next words. "But a delightful one. Thank you." His gaze softened as it landed on Junior, a silent acknowledgment of the effort and thought that had gone into the elaborate Christmas display.

Just then, the door to the stairs leading up from downstairs creaked open, and Brian and Seo-Yeon emerged, blinking in the sudden brightness of the decorated living room. Brian's jaw dropped. Seo-Yeon gasped, covering her mouth with her hand. "Holy mistletoe!" he exclaimed, his eyes darting from the myriad of stockings on the fireplace to the twinkling lights draped across the archways. "What... what is all this?"

Seo-Yeon simply raised an eyebrow, but a small smile tugged at the corner of her lips. She knew Brian, even if he acted like a gruff gardener, was a big softie inside. "It seems someone's been busy while we were underground, Thìrak." Junior, still basking in David's approval, puffed out his chest slightly. "We thought we'd bring a little cheer into the place. You know, fight off the December gloom." He gave Brian a playful nudge. "You look like you could use some cheer. Those tomatoes giving you trouble again?"

Brian chuckled, shaking his head. "Always. They're divas, I swear. But this…" He gestured around the room, taking in the sheer scale of the decorations. "This is something else. Seriously, Junior, good job. You and the team really outdid yourselves." Still goggling at the decorations, he suddenly puffed up his chest, a mischievous glint in his eyes, then cleared his throat and announced, "Actually, there's something else that's germinating around here. A new sprout, if you will. One that requires... a little more care than tomatoes."

Jennifer, perched on the arm of David's chair, tilted her head, her brow furrowing slightly. "Oh? What kind of new vegetable have you decided to torture now, Brian? Brussel sprouts? I still remember that year you tried to grow artichokes..." She shuddered dramatically. "Never again." Seo-Yeon, standing beside Brian, let out a soft, throaty giggle. She placed a hand on her stomach, subtly rubbing it in a circular motion. Her smile was widening, almost wickedly, as she looked at Jennifer with knowing eyes. "Perhaps, Jennifer, it's not quite a vegetable. Maybe something... a little sweeter."

The penny dropped for Jennifer, her eyes widening in realization. She gasped, clasping her hands to her chest. "Oh my GOD! Seo-Yeon, darling, are you...?" She squealed, jumping off the arm of the chair and rushing towards Seo-Yeon, throwing her arms around her in a tight hug. "Oh, honey, congratulations! That's wonderful! We're going to have a baby!" She turned to Brian, a huge grin plastered on her face. "And you, you sneaky gardener, keeping this a secret!"

Elena, who was standing in the doorway to the dining room, looked from Seo-Yeon to Alissa, then to Taylor, and finally to Jessica, bouncing Poppy in her arms. Considering the sheer volume of pregnancies in the family, she took a tentative sniff of her coffee. The aroma of Christmas spice seemed somehow...threatening. She sighed, a dramatic flourish, and poured the steaming liquid down the drain.

Tiffany, ever observant, noticed Elena's coffee disposal. She frowned slightly, concern etched on her face. "Elena, dear, are you feeling alright? You seem a little…off." She paused, placing a gentle hand on Elena's arm. "Is it the decorations? I know the tinsel can be a bit overwhelming." Elena sighed again, a theatrical edge to it. She gestured vaguely towards the pregnant women in the room, a conspiratorial look in her eye. "Oh, I'm perfectly fine, Tiffany. Physically, at least. But…let's just say I don't trust the coffee around here anymore." She lowered her voice, leaning closer to Tiffany. "It's probably got subliminal baby-making additives. David's probably orchestrated the whole thing!" she whispered suspiciously.

Jennifer cackled, releasing Seo-Yeon from her enthusiastic embrace. "Additives! Oh, Elena, you always know how to make me laugh. David doesn't need additives! The man's got pheromones potent enough to fertilize a cactus! Besides, it's Christmas! It's a time for miracles, and babies are definitely miracles!" She winked suggestively at David, who was watching the spectacle with an amused glint in his eyes. "Speaking of miracles, Master, when are you going to work your magic on me again?" she purred, sauntering back towards him and playfully tugging on his sleeve.

David chuckled, catching Jennifer's hand and giving it a gentle squeeze. "Patience, my dear. Christmas is a time for giving…and receiving. There's plenty of time for miracles, both big and small." He turned his attention to Brian, clapping him on the shoulder. "Congratulations, son. Seo-Yeon, welcome to the club. Life is certainly never dull in this family, especially with little ones around." Brian beamed, a genuine happiness radiating from him. "Thanks, Dad. Seo-Yeon and I are really excited, though slightly terrified. This whole…apocalypse baby thing is a little daunting." Seo-Yeon, nestled beside him, squeezed his hand reassuringly.

Just then, Kyle strolled in, his usual stoic expression softening slightly as he took in the sheer volume of Christmas cheer. Grace, after spotting him, let out a squeal of delight and launched herself onto his back, wrapping her arms around his neck. "Kyle! You're finally here! Merry Christmas, my love!" She peppered his cheek with kisses, completely unfazed by the amused glances from everyone else. Kyle grunted, a barely perceptible smile tugging at the corner of his lips. "Alright, Grace, easy there. You'll choke me." He gently peeled her off his back, setting her on the ground.

Grace, undeterred by his mild protest, beamed up at him with an innocent, yet knowing, smile. "But Kyle, don't you want lots of kisses?" She tilted her head. "When we're married…" She trailed off, then leaned closer to Kyle, gesturing with her hand and her tongue against the inside of her cheek, insinuating lots of blowjobs. The room went silent, save for the crackling fire in the hearth. Even Jennifer, usually the queen of innuendo, seemed momentarily speechless. A few people choked on their coffee.

David's laughter boomed, breaking the awkward silence. He clapped his hands together. "Alright, alright, settle down everyone! Grace, darling, while I appreciate your…enthusiasm for the future, let's maybe keep it PG-13 for the audiences." Kyle coughed, his face reddening slightly despite his best efforts to maintain his stoic facade. He glared playfully at Grace, ruffling her hair. "You're never going to let me forget, huh?"

Nicole, still recovering from her laughter fit, managed a weak, "Sorry, Kyle. She gets it from…somewhere." She shot a pointed look at Jennifer, who simply shrugged with an innocent smile. Just then, the door swung open, and Andrea, Janet, and Eric shuffled in, their arms laden with children. Mike, Bonnie, Lori, and Beth trotted in behind them, their eyes wide with Christmas excitement. Sara, looking slightly harried but radiant nonetheless, trailed behind pushing Jake's stroller.

The sound of a baby's gurgle filled the air as Sara wheeled Jake's stroller further into the house. Marvin, ever vigilant, hovered nearby, his eyes scanning the room. "Merry Christmas, everyone!" Sara called out, her voice a little tired but full of cheer. Jake, oblivious to the surrounding festivities, waved his tiny fists in the air, his eyes fixated on the twinkling lights of the Christmas tree.

Bonnie, however, was not interested in babies or Christmas trees at the moment. Her eyes were glued to Seth, who was busy writing his Christmas list on one of the provided sheets. She bounced on the balls of her feet, trying to catch his attention. Grace, catching Bonnie's lovestruck gaze, giggled conspiratorially. "Don't worry, Bonnie! He'll come around. Just give him time. Kyle is still playing hard to get too." She winked, then returned her attention to Kyle, who was now standing beside David, taking in the scene with a mixture of amusement and guarded approval.

"Impressive," Kyle finally said, his voice low and gravelly. "Junior's team went all out." David nodded, his eyes twinkling with pride. "Indeed. They certainly have a knack for…excess. But, in times like these, a little excess is a welcome distraction, don't you think?" He clapped Kyle on the shoulder. "Speaking of distractions, I believe there's a mistletoe strategically placed above the doorway. Don't let Grace catch you standing under it, you know how sneaky she can be."

The chaotic, yet heartwarming, atmosphere of Christmas was in full swing. Children were scattered around the lower living room, hunched over the letter-writing station, tongues sticking out in concentration as they meticulously crafted their wish lists. Bonnie, however, was employing a more direct approach. She'd abandoned the craft table and was now perched precariously close to Seth, practically breathing down his neck as he wrote. "Seth, Seth, Seth!" she chirped, her voice filled with an eagerness that bordered on desperation. "Are you asking Santa for me? I want a unicorn, and a diamond ring, and light up house slippers!"

Seth, barely lifting his head from his writing, sighed dramatically. "Bonnie, for the last time, Santa isn't real. And you're eleven. Plus, what would you do with a diamond ring?" He underlined a word on his list with exaggerated force. "Besides, I'm making my own list." Bonnie scowled, but resolute, leaned close. "If Santa isn't real, who are you writing the letter to?"

He carefully capped his pen, turning slightly towards Bonnie. "Okay, look," he said, his voice softer now. "Santa… well, Santa might not be exactly real in the way you think. But someone like Santa is helping out this year." He glanced around conspiratorially, lowering his voice even further. "Junior is basically Santa this year."

Bonnie's eyes widened, her earlier frustration completely forgotten. "Junior? Really? Junior is Santa?" The thought was both exciting and strangely plausible. She scrambled up, practically vibrating with renewed enthusiasm. "Okay, okay!" She bounced off towards the letter-writing station, grabbing a fresh sheet of Christmas-themed paper. Returning to Seth, she plopped down beside him, pen poised, eyes shining. "If Junior is Santa, then I really need to make a good list. What do you think he can get? Can he get a real unicorn? Or just a really good fake one?"

As David ate, his gaze drifted towards the lower living room, where the cacophony of children scribbling and chattering filled the air. He watched, amused, as Bonnie launched her relentless assault on Seth, her youthful exuberance a stark contrast to Seth's exasperated patience. Suddenly, his eyebrows furrowed slightly. He noticed a few of the adults discreetly approaching the mailbox set up for the letters. Eric, looking sheepish, slipped a folded piece of paper inside. Then Lily, a mischievous glint in her eyes, followed suit. Even Kyle, usually stoic and reserved, quickly scribbled something down and deposited it in the festive box.

David nudged Tiffany, a silent question in his eyes. "What's going on with the letters, dear?" Tiffany smiled knowingly. "Junior's team has been planning something special for Christmas," she explained. "Apparently, the adults are getting in on it too. It seems the Christmas spirit is contagious, even in the apocalypse." Jessica snorted. "I bet half of them are asking for more ammo. Or maybe a lifetime supply of bubblegum. Who knows what goes on in those heads?"

David chuckled, shaking his head. "Whatever it is, it's good to see them having a little fun. They deserve it." He paused, considering. "Perhaps I should write a letter too." Elena, ever perceptive, raised an eyebrow. "Oh? And what would you ask for, David?" David smiled enigmatically. "That, my dear, is for Santa... or rather, Junior... to know." Jessica's eyes narrowed, and her petite frame seemed to radiate a surprising amount of menace. "Don't you dare ask for another wife, David," she hissed, her voice surprisingly sharp. "I swear, if you do, I'm going to bite your dick. And I'm not kidding." David raised his hands in mock surrender. "Duly noted, my dear. My Christmas wish remains a secret... for now." He winked.

Meanwhile, completely unbeknownst to David and his wives, Junior had slipped away from the Christmas bustle upstairs and descended into the depths of the bunker network. He found Olivia, Riley, Kathy, Andrew, Susan, Caleb and Darrel, lounging at the pool, enjoying a refreshing break after their hard work. Olivia, sleek in her swimsuit, surfaced from a dive, water cascading down her face. "So," she said, pushing her hair back, "How'd everyone react to the decorations?"

Junior grinned, plopping down on a lounge chair. "It was an even bigger success than I hoped. David looked genuinely surprised; even Jessica seemed impressed, though she'd sooner wrestle a bear than admit it out loud." Riley, ever sarcastic, smirked. "Surprised, huh? I bet he thought the elves were snorting pixie sticks with all the tinsel we put up." "Speaking of which," Andrew interjected, glancing at Junior, "Did you get all the intel you needed from everyone about what they want?"

Junior chuckled. "Working on it! David is being pretty coy about his letter, though." Darrel, ever witty, piped up, "He probably wants a jetpack. Or maybe a solid gold toilet. The man has everything else." "More likely," Caleb mused, adjusting his sunglasses, "He wants everyone to think they're content. It's the illusion of happiness that's the killer app."

Junior considered Caleb's point, a flicker of seriousness crossing his face. "Maybe. But I genuinely think he just... wants us all to be okay. Which, honestly, makes my job a lot harder. How do you shop for 'contentment' at the end of the world?" Riley, who was lounging nearby, patted over to Junior, carefully resting her body against his. "Whatever he wants, he'll write it down."

Just then, Noah and Sophia approached the poolside, still slightly damp from their breakfast stint. Noah, ever enthusiastic, practically bounced as he spoke. "Junior, you made David's day! He hasn't stopped talking about the decorations since he saw them. He keeps saying how much it means to him that we're keeping the spirit alive." Noah turned to the others, beaming. "He said it's the best Christmas in years, and that's saying something coming from him!"

Sophia, more reserved but equally sincere, nodded in agreement. "He really appreciated it. He was also very impressed with the letter-writing station. Called it 'a brilliant way to connect and share our hopes in these trying times.'" Junior felt a warm rush of pride hearing Noah and Sophia's words. He'd been working tirelessly with the others, under the cover of their assigned tasks, to bring some semblance of holiday cheer to their little community. To know it had truly resonated with David… it was more rewarding than any successful training exercise.

Riley, sensing his satisfaction, leaned in and pressed a kiss to his cheek. "See? You probably gave him the best gift of all, proof that his efforts haven't been in vain. He worries about everyone so much; knowing we're still finding joy, still connecting, that's gotta mean the world." Junior wrapped an arm around her, pulling her closer.

"Maybe you're right. I still feel like I gotta get him something, though. Something…tangible."

Chapter 46:

The Christmas Scavengers

Inside the main house, David sat at the table, eating dinner with his wives. Kayla thought hamburgers would be a nice change of pace and nobody was complaining. "Master, what do you think everybody else is doing with the weather?" Jennifer asked, her eyes sparkling with mischief as she dangled a crispy French fry in front of Poppy.

David, methodically constructing his twin hamburger masterpiece, finally looked up. His gaze swept across the faces of his wives. "Well, Darling, this is the first cold winter of the apocalypse, so I hate to say, but most people are probably freezing to death." He stated bluntly, a flicker of sadness in his eyes before returning to his culinary task.

Taylor, carefully stacking a second layer of pickles onto her hamburger, furrowed her brow slightly. "David, how did you even get through the first winter? Especially since you were stuck up in the Pacific Northwest? I imagine that was a lot worse than central Texas." She leaned forward, genuinely curious.

David set down his half-assembled burger, a distant look in his eyes. "That was... an experience, to say the least." He chuckled dryly, a hint of steel in his voice. "I had rendezvoused with my coworkers, remember? We were all pretty resourceful. We managed to cobble together an old immersion heater using ventilation pipes, scrap metal, and a couple of old water tanks." He paused, marveling at his own ingenuity. "It wasn't pretty, but it kept us from turning into popsicles."

Jessica raised a skeptical eyebrow. "Where did you even learn to do that, Daddy?" She asked with a touch of incredulity. "Turning ventilation pipes into a heater sounds like something MacGyver would do." David chuckled, picking up his burger again. "Well, Baby, back in the day, when I was in training, a democrat was president. Which meant we were all training on World War II-era equipment. And I had a vague idea of how they worked.!" He winked. "It helped keep the water warm too. Plus, they could run on anything flammable."

Tiffany shook her head with a fond smile. "Only you, David. You can turn the apocalypse into a history lesson." David took a big bite of his hamburger before continuing. "Luckily, we had enough food to get us through the winter. We mostly just hunkered down." He paused, his expression turning grim. "But once the snow thawed… that's when things got truly nasty."

Aidan, who had been quietly listening while helping Alissa load her plate with a mountain of tater tots, perked up. "Nasty how, Dad?" David sighed, setting down his burger again. The jovial atmosphere of the room seemed to dim a fraction as he spoke. "The thaw revealed… well, the remains of countless people who hadn't made it. Freezing wasn't the nicest way to go." He rubbed his temples. "And those bodies... they became a feast for the feral animals. Dogs, cats, even rats grew bold. They were starving, and they spread disease like wildfire."

Tanya leaned forward, her dark eyes sharp with concern. "What kind of diseases, David? Was it rabies? Something like that?" David shook his head, a slight grimace on his face. "Mostly stuff like hepatitis. The real problem was the sheer volume of it. Apparently, humans are the most diseased; animals just carry it around like bees carrying pollen." He paused. "That's when we started focusing on sanitation, on burning the dead, on securing clean water sources. It was a brutal learning curve."

Alissa, who had been happily munching on her tater tots, suddenly lost her appetite. The thought of feral animals feasting on frozen corpses made her stomach churn. She pushed her plate away slightly, reaching for Aidan's hand. "That sounds... awful," she whispered, her voice barely audible. "Did you... did you ever get sick, Dad?" Aidan asked, squeezing Alissa's hand. "I had some nausea here and there, nothing a little charcoal couldn't fix. We had to be careful, and we didn't just go around trapping any animal for food. But the most challenging part was the loneliness." He sighed, his gaze drifting towards the Christmas tree. "Being isolated like that, not knowing if anyone else had survived... it takes a toll on the mind."

Seth, pausing mid chew, looked around the table. "Are we going to have that problem here, Dad? You know, with the cold weather?" He gestured vaguely towards the windows. "I mean, we've been pretty isolated, but..."

David took a long swig of his tea. "Probably not," he said, his voice regaining some of its usual firmness. "We've got the valley pretty well secured. As long as it doesn't snow enough to bury bodies, we should be okay. The dogs will give us a heads-up anyway."

Kayla, chimed in. "What do we do if we end up coming across bodies then, are we just going to burn all the bodies we find?" David shook his head thoughtfully. "That only really works if there isn't a better option. Ideally, we should bury the bodies if we can, but it's also unreasonable to think we could really make a difference," David said, his tone hardening. "We'll prioritize those closer to the house first and foremost, and if the ground is frozen or we're low on time, we'll do what we must. Hopefully, we won't have to deal with any of that."

Meanwhile, in the work shed, Parker was helping Junior pack the Behemoth for their run to Cleburne. "Junior, are you sure you can drive this thing? I mean, it's a lot bigger than the van." Parker asked, pushing the heavy door to the back of the truck closed. Junior grinned. "Relax, Parker. I'm not planning on causing havoc. Just wanna do some shopping and get back as quick as possible." He patted the Behemoth's armor plating affectionately. "Besides, it's the closest thing we have to a sleigh this year. Gotta bring back the Christmas spirit, right?" Parker eyed the reinforced steel and bulletproof glass. "Christmas spirit, or another dent in the shed?" he teased, though a hint of worry still clung to his voice. He knew Junior was a skilled driver, having trained him extensively himself, but the Behemoth was a beast of a different caliber. His beast, and he still worried when somebody else used it. Junior chuckled. "Don't worry, I'll be extra careful. Besides," he winked, "I've got Olivia and Riley to keep me grounded." He hopped into the driver's seat, the engine roaring to life with a satisfying rumble. "See you later, Parker. Wish us luck!" Junior, Olivia, Riley, and Caleb crammed into the crew cab, the air filled with nervous excitement and the faint scent of Riley's fragrant conditioner. While Darrel, Noah, and Andrew sat in the back, perched on the bench in the front of the space.

"Alright, team, let's make this quick and clean," Junior announced, adjusting the rearview mirror. "Olivia, navigation. Riley, comms. Caleb, eyes peeled. Everyone else, stay sharp." Olivia nodded, unfolding a map of Cleburne. "The distribution center is our primary target. Looks like a clean shot up Highway 281, but we should still be cautious. There could be roadblocks."

Riley fiddled with the radio, scanning for any signs of activity. "Quiet so far. But you know how that goes. Always expect the unexpected." Caleb, leaning forward in his seat, peered through the side window. "The roads are clear. Let's go get our Christmas on!" In the back of the truck, Darrel, opened the port between the crew cab and the compartment in the back, revealing a small rectangular hole, just large enough to pass a machine gun through.

David watched the Behemoth rumble past the house, a proud smile stretched across his face. Seeing Junior taking the lead, especially with such a special mission, filled him with a sense of pride and accomplishment. He knew the team Junior was leading was capable, but the world was still a dangerous place, especially with everything frozen outside. A tap on his shoulder drew his attention.

"Thinking about them already, Daddy?" Jessica asked softly. She stood beside him, Poppy cradled in her arms. The baby watched, reaching out a tiny hand toward David. He chuckled, leaning down to kiss Poppy's forehead. "Always thinking, Jess. Especially when they're heading out into the unknown. But I trust Junior. He'll bring them back safe." He straightened, turning to face Jessica. "Lets not waste a good night by worrying," he said.

Inside the Behemoth, an important mission briefing was underway. "Seriously, man, this thing could probably pull a small house off its foundation," Andrew said, kicking at the metal floor of the Behemoth. The metal thump echoed through the cargo area. "Junior said it can haul seventy tons." Darrel leaned back against the wall, arms crossed, a smirk playing on his lips. "Seventy tons? That's like, what, fifty cars? A hundred?" He scratched his chin, feigning deep thought. "I bet we could tow the whole damn distribution center back here if we wanted to."

Noah chuckled, shaking his head. "Don't give Junior any ideas. He'd probably try it." He ran a hand along the smooth, reinforced plating of the wall. "It's insane. You think they just found this thing in a surplus yard?" Andrew shrugged. "He said his brothers rebuilt the engine and fixed the working systems, but Parker and his men made the armor plating and this fine cargo compartment."

Darrel whistled. "No way. That's some serious dedication. Those guys have skills." He poked his head through the opening to the crew cab, shouting over the engine noise. "Hey, Junior! How much horsepower this thing got?" Junior's voice muffled back. "What's that, Darrel? Can't hear you over the sweet sound of freedom!" "The engine," Darrel repeated. "How much horsepower this thing got?"

Junior pumped the accelerator, the Behemoth shuddering with restrained power. "Alright, alright! Hold your horses… literally. After Aidan's quad compound turbo upgrade? I'm guessing this beauty's pushing around… eight hundred horsepower, give or take. And… hold on, hold on… more importantly, it delivers over twenty-five hundred foot-pounds of torque. So, yeah, we could definitely pull a lot. Why? You got any interesting ideas?" he asked, grinning like a kid on Christmas morning.

Olivia rolled her eyes, but a smile played on her lips. "Don't encourage him, Junior. Please." Riley snorted with laughter. "Encourage him? You think anything can discourage Darrel?" She leaned over, bumping Junior's seat playfully. "Eight hundred horsepower, huh? You gonna show off for us, Junior? Maybe run over a roadblock or two?" Caleb cleared his throat, looking slightly uncomfortable. "Guys, maybe we should focus on the mission? We need to be quick and efficient. Get in, get the supplies, get out."

Darrel turned back to Noah and Andrew, a wide grin splitting his face. "Eight hundred horsepower, baby! And twenty-five hundred foot-pounds of torque!" Noah raised an eyebrow. "Okay, I've seen cars with a thousand horsepower. So what? Is this all you ever think about?" Darrel scoffed. "Yeah, but this beast probably idles in the hundreds. Most cars only hit that if their pushing serious boost." He looked over at Andrew. "Horsepower… Horsepower is how hard you hit the wall. But torque, my friend, torque is how far you take the wall after you hit it." He punctuated his statement with a theatrical air punch. "We can bulldoze through anything."

Andrew, who'd been unusually quiet, finally spoke up, running a hand thoughtfully over his chin. "So, hypothetically speaking, we could technically drive through anything between here and Cleburne?" Junior chuckled, glancing at Andrew in the rearview mirror. "Well, technically speaking, yeah. But I'd rather not test the Behemoth's limits on, say, a building. But seriously, stick to smaller stuff. Fallen trees? No problem. Abandoned cars? We'll make 'em into speed bumps."

He paused, his expression turning serious. "Alright, before we get too carried away with vehicular manslaughter fantasies, let's talk lists. Now, most of these items are pretty self-explanatory – maternity clothes for Alissa, sex swing for Jennifer, pasties for Jessica… I'm not even gonna ask about the pasties. We just grab what's on the list, no judgment, and try not to think about why David needs so many travel mugs."

He scanned the faces in the cab. "Are there any questions? Anything you guys are unsure about, or think we might have trouble finding?" He drummed his fingers on the steering wheel. "I suspect a lot of the adults just put stuff on there to see if we could find it. Like, who seriously thinks we'll find a sex swing in a distribution center?"

Riley snorted. "Knowing Jennifer, she probably expects us to make a sex swing out of scavenged materials. Which, honestly, isn't the most outlandish thing we've done this year." "Point taken," Junior conceded. "Okay, first things first, let's be realistic. We're not going to find everything on these lists in one trip, or even at the distribution center. This is a recon run, a supply gathering mission, and a potential looting opportunity all rolled into one festive package. We're going to have to make multiple trips."

Caleb piped up, "What about the PS5? I mean, finding one is a long shot, but even if we do, won't it need updates?" Junior nodded. "Good point, Caleb. Let's cross off anything that's going to be reliant on the internet. That means no brand-new gaming consoles. Look for used or older models, and games that don't require updates."

Darrel groaned from the back. "So, my Xbox Series X is out?" "Not if we can find a used one with the blu-ray drive," Junior replied. Noah sighed. "And my model train set? Will we even find anything like that?" "Definitely," Olivia interjected, "but probably not at the distribution center. We'll have to hit up a hobby shop. There has to be a lot of those close to Dallas."

Junior nodded. "See? Teamwork. We'll prioritize the distribution center first, then branch out based on what we find. Remember, our main goal is to make Christmas happen. Small victories count." "What about Bonnie's real diamond ring?" Andrew asked, finally sounding a little less like he wanted to stage a demolition derby and a little more like he was actually thinking about the task at hand. "That's going to be a jewelry store run," Junior said. "Thankfully, those are typically easier to find intact than, say, a grocery store. A diamond ring, surprisingly, is easier to come by than batteries these days. We'll keep an eye out."

Riley chuckled. "Alright, so we're basically playing apocalypse Santa, but instead of a sleigh and reindeer, we have the Behemoth and the looming threat of bandits." "Pretty much," Junior confirmed, grinning. "But the bandits don't know what's coming. Now, let's get this holiday cheer on the road!"

Darrel leaned against the cold metal of the Behemoth, his breath puffing out in white clouds. "Think we'll find anything good in this wasteland of shattered dreams, Junior?" he asked, gesturing towards the hulking distribution center in the distance. Junior tightened his grip on the steering wheel, his eyes scanning the horizon. "We're scavengers now, Darrel. Hope is our best weapon. Just remember the list. And try not to break anything too expensive."

Olivia adjusted her tactical vest, her brow furrowed. "This place looks picked over. We need to be systematic. Riley, you, Darrel and Noah take the left side.

Caleb, Andrew, you're with me on the right. Darling, can you support us from the middle?" Junior nodded. Riley flashed a grin. "Roger that, boss lady. Let's go get some loot!" After mounting her night vision, she, Darrel and Noah moved into a loose formation, weapons at the ready, heading towards the opened loading door on the west side. Olivia, Caleb, and Andrew mirrored their movements on the other side.

Riley chuckled, her night vision goggles giving her an eerie glow. "This is nothing like those 'clean sweep' shows, is it? More like 'dusty sweep'." She looked at the signs on the racks. "This isn't Costco, we aren't going to find the housekeeping section organized by item. Think, a pallet box full of stuffed bears, or an entire pallet of various model toys, all shrink wrapped together." Noah surprised them. "Think of it like a giant, deconstructed advent calendar. We just have to find the right doors." He adjusted his goggles and began carefully examining the pallets. They fanned out, carefully searching the isles. They were going to have to unpack one pallet at a time.

Noah, diligent as ever, located a promising pallet, marked with a cryptic barcode and the word "Toys" in faded ink. He strained to move the pallet. "Jackpot! Maybe? I can't tell what's inside." Junior swaggered over, his combat boots crunching on the dusty concrete. He assessed the situation with a practiced eye. "Stand back, rookies. Let's see what Santa's got for us." Without a word, he grabbed the pallet with both hands and heaved. The entire thing, a solid mass of cardboard, wood, and untold treasures, shifted, groaned, and then, with a deafening crash, toppled to the concrete floor. The impact sent a cloud of dust billowing outward.

As the pallet slammed onto the warehouse floor, he reached out and lifted off the top. The dust swirled, settling on the faces of the scavenging team. Caleb coughed, waving a hand in front of him. "Well, that was... dramatic." Junior, unfazed as always, dusted off his tactical vest. "Dramatic is my middle name. Besides, look!" He reached out and lifted off the top of the damaged cardboard box.

The pallet was full of assorted stuffed animals. Not vintage gaming consoles, not rare jewelry, just...plushies. A groan escaped Darrel's lips. "Seriously? An army of bears and bunnies? This is what we risked our necks for?" Riley, ever the pragmatist, surveyed the situation with a raised eyebrow. "Don't be so quick to judge. Remember, this is just one pallet. We have an entire warehouse to go through." As the group rummaged through the box of stuffed animals, David went to look for a forklift. This whole process would take days if they didn't get a move on.

As Junior disappeared into the cavernous warehouse, the others began sorting through the plushie pallet. Noah, surprisingly, perked up. "Hey, this unicorn looks kinda cool." He held up a pastel-colored unicorn with rainbow hair. "Bonnie would flip for this." "Yeah, well, Bonnie's not here," Darrel grumbled, kicking a discarded teddy bear. "I came for an Xbox, not a cuddle buddy." Olivia finally snapped. "Darrel, quit being a bitch and just grab some stuffed animals and get over yourself. This isn't about you. It's about making people happy. Now, are you going to help or are you going to whine while the rest of us are getting work done?"

Darrel, momentarily taken aback by Olivia's fiery outburst, cracked a mischievous smile. "Woah, okay, okay! Feisty. You're right. Besides, I bet they have a lot of games hidden in a crate here somewhere." He started rummaging through a box of oversized plush dogs with renewed enthusiasm. "Gotta find something to keep Marvin from getting all mopey about missing internet raids."

Caleb pulled out a stuffed golden retriever with floppy ears. He hesitated for a moment, then a faint blush crept up his neck. "You know, Sophia always liked dogs..." He trailed off, clutching the plushie a little tighter. "Maybe she could use a little cheering up. It's been rough on her since… y'know." Andrew, fiddling with the control panel on his night vision goggles, piped up, "Speaking of things we like, I haven't seen any music shops on the map. Are we even going to find an electric guitar?"

Riley, ever prepared, pulled out her own map, a tattered relic from a long-forgotten gas station. "The original plan had us hitting the outlet mall after this. should be a good place to find jewelry stores and video game shops. Music shops will be deeper in the city, we might have to do that another day. If you want to find a Les Paul, that is." She grinned, knowing how serious Andrew was about his rock star dreams.

As they squabbled, Olivia pulled out a box of miniature chem lights. "Okay people, let's keep the focus. We're dividing and conquering. Caleb and Andrew, dump this pallet and put what we keep in here. The rest of you, take these chem lights."

Just then, a low rumble echoed through the warehouse. The team tensed, their hands instinctively reaching for their weapons. But then, Junior's voice boomed, amplified by the warehouse's acoustics, laced with a hint of crazed glee. "Alright team, forklift's here! Let's get this Christmas miracle rolling!" The sound of strained gears and squealing tires filled the air as Junior navigated the behemoth of a machine through the aisles.

"Alright, team, listen up!" Junior boomed from the forklift. "The automated warehouse management system is about as useful as a screen door on a submarine. But! After sorting the plushies, all six of you use those mini chem lights to mark the areas needing a forklift." "Darling!" Olivia interrupted, a playful glint in her eyes. "We got that sorted. We'll need three more pallet boxes for our haul though, so bring those here if you find them," she said, a hint of playful authority in her voice.

Junior, momentarily surprised and genuinely impressed by Olivia's initiative and interruption, beckoned her closer with a flick of his wrist. Olivia grinned, a spark of anticipation dancing in her eyes. She nimbly climbed onto the forklift, balancing herself against the metal frame. The roar of the engine momentarily masked their hushed conversation.

He lifted his night vision goggles from his face, revealing his dark eyes, gleaming with mischief in the dim light. Leaning close, he whispered, his breath warm against her ear, "I'm going to fuck you for that later." Olivia's smile widened, a blush rising on her cheeks. "Promises, promises," she murmured back, her voice a low purr. She gave him a playful shove, then gracefully climbed down from the forklift, returning to the task at hand, leaving Junior grinning like a Cheshire cat.

As the team disbursed, Junior went from aisle to aisle, bringing down pallets and moving merchandise as his team filled the boxes laid out for them. Darrel, ever the comedian, was the first to pipe up. "Yo, Junior, you see the look on Noah's face when Olivia took charge? Dude looked like he'd just seen a unicorn riding a skateboard!" Junior chuckled, maneuvering the forklift with practiced ease. "Noah's simple. Plus, he's probably use to me giving orders. Besides, Olivia's got a way of… motivating people."

Hours melted away as they navigated the cavernous distribution center, their night vision goggles cutting through the inky blackness. Pallets groaned under the weight of their chosen treasures, destined to bring a flicker of pre-apocalyptic joy to their loved ones back home. Every so often, someone would peel off for a quick, shivering break, the biting cold proving stubbornly insistent on clinging to the warehouse's unheated interior.

"Found something for Alissa!" Riley called out, emerging from behind a towering display of what used to be inflatable holiday decorations. She held aloft a surprisingly intact candle-making kit, complete with various scents and molds. "Think she'll like it?" Junior, expertly stacking boxes of clay pigeons and golf balls onto a pallet, gave a nod. "She will. She's been talking about wanting to make something for the baby. Good find, Riley."

Caleb, his face flushed from the cold, shuffled over, clutching a slightly dusty PlayStation 5 box. "Score! Found one. Think Sophia will actually stop talking to me if I get her this?" "Only one way to find out," Darrel quipped, reappearing with an armful of anime Blu-ray box sets. "But if she does, I'll gladly take it off your hands. Cause, you know, I'm a good friend." He winked, earning a playful shove from Caleb.

As the night wore on, the Behemoth began to fill. The team worked with a focused energy, their individual tastes and desires blending into a collective mission: to create a Christmas that transcended the bleak reality of their world. Around 10:00 pm, stomachs started to rumble, a symphony of growls echoing in the vast space. Junior called for a halt. "Alright, chow time! Andrew, you and Noah go ahead and get that kerosene heater in the Behemoth going. The rest of us will be there in a bit."

Minutes later, they were huddled inside the back of the Behemoth, sipping lukewarm coffee and munching on David's signature oatmeal 'cookies'. The air filled with the low hum of conversation, punctuated by the occasional crackle of the heater. "Anyone else feel like they're living in a post-apocalyptic shopping spree movie?" Darrel asked, his breath misting in the cold air. "Like, 'Dawn of the Discounted Blu-rays' or something?"

"More like 'Night of the Night Vision Ninjas,'" Olivia countered, earning a round of laughter. "I'm just picturing us all back at the compound, opening presents like it's Christmas morning, except we're all packing heat." As the group finished their break, Caleb and Darrel remained in the truck as Junior loaded the now full pallet boxes into the back of the Behemoth with the forklift. "It's gonna be real tight back here. Hopefully nothing moves around," Darrel commented incredulously. As the words left his mouth, Riley threw them several packages of ratchet straps. "Here guys, tie those down, so ya don't get squished."

As Junior secured the back of the Behemoth with Darrel, Noah and Andrew in the back, everyone else climbed in the cab. "Right, all presents safely secured, next stop, Wedgwood," Junior announced, hopping into the driver's seat of the Behemoth. "Riley, you want shotgun?" Riley grinned, adjusting her seatbelt. "Wouldn't miss it. Besides, someone's gotta navigate and keep you boys from getting us lost."

As the massive vehicle rumbled back onto the road, the conversation inside, already buzzing, picked up steam. "Wedgwood, huh? Sounds fancy," Andrew mused. "Hopefully, they've still got a decent selection of guitars to pick from. Maybe a few." Caleb, nursing the last of his coffee, chimed in, "And another PlayStation 5, preferably one that doesn't have a family of cockroaches living inside. That would be a Christmas miracle in itself."

"Alright, team, report," Junior commanded, his voice booming slightly in the cab of the Behemoth. "What did we snag at the distribution center? Let's hear it." Riley pulled out a crumpled piece of paper. "Okay, so we hit a good chunk of the list. Thanks to you, Darrel, Noah, and Andrew, we managed to load a whole lotta tools. Aidan's gonna be ecstatic. We also got clothes, shoes, enough to outfit a small army, I think. A few bicycles for the kiddos, and a mountain of stuffed animals. Enough to last for years."

"Video games!" Caleb exclaimed from the back. "We got a bunch of games. Plenty of controllers too, hopefully enough variety for everyone. And movies! Brian's anime obsession is about to be fed for a month straight." Noah, usually quiet, spoke up. "Got some headsets too. Decent ones, I think. Should keep Caleb and Darrel from yelling at each other while they're gaming." He grinned, earning a playful shove from Darrel.

"And Andrew grabbed enough golf balls for Eric to lose a thousand in the valley," Riley added, earning a snort of laughter from Andrew. "Clay pigeons, paper for Sara and Nicole, blankets for everyone, knives for Lily and Scott, house shoes for Summer and Bonnie, a fitness ball for Tiffany, goggles for everyone, and steel targets." She paused, scanning the list. "Oh, and dolls. Lori's getting a dollhouse and dolls. I think we cleaned them out."

Junior leaned back in his seat, a satisfied smile spreading across his face. "Sounds like you guys went 300% on the list. I'm impressed." Caleb chuckled. "We were thinking about the future, not just Christmas, Junior. I mean, maybe only two people asked for goggles, but everyone swims. Might as well stock up." "Exactly! And those tools? You can never have too many," Darrel chimed in.

Junior nodded, his smile widening. "Alright, alright, I get it. Strategic gifting. Future-proofing the Christmas spirit. I'm proud of you guys. Seriously. We're gonna make this the best damn Christmas anyone's ever seen." He glanced at Olivia briefly. "Okay, Wedgwood is our next stop. Super Walmart first. Here we come!"

Chapter 47

The Hulen Holiday Looters

The Super Walmart loomed in the distance, a few figures milled around the entrance, their faces etched with the weariness of survival. "Looks like we're not the only ones with Christmas shopping on their minds," Caleb quipped, earning a nod from Riley. "Relax, I'm just sayin'. They don't look like trouble." Riley snorted. "Famous last words, Caleb. Remember the last time you said that? We almost got ambushed by those feral kids with shopping carts."

Junior slowed the truck to a crawl. His eyes, sharp and observant, swept over the other scavengers. Their worn clothing, their nervous postures, the weapons they clutched, they painted a picture of desperation, not aggression. "Alright, let's keep it professional," Junior commanded, his voice calm but firm. He parked the truck near the door, the squeal of the brakes echoing in the still night. "Olivia, Riley, you're with me. Caleb, Darrel, grab a couple of carts. Noah and Andrew, keep an eye on the perimeter. I'm gonna go talk to them first. After all, they probably need supplies a lot more than we do."

The team dismounted quickly, moving to their positions as Junior climbed out of the truck. Olivia, her lithe form radiating an unexpected air of confidence, fell into step beside Junior. Riley, in typical form, scanned the surrounding area, her red braid a stark contrast to her white jacket. Caleb, Noah and Andrew, armed with their rifles, positioned themselves strategically, their eyes constantly moving, watching for any sign of threat.

Junior approached the small group of scavengers. Two men, grizzled and sporting the kind of beard growth that suggested razors were a luxury, and a woman, clutching a shotgun with a white-knuckled grip. They were apprehensive, their eyes darting between Junior and his team like cornered rabbits. He stopped a few feet away, raising his hands in a gesture of peace, his own rifle slung casually over his shoulder. "Evening," he said, his voice friendly. "Name's David. We're just passing through, doing a little scavenging. You folks alright?"

The woman, her eyes narrowed, finally spoke. "We're...fine. Just looking for some supplies." Her voice was rough, betraying a life lived hard. "Anything specific?" Junior asked, genuinely curious. "Maybe we can help. Make this little trip a bit quicker for you folks." One of the men, the taller of the two, stepped forward, his gaze flickering to Olivia and Riley. "Don't need your charity," he grunted, but there was a flicker of something in his eyes, maybe hope, maybe just plain hunger.

Junior chuckled softly. "Whoa there, partner. Charity's got a funny smell to it these days, I agree. We ain't here to take your stuff, and we ain't here to give you a handout. We're just... resourceful, that's all. See, we're stocking up for the winter, but we're probably not looking for the same thing." He glanced at his team, a silent communication passing between them. "Truth is, we're looking for specific things. Stuff you probably wouldn't even want. So how about this? We work together, so what are you looking for?"

The woman seemed to consider this, her grip on the shotgun loosening slightly. "Food. Medicine. Anything to keep us warm." Junior nodded. "Alright. We can do that. How many of you are there?" "Five. Us three and two more inside," the taller man replied, his tone still wary. Junior's mind raced, calculating the best way to handle this. "Alright, here's the deal. We split into pairs. Andrew, Noah, Caleb, Darrel, you each take one of these folks with you. They can guide you to what they need, and you make sure they get it. One of our people goes with one of yours. Clear?" He waited for confirmation, then continued. "Olivia, Riley, and I will stay here with...uh..." He looked at the woman expectantly. "Janice," she supplied gruffly. "Right, Janice. We'll stay here with Janice, keep an eye on things. Sound good?"

The taller man, who Janice introduced as Jake, grudgingly nodded. The younger one, Marcus, just stared blankly, his eyes wide with a mixture of fear and awe. Okay, Andrew, you're with Jake. Noah, take Marcus. Caleb, Darrel, you're with the guys inside. Everyone clear on their objectives? Let's move!" Before the scavenging teams could disperse, Janice stopped them. Her voice, though raspy, held a note of urgency. "Hold up," she said, gesturing with the shotgun. "We've only got two flashlights, and the batteries are practically dead."

Junior raised an eyebrow, then rummaged in his backpack, a grin spreading across his face. "No problem. I came prepared. Figured someone might need a little extra light." He tossed Janice a couple of packages of batteries. "Here you go. Enough juice to power a small city…well, if that city was made by fisher price." He then pulled out two more flashlights, sleek and military-grade. "Consider these a Christmas bonus."

Janice looked surprised, a look of something akin to gratitude in her eyes. "Thanks," she mumbled, handing the batteries and flashlights to the others. "Don't mention it," Junior replied with a wink. "Now, let's get this show on the road. Remember, keep close, stick to the plan, and if you see anything…or anyone…that looks even remotely sketchy, hit 'em with your flashlight."

Not even half an hour later, the first team returned, then another, and finally, the last emerged from the darkness. "Alright, everyone back?" Junior scanned the faces, then counted heads, mentally ticking off names. "Good. Nobody got lost in the toy aisle." Caleb, clutching a nearly overflowing basket of toilet paper and video games, looked slightly overwhelmed. "So…did we get everything? I think I accidentally grabbed two copies of the new Avengers game."

Noah, who had been unusually quiet, finally spoke, his eyes still wide. "Marcus keeps asking if you're…like, a superhero." He gestured towards the younger stranger. "He thinks the tactical gear is a costume." Noah, nudged

Marcus forward slightly. "He's been asking ever since we left the truck. He's impressed with the vest."

Junior knelt to be eye-to-eye with the younger man. His expression was as gentle as his words. "Marcus, my name is David." He tapped his tactical vest. "This is just body armor, plus it helps me carry my tools. I'm not a superhero, I'm just a man. But I am a combat trainer and I do have other skills that may seem amazing, but that's all."

Olivia, leaning against one of the trucks, snorted softly. "Yeah, just a regular guy who can deflect bullets with a sword and speak five languages." Riley, ever the show-woman, theatrically gasped and clutched her chest. "He's so humble! It's endearing." Junior shot them both a look that bordered on exasperated affection. "Alright, alright, enough with the embellishments."

Janice stepped forward, her face etched with a mixture of curiosity and apprehension. "Okay, look, I gotta ask. Who are you guys? With the polar gear and all the…" She trailed off, gesturing vaguely at Junior's team. "…equipment. You look like some kind of…mercenary squad." Darrel chimed in before Junior could fully formulate a response. "Well, Janice, you're not entirely wrong. We kinda are a mercenary squad. Junior here is our commander, more or less."

Olivia pushed herself off the truck, her voice smooth and reassuring. "Look, Janice, we're a small piece of a bigger...community. And yeah, some of us are trained. But tonight? Tonight, we're just here for Christmas. Think of us as… extremely well-equipped elves." She gave Janice a small, almost apologetic smile. "We're not looking for a fight, or anything like that. Just trying to make things a little brighter for the people we care about."

Janice nodded as she turned toward her four shopping carts. Suddenly, Junior began barking orders. "Olivia, Darling, bring me our carts, Riley, Baby, open the truck. The rest of you, help Janice and her family get their stuff loaded, I want it nice and neat too." Janice and Marcus watched their approach with a mixture of awe and apprehension. The quartet moved quickly, and with a purpose, an efficiency that spoke of rigorous training. It was a far cry from the usual chaotic shopping spree. "Wow," Marcus breathed, his eyes wide as he stared at the approaching figures. "They're… organized."

Janice nodded slowly, her gaze fixed on Andrew, who was straddling the bed of a pickup truck, quickly stacking boxes of dry food as they were thrown to him. "Organized and…intense. You don't get that kind of focus just from playing video games, Marcus." Beside the truck, Olivia leaned against the shopping carts and grinned as Riley hopped onto the back of the truck to open the door. Meanwhile, Junior approached their own shopping carts with a casual, almost arrogant ease. He surveyed the piles of toilet paper, movies, games and bagged dog food. Carefully cataloging each cart's contents.

Then, with a grunt, he started lifting. One by one, the shopping carts, overflowing with Christmas booty, were effortlessly hoisted and dumped into the massive boxes filling the Behemoth's cargo space. Each cart landed on the ground with a resounding thud, as he emptied each one. "He… he just lifted all of that?" Marcus stammered, his voice getting progressively higher. He'd been impressed earlier when Junior had casually commanded his team, but this? This was a whole new level of "WTF."

Olivia chuckled. "Show off," she teased, her eyes twinkling as she watched him casually jump from the back of the truck. "Remember when you told Marcus you were 'just a man'? Well, he's about to have a crisis of faith." She gestured towards the awestruck teenager, who was currently staring at Junior as if he just landed from Mars.

Junior, oblivious to the existential turmoil he was causing, grinned, a flash of teeth in the dim light. He sauntered over to Riley, who was wrestling with the cargo door, and gave her a playful slap on the rear. "Need a hand, babe?" Riley swatted his hand away, a smirk playing on her lips. "I got it, show-off. But if you're offering to use your…talents…to help me with something later, I might consider it."

Janice watched, a subtle furrow forming between her brows as Junior, with inhuman ease, emptied the shopping carts. Marcus' slack-jawed awe was almost contagious, but something else caught her attention. Olivia's playful ribbing, the easy banter, and then the casual, almost proprietary way Junior slapped Riley's rear as she secured the truck's cargo door. It was… domestic. It was a sharp contrast to the grim reality they were all living in.

"He's…efficient," Janice mumbled, more to herself than anyone else, her gaze flickering between the trio. These young people, barely out of their teens, were moving with a practiced coordination that hinted at a much deeper connection than just scavenging partners. And the flirting… it was almost brazen, a defiant act of joy in a world desperately devoid of it.

Her husband, Jake, nudged her gently. "They seem to know what they're doing, Jan. Let's just be grateful they offered to help us out." Janice huffed a small laugh. "Talents is one word for it. But… they all look so young." It wasn't just their age, it was the confidence, the surety in their movements. It was the way they carried themselves, like they were playing a game, a dangerous and complicated game, but a game nonetheless.

"Alright, everyone in!" Junior clapped his hands together, the sound echoing in the darkness. "Game consoles are next!" As the others piled into the Behemoth, Janice lingered, watching them. This giant vehicle, this operation, it was all so… organized. What kind of community would have a private army for Christmas shopping? Most people struggled to survive one more day in this cold, and Junior and his group were going midnight Christmas shopping, in a truck that probably chugged fuel like a frat house chugs beer.

She couldn't help but wonder about the cost. What did it take to maintain this level of self-sufficiency? What were the sacrifices they had to make? What kind of world did they live in, back wherever they came from, that allowed them to seemingly thrive while the rest of the world crumbled? "Everything alright, Janice?" Jake asked, his hand resting on her shoulder. "Yeah, just…thinking," she replied, forcing a smile. "They're good kids, aren't they?"

Jake shrugged. "Seem like it. Though, I wouldn't want to get on their bad side." He glanced at Junior, who was now meticulously checking the truck's mirrors. "That one…he's got a look in his eyes. Like he's seen things. Done things." Janice shivered, despite the wool coat she was wearing. "Let's just hope we don't find out what those things are."

After several stops and nearly an hour later, Junior pulled the Behemoth in front of the massive liquor store. The north side of the outlet mall loomed, the place was looted, badly. Shattered glass crunched under the Behemoth's tires as Junior parked, the armored beast looking oddly out of place beside the ravaged storefront. "Okay, people! Kayla's Christmas mission starts now!" Junior announced, hopping out of the driver's seat. Olivia and Riley followed close behind, weapons at the low ready.

Darrel, Caleb, Noah, and Andrew trailed, looking more like college kids on a field trip than a scavenging squad in a post-apocalyptic wasteland. "Anyone see any obvious threats?" Junior asked, scanning the area. "Looks clear, mostly," Riley said, her eyes narrowed as she surveyed the shadows. "Just the usual rats…and maybe a couple of bigger ones." "Alright, let's move smart," Junior said, his voice serious. "Darrel, Caleb, scope the perimeter, make sure no one's decided to set up shop in here. Noah, Andrew, you're with me. Olivia, Riley, you're on overwatch. We're looking for anything salvageable, high-end stuff preferred. Kayla deserves the best."

He pushed open the battered doors of the liquor store, stepping into a scene of utter chaos. Shelves were overturned, bottles lay shattered, and the air reeked of stale alcohol. "Great," he muttered. "Looks like a frat party after a zombie apocalypse… oh wait…" Andrew interjected, "Hey, maybe there's some hidden gems! People usually just grab the easy stuff, right?" "That's the spirit," Junior said, a hint of a smile on his face. "Alright, let's start digging. I'm thinking we should look for intact bottles of whiskey, scotch, maybe some tequila. And don't forget mixers - bitters, vermouth, the fancy stuff."

Noah, who'd been quietly observing the scene, pointed to a far corner. "Hey, I think I see something back there. Looks like a storage room." "Good eye, Noah," Junior said, heading towards the back. The storage room door was partially open. He kicked it the rest of the way, revealing a surprisingly organized space. Rows of shelves lined the walls, stacked with boxes and crates. "Jackpot!" he exclaimed. "Looks like the looters were too lazy to check back here, for now."

Olivia and Riley cautiously entered, their guns raised. "Still clear," Olivia said. "But stay sharp." They began opening boxes, revealing a treasure trove of untouched alcohol. "Holy crap," Andrew breathed, pulling out a bottle of what looked like premium single malt scotch. "This stuff costs a fortune!" Junior grinned. "Kayla's gonna love this. Okay, let's load up! Careful with those bottles; we don't want any accidents."

Olivia snuggled up to Junior, her voice soft amidst the bustling activity. "Hey, babe? What happens when everything is looted? When there's nothing left in stores, not even the back rooms?" Junior wrapped an arm around her, kissing her forehead. "That's when scavenging gets… personal." He sighed, his eyes hardening. "People start going house to house. And that's where you find some weird stockpiles, things people clung to. Things people looted from the stores."

He picked up a bottle of rare Bordeaux, examining the label as if it held the secrets of the post-apocalyptic world. "Just because most of the alcohol is gone doesn't mean it's been drank or burned. It's probably sitting in some guy's bedroom, with his frozen body stuck on the couch, a half-empty bottle clutched in his hand." He paused, a slight grimace crossing his face. "Dad told me a story, you know. He said he once found cases and cases of cat food in a guy's house, but the guy starved to death long after eating his own cat."

A hush fell over the group as Junior recounted David's morbid discovery. The image of a man surrounded by enough cat food to survive for months, yet choosing starvation after consuming his pet was unsettling. It was a stark reminder of the psychological toll the apocalypse took on people, driving them to irrational and ultimately tragic choices. "Jesus, Junior," Caleb said, breaking the silence. He shuddered. "Thanks for the bedtime story. I'm actually gonna need a drink after that."

Olivia shivered, pulling her jacket tighter. "That's... cheerful," she muttered. "Let's just focus on the presents, okay? Maybe some glitter glue and model trains will scrub that image from my brain." Junior chuckled, squeezing her hand. "Right, looter therapy." He clapped his hands together. "Alright, team, God's craft store is next! Let's get Aidan his model kits and Alissa her candle-making dreams. And someone keep Darrel away from the bedazzling station."

After a frantic final sweep of the liquor store, they crammed their haul into the back of the truck, Darrel narrowly avoiding a collision with a display of discounted wine charms. The short drive to God's craft store was filled with nervous laughter and Caleb's increasingly desperate pleas for a stiff drink.

The bell above the door jingled as the group filed into the door. The lack of electricity has rendered the store silent, save for the crunch of their boots on the dusty floor. Moonlight streamed through the large windows, casting long, eerie shadows across aisles overflowing with crafting supplies. "Holy craft-pocalypse!" Andrew exclaimed, his eyes wide. "It looks like we broke in on a Sunday, not ten months after the collapse of society."

Riley snorted. "Yeah, because everyone's dying to bedazzle a picture frame these days. I'd say arts and crafts don't seem to be the priority anymore." Junior clapped his hands together, his breath fogging slightly in the cold air.

"Alright, people, focus! Remember the mission. Aidan needs his model kits to keep him from tinkering with the generator again. And Alissa is relying on us to fuel her candle-making obsession."

"What exactly is candle making, anyway?" Caleb asked, his brow furrowed in confusion. "Is she trying to start her own medieval lighting company? Are we going to have a town crier soon? 'Hear ye, hear ye, the Duke of Alissa has lit a new citronella, warding off mosquitoes and despair!'" Olivia elbowed him sharply in the ribs. "Just get the wax, Caleb. And maybe try not to be a total idiot for five minutes."

Junior pulled out a small, handwritten list. "Okay, model kits, train sets, and other art supplies are in the back. Scrapbooking and candle-making stuff is on the back left. And fabrics are on the right. Everyone knows what they need to get?" He pointed to the back of the store. "Don't be shy now! Fill your carts generously."

He gestured towards the checkouts. "Alright, first grab some bags from the front. Preferably the ones that say 'Hobby Lobby' on them and get a cart. We're not carrying all this crap." A flurry of movement followed as everyone grabbed a cart and a handful of bags. The dull thud of plastic against plastic echoed in the silence. Then, they scattered, armed with rifles, night vision, and their assigned shopping lists, disappearing into the dimly lit aisles. Junior watched them go, a small smile playing on his lips. Scavenging for Christmas presents in a deserted craft store? This was definitely a new one.

Twenty minutes later, they reconvened at the front of the store. Miniature shopping carts, overflowing with an odd assortment of arts and crafts supplies, were parked haphazardly by the abandoned checkouts. Noah's cart looked like a miniature train depot exploded. Model train cars, track sections, tiny plastic trees, and bottles of 'realistic water effects' teetered precariously. "I might have gone a little overboard with the diorama stuff," he admitted sheepishly, adjusting his night vision goggles.

Darrel rolled his eyes, his cart overflowing with yarn in every conceivable color and texture. "Overboard? Look at me! I'm practically drowning in sheep fuzz. Susan's going to be crocheting us all sweaters until forever." Caleb pushed his cart, which held an impressive array of candle-making supplies: paraffin wax, beeswax, soy wax, wicks of all sizes, essential oils, dyes in every shade imaginable, and a small mountain of decorative molds. "Alissa's going to be so happy."

Olivia, trailing behind Caleb, had a cart overflowing with scrapbooking paper, stickers, stencils, and an assortment of decorative punches. "Kathy is going to be obsessed. I got her a bunch of double sided sticky tape too, that stuff will come in handy." Junior surveyed his group. There were enough craft supplies here to keep them all busy for a long time.

The team efficiently unloaded the carts, carefully packing the art supplies into sturdy box crates in the back of the Behemoth. The cargo space was already near capacity, a testament to their earlier stops. "Alright, that's a wrap here!" Junior declared, wiping his hands on his pants. "Next stop: the mall. Let's see what we can find there."

Junior settled into the driver's seat, the engine rumbling like a sleeping bear. Darrel was half-buried in a mountain of yarn, looking like a disgruntled Yeti. Olivia was sitting on her hands, and Caleb stared out the window from the back seat. "Alright, chuckleheads," Junior announced, his voice amplified by the Behemoth's surprisingly good acoustics. "How are we doing? Any complaints? Anyone need a blankie and a hot cocoa before we hit the mall? Riley, you look like you're about to turn into an icicle."

Riley, snuggled in the passenger seat, blew on her hands and rubbed them together. "Baby, it's fucking freezing out there," she shivered dramatically, her eyes twinkling mischievously. "I'm just looking forward to getting you back into bed. Where you fucking belong." She said, earning a playful swat from Olivia.

Darrel dramatically coughed up a puff of yarn. "For real man, this is some hard-core shit. It's been fire the entire time." Caleb cleared his throat, his usual jovial tone replaced with something more serious. "Hey, Junior," he said, his voice a little softer. "I just… I wanted to say thanks. For real. For picking us up when you did, Nicole, too. I know it's cheesy but, well… If you guys hadn't come, honest to God I don't think half of us would have survived."

"Actually, I was wondering…" Andrew added, his voice hesitant. "Do you guys ever think… do you think there's anyone else still back there? From the base, I mean. Did anyone else get away?" He bit his lip, suddenly feeling foolish for asking. Noah, who'd been silently fiddling with a Rubik's Cube he took from the Walmart, looked up, his brow furrowed. "Honestly, I've thought about it. But… realistically? We were maybe the only ones who got out early enough. Everyone else… who knows. I mean, we all thought Junior was nuts. We were just crazy enough to give it a chance."

"But we were a big group," Andrew persisted, his voice gaining a little more conviction. "Seven others, plus Sergeant Miller and his crew. Were they better off with us leaving? Or did we leave them behind to die?" The question hung heavy in the air, a dark cloud threatening to overshadow their meager joy. Junior gripped the steering wheel, lost in thought. He had wrestled with this question himself, countless times. Every decision he made was a gamble, a balancing act between survival and morality. He'd chosen to save those he could, but the cost was the unknown fate of those left behind.

Olivia, sensing the shift in mood, quietly leaned close to Junior's ear and kissed him, her lips soft and reassuring against his skin. "Just drive, honey." Her voice a low, comforting hum. He took a deep breath, letting Olivia's touch ground him. He knew the unspoken fear in their eyes, the guilt that gnawed at their conscience. "Okay," he said, his voice firm, "let me ask you this. Would you be willing to give up your share for another? I mean, Dad's resources are abundant, but they're not unlimited."

A collective sigh passed through the space as Junior pulled into the mall parking lot. After turning off the engine, he turned back in his seat, facing the rest. "The most difficult part of charity is knowing when to cut them off. Plus, not everyone would be able or willing to get in step." Olivia placed her hand on his shoulder before adding her two cents. "We can go back, but we can't help everyone, nor is that always the responsible thing to do. Junior's dad worked his entire life to prepare for this, and we're still guests in his home. So, we need to be courteous to our benefactor."

"Okay," he began, his voice resonating with newfound resolve. "So, here's the truth. We can go back. We can try to help everyone we see. But Dad always says, 'You can't save the world, but you can make a world of difference.' And let's be real, we're already making a massive difference just by keeping our little community strong."

Olivia squeezed his shoulder gently. "Junior's right. We have a responsibility to the people who are counting on us back home. David's made sure we are all ready for this world, and he didn't do it for us to throw it away." Darrel, ever the pragmatist, chimed in, "Exactly. David's got a system, and we're part of it. We can't just go rogue, handing out resources to every Tom, Dick, and Harry. It's not sustainable."

Noah, who had been unusually quiet, spoke up, his voice laced with a childlike curiosity that often surfaced despite his age. "Junior, did your dad ever have to deal with, like, insurrection? Or betrayal? Like, people trying to take what he's built?" "Yeah, Noah," Junior said, the playful edge gone from his voice. "Dad's seen it all. He's always said that the hardest part about building something worthwhile is protecting it. There are always going to be people who want what you have, who think they deserve it more, or who just want to watch it burn."

He paused, his gaze sweeping over the faces of his companions. "He's had to deal with... let's just say he's dealt with threats. Intimidation, theft, outright attacks. And, yeah," he admitted, his voice dropping, "betrayal." The jovial atmosphere of their mission was momentarily eclipsed by the stark reality of the word, betrayal. It was a chilling word, especially in a time when trust was a rare and precious commodity.

"He's very protective," Olivia elaborated, her voice soft but firm. "Of his family, his wives, his children, his home… everything he's built. He wouldn't hesitate to eliminate someone who posed a threat." Darrel whistled softly. "Damn. I knew he was hardcore, but 'eliminate' is a strong word." Junior nodded grimly. "It is. But Dad doesn't take chances when it comes to family. He learned that lesson the hard way." He hesitated for a moment, chewing on his lip. "There was... one person," he finally said, his voice tight. "Someone on the inside. Trusted." Andrew leaned forward. "What happened?"

Junior sighed, raking a hand through his hair. "It was a while back, just a couple of weeks after the Blackout. A woman named Kris. Dad took her in, like he's done with a lot of people over the years. She wanted to become one of his wives, desperately so. But she gave away secrets. About our security, about the layout of the house, about... us." "What did she tell?" Caleb asked, his eyes wide.

"Enough," Olivia answered, her face grim. "Enough to put everyone at risk. Luckily, David found out before anything serious could happen. He discovered her betrayal while he was out on a run rescuing Clarence and Margaret." "So he kicked her out?" Noah asked naively. Junior's expression hardened. "No. He didn't. He... eliminated her." He looked directly at Noah, his eyes conveying the full weight of the statement. "With his bare hands. No hesitation. No second chances. She didn't intend to physically harm anyone, but the implications were deadly serious."

A shiver ran down Olivia's spine, despite the fact that she'd heard the story before. David's protective nature was one of the things she admired and feared most about him. Darrel swallowed hard. "Damn. He really doesn't play." Parked in front the main entrance, Junior and his team dismounted. "Alright, team," he announced, "We're here for a purpose. Remember the list, stick together, and be vigilant. This place is a tomb, but tombs can still have traps."

He glanced at Darrel and Andrew, who stood ready near the Behemoth. "Darrel, Andrew, you two are on truck watch. Anyone gets close, you fire. No questions asked. Understood?" Darrel, ever the wisecracker, gave a crisp salute. "Understood, sir. Anyone looking to steal our sleigh is gonna have a really bad day."

Andrew, more reserved, simply nodded, his hand resting on the grip of his rifle. "We got it, Junior. Truck's safe with us." Junior nodded in satisfaction, then turned to the rest of the group. "Olivia, you're with me. Caleb, Noah, you two sweep ahead, eyes peeled for anything out of place. Remember our signals. We're in and out, quick and clean." He led the way into the mall, the others falling into formation behind him.

Chapter 48:

The Great Mall Haul

As they moved deeper into the mall, Olivia and Riley stuck close to Junior, navigating the maze of darkened storefronts, while Caleb and Noah, true to their assigned task, lead the group keeping an ever-watchful eye. It wasn't long before an uncomfortable silence took hold, the echoes of their footsteps and occasional whisper seemed to scream against the quiet. As they moved into the dim interior, Caleb whispered. "Hey, Junior... about what you were saying... about David and that Kris chick... he...he killed her with his bare hands? What... what does that even look like?" He looked genuinely disturbed, imagining some kind of brutal, drawn-out fight.

Junior didn't flinch. He kept his eyes moving, scanning the shadows. Olivia, walking close behind, winced slightly at the question. He turned to Caleb, his tone flat. "It wasn't a fight, Caleb. It was... clinical." He paused, searching for the right words. "He hugged her. Crushed her ribcage, collapsed her lungs. It was over in seconds. No screaming, no struggle. Just... silence." Noah gasped softly, his youthful complexion paling. "Damn," he muttered, "That's... intense."

Riley, who had been silent until now, finally spoke, her voice low and laced with a hint of playful challenge. "So, Junior, be honest. If someone tried to, say, steal my last pair of sexy boots, would you... you know... clinical hug them?" She batted her eyelashes, a mischievous look in her eyes. Olivia gently elbowed Riley, a small smile playing on her lips. "Riley, seriously?" But the question was out there, lingering like the scent of gasoline.

Junior stopped walking." Is that what you think of me Riley? Do you honestly think I'm going to hug people to death? Is that what you're fishing for?" He sighed, his eyes softening as he looked at Riley and Olivia. "Look, what happened with Kris was... unique. Dad trusted her and I really believe she loved him. And yeah, if protecting you two meant doing the same... I wouldn't hesitate." He paused, letting the weight of his words sink in. "But if someone hurt you, it wouldn't be clinical. It would be personal." Olivia stepped forward, placing a hand on Junior's arm. "We know you would, Junior. We trust you."

The tension in the air eased, replaced by a quiet understanding. Junior offered a small, genuine smile, then turned back to the task at hand, pushing open the doors to the dim interior of what used to be a Macy's. They stepped inside, the cavernous space echoing with the ghosts of shoppers past. Racks of clothes stood like silent sentinels, picked over but still holding treasures for those willing to look.

"Alright, ladies," Junior announced, his voice regaining its usual confident tone. "Let's find some clothes." He winked. "And anything else that catches your fancy. Olivia, you and I will stick together and make sure none of these hooligans get lost; Caleb, your job is to find the fancy clothes for the wives, so stay on that mission."

As the group dispersed, Noah, ever the curious one, fell into step beside Junior. "Hey, Junior," he asked, his voice a little hesitant, "About your dad... and you. Who's stronger? Like, physically?" Junior considered the question for a moment, his gaze sweeping across the department store. "That's a good question, Noah. The answer is complicated." He chuckled softly. "I'm physically stronger, that much is true. Thanks to, let's say, a lifetime of training. I can lift more, hit harder. Numbers-wise, I have him beat." He lowered his voice slightly. "He doesn't need to be the strongest or the smartest, because he has all of us. He cultivated us, trained us, gave us the tools to survive. He gave us a purpose. That's a power greater than any amount of brute force." "So, in a straight-up arm wrestling match," Noah pressed, a glint of amusement in his eyes, "You'd win?"

Junior grinned, a flash of white teeth in the dim light. "Absolutely. No question. But strength isn't everything, Noah." He clapped Noah on the shoulder. "There is this thing called 'leverage,' and Dad is a master." He winked. Olivia, her arms overflowing with lace and silk, sauntered over, a mischievous sparkle in her eyes. "Speaking of strength," she purred, gesturing to the overflowing cart, "are you two going to stand here chatting all day, or are you going to help me load up these... essentials?" Junior chuckled, taking the lingerie from her and carefully placing them in the cart. "Essentials indeed.

For whom, exactly?" he teased, raising an eyebrow. Olivia batted her eyelashes dramatically. "For surviving the apocalypse in style, darling. What else?"

Caleb, looking frazzled but triumphant, pushed another cart laden with brightly colored dresses and silky blouses toward them. "Mission accomplished!" he announced. "I think I found something for every wife. Though I'm a little worried I might have accidentally grabbed ten of the same dress for Summer. They all look good on her." "Ten of the same dress is fine," Junior said with a dismissive wave. "Plus, someone else might want one." He glanced over at Riley, who was tossing another pair of boots into the already overflowing cart. "Riley, are you planning on opening a shoe store back at the ranch?"

Riley shrugged, a sly grin on her face. "Gotta have options, Junior. Can't go wrong with good boots. Besides, who knows when we'll get a chance to go shopping again? Might as well stock up." She paused, "And some of these heels... well, they're for special occasions." Noah, returning with his armful of down jackets, barely managed to keep them from tumbling to the floor as he nearly crashed into Riley. "Whoa! Sorry!" he exclaimed, struggling to regain his balance. "Almost lost the entire winter wardrobe there."

Junior laughed. "Okay, team, let's start moving these carts toward the exit." He clapped his hands. "No dilly-dallying." Riley, Caleb, and Noah began pushing the three carts burdened with gifts and essentials as Junior and Olivia picked up two empty carts, ready and eager for their next round of scavenging. As the group approached the mall door near the Behemoth, they carefully pushed the full carts outside. Andrew and Darrel giving subtle thumbs-ups from their vigil.

As Darrel and Andrew efficiently transferred the contents of their full carts into the Behemoth, Darrel cracking jokes about the sheer volume of stuff they were acquiring. "I swear man, it's going to take us till Christmas, just to get everything sorted." Andrew snorted with laughter, carefully stacking the down jackets Noah had acquired.

With the Behemoth momentarily restocked, the team plunged back into the mall's echoing corridors. Their next destination: the anime store, a quest spurred by Brian's deep love for 'culture'. As they walked, Junior grinned at Olivia. "Alright, what intel do you have on this anime store, O wise one?" Olivia consulted her mental map. "It's upstairs, and it's in the north wing. They have everything: Blu-rays, manga, figurines, wall scrolls… the works. Word on the street is they have an impressive collection of limited-edition box sets. Brian is going to lose his mind."

Junior nodded thoughtfully. "Limited-edition box sets...sounds promising. We grab everything we can." He glanced around at his team. "Remember, folks, think long-term strategy. Christmas is just the beginning. We need a stockpile for birthdays, anniversaries, Tuesdays...you name it." Caleb, suddenly turned. "There's a jewelry store over there," he said, as he pointed toward the left. "We still need to get those rings and stuff, right?"

As they approached the jewelry store, the heavy metal security cage loomed before them. Riley sighed dramatically, placing her hands on her hips. "Well, that's just great. Looks like someone didn't want anyone getting in. That thing is locked up tighter than Fort Knox."

Caleb grunted, the muscles in his arms straining as he tried to lift the metal cage. It was useless. The security cage, designed to thwart even the most determined thieves, remained stubbornly in place. "Damn it," he swore, wiping sweat from his brow. "This thing is heavier than it looks." Noah circled the cage, his eyes scanning for weaknesses. "Looks like others have tried their luck," he said, pointing to a series of mangled edges and pry marks near the base. "But they didn't get very far. This steel is pretty thick." Noah tapped the bars again. "Hear that? Solid. This isn't just your average cage, guys. Someone really didn't want anyone getting their hands on what's inside."

Junior stepped forward, his expression determined. "Alright, enough complaining. We knew this wouldn't be easy. Caleb, Noah, take the edges. Riley, keep watch at the door. Olivia, keep an eye on the machinery so nothing comes crashing down." Junior then leaned back against the cage, finding purchase. "On three. One...two..." Taking a deep breath. "...THREE!" Junior strained, his face reddening. The muscles in his legs and back bulge as he heaved with incredible force. The sound of ripping metal fills the room, followed by a loud "POP!" The cage jerked upward, free from the floor. "Clear!" Riley announced, glancing nervously towards the front of the store. "Someone could've heard that."

Noah wedged the overturned display frame under the cage, keeping it propped up. "Just buying us a little time, but it's time nonetheless." Olivia stared at the jagged hole in the floor where the locking mechanism used to be. Her gaze lingering on Junior, a strange mix of awe and... something else, swirling within her. She cleared her throat, trying to regain her composure.

"Alright, alright, settle down, everyone," Junior said, panting slightly, but already regaining his composure. He wiped his brow with the back of his hand. "Cage is open. Now let's find that diamond ring for Bonnie. And try not to attract any unwanted attention. We don't need any... complications." He glanced at the empty display cases, then at Olivia, who was still staring, a strange expression in her eyes. "Olivia, you okay? You look like you've seen a ghost."

Olivia snapped back to reality, a faint blush rising on her cheeks. "I... I'm fine," she stammered, quickly diverting her gaze. "Just... impressed. That was... impressive." She busied herself with checking the structural integrity of the ceiling above, though her mind was far from the task at hand. The sheer, raw power Junior had displayed left her reeling.

"Impressed is an understatement," Riley muttered under her breath, a playful smirk dancing on her lips. She elbowed Olivia lightly. "Admit it, you're practically drooling." Olivia glared at her half-heartedly, but the flush on her cheeks deepened. "Shut up, Riley," she hissed. "Just help me look for the ring. And try to be discreet, unlike some people." She shot a pointed look at Junior, who was already rummaging behind the counter, trying to find a way to access the back room.

Junior, oblivious to the simmering tension, grunted in frustration as he tugged on the stubborn counter door. "Damn thing's locked tight. Noah, you're the lockpicking guru, right? Get over here and work your magic." Noah stepped forward, picks in hand. "On it. But don't expect miracles. This doesn't look like an ordinary deadbolt." He knelt down, his fingers already dancing over the lock, tiny instruments clicking and whirring. "Could take a few minutes."

Caleb, who'd been lingering near the entrance, suddenly perked up. "Wait a minute... I think I saw a key rack near the register when I came in. Maybe they left something behind?" He darted behind the counter, rummaging through drawers and shelves. After a moment, he emerged, a triumphant grin on his face and a small key ring dangling from his fingers. "Bingo! Looks like our lucky day."

Junior snatched the keys, his eyes gleaming with anticipation. "Alright, Caleb, you just saved us some serious time. Let's see if these bad boys work." He inserted a key into the lock, turning it gently. Click! The door swung open with a soft creak. "Jackpot! Now, let's get this show on the road." He pushed through the door, disappearing into the back room. Olivia, shaking off her reverie, followed close behind, Riley hot on her heels. Noah and Caleb brought up the rear, ensuring no one disturbed them.

The back room was small and cramped, filled with metal shelving and filing cabinets. But the centerpiece was undoubtedly the ominous-looking locking cabinet. It stood taller than Junior, its numerous drawers secured with individual locks. A small, printed label was taped to each drawer: "Diamonds," "Emeralds," "Rubies," "Saphire," "Topaz," and so on.

Junior whistled. "Well, well, well. Now that's what I call job security for a locksmith. Where do we start?" Riley pointed to the "Diamonds" drawer. "Seeing as we're looking for a diamond ring, maybe that should be our first stop?" "Good call, Riley," Junior agreed, already reaching for his lock picks.

Junior, his focus unwavering, made quick work of the locks. His fingers danced over the intricate mechanisms, the subtle clicks and scrapes music to his ears. One by one, the tumblers fell into place, and the drawers sprang open with a soft thunk. Soon, the entire cabinet stood unlocked, a treasure trove revealed. He grinned, a flicker of pride in his eyes. "Alright, team. Let's see what Santa's elves left behind."

He pulled open the "Diamonds" drawer, his eyes widening slightly. Inside, nestled in velvet trays, were rings of all shapes and sizes. Solitaires, clusters, bands adorned with stones of varying cuts and clarity. "Damn," he breathed, "Bonnie's gonna love this." Olivia, ever practical, leaned closer. "Okay, but which one is 'Bonnie' worthy? We need something that says 'eternal love,' not 'I found this in a raided jewelry store.'" Riley snorted. "Isn't that all of them, technically? Unless you think we're going to find a receipt hidden in here." She winked at Junior. "I say, go big or go home. The girl is crushing hard." "Alright, team," he announced, gesturing towards the open drawers with a sweep of his hand.

Olivia, her dark eyes narrowed in concentration, started meticulously examining each ring. "Alright, alright, let's see what we have... Oh, that's way too gaudy. This one looks like it came out of a gumball machine. Seriously, who buys this crap?" Riley picked up a sizable solitaire. "This one's got some heft to it... But is it too... traditional for Bonnie? She's a cool kid, you know?"

Junior, ignoring their debate, grabbed a handful of empty jewelry gift boxes and began scooping gems into them with surprising delicacy. Diamonds glittered, emeralds flashed, and rubies pulsed with inner fire as he filled the boxes with an almost reckless abandon. "Alright, alright," he said, his voice brooking no argument. "Enough window-shopping. Olivia, Riley, you two pick something simple, elegant. A two-carat princess cut, maybe? Something that screams 'forever' without screaming 'I robbed a jewelry store during the apocalypse.'" He said, adding, "Although, technically..."

Olivia, momentarily distracted by the sheer audacity of his gem-grabbing operation, regained her composure. "Princess cut, huh? Practical. I like it." She resumed her search, now with a more focused intensity. Riley, still slightly dazed by the glittering spectacle, nodded in agreement. "Yeah, something classic. Can't go wrong with a princess." Junior, his task nearly complete, rummaged further, his brow furrowed in concentration. "Okay, next up: Grace. Needs something...sweet. Innocent. But with a little hidden strength. And Kyle..." He chuckled, a low rumble in his chest. "Kyle needs something that says, 'I'm a badass, but this girl's got me whipped'."

He extracted two more rings from the overflowing drawers. One, a delicate silver band with a small, sparkling aquamarine. The other, a black titanium ring with a single, embedded ruby. He placed them carefully into separate ring boxes, a satisfied grin spreading across his face. "Alright, team," he announced, holding up the small boxes. "Bonnie's, Grace's, and Kyle's are secured. Now, let's move on to the really fun stuff."

As they exited the jewelry store, Junior whistling a tuneless melody, Olivia was practically vibrating with barely suppressed energy, and Riley was still slightly cross-eyed from the sheer bling, Caleb and Noah exchanged knowing glances. They had seen Junior's brand of "shopping" before. It was efficient, to say the least. "Anime store, here we come!" Noah declared, pumping his fist. "Brian's gonna freak when he sees what we got him."

"So, Junior," Olivia began, "about those 'raw materials' you liberated from the jewelry store... care to elaborate?" Junior shrugged, his expression nonchalant.

"Jewels are pretty much useless now, right? I mean, yeah, they're shiny and pretty, but you can't eat 'em. But the materials? Gold can be melted down, turned into wiring, used for repairs. Platinum is super durable. Diamonds... well, diamonds are forever. We can use them for cutting tools, abrasives, all sorts of stuff. Plus," he added with a wink, "when society starts to rebuild, who knows? Maybe they'll be worth something again. We'll be holding onto a little piece of the old world, a reminder of what once was. Like a shiny, sparkly time capsule."

Riley snorted. "You make it sound so practical. I thought you just wanted to hoard shiny things like a dragon." Junior shook his head. "I could really care less. But someone will get it eventually and it might as well be us. Plus, we're already here." Caleb, who had been lagging slightly behind, finally caught up. "Anime store's just a few stores down," he said, pointing further into the mall. "I see a bunch of figurines and stuff in the window. Should be easy pickings."

Noah, with his encyclopedic knowledge of anime, immediately zeroed in on a stack of Blu-ray box sets. "Attack on Titan! Full Metal Alchemist! Oh man, Brian is gonna lose it!" He began frantically stacking the sets in his arms. Olivia leaned closer to Junior, her voice a low, sultry whisper that only he could hear. "Junior," she murmured, her hand lightly tracing the outline of his jaw, "I need to use the bathroom. Badly." She gave him a look, a mixture of urgency and something more... intimate. "Would you... mind coming with me?"

Junior tilted his head, a flicker of amusement in his eyes. "Escorting you to the restroom? Is that a new tradition for our scavenging trips?" Olivia blushed slightly but held his gaze. "Not exactly escorting. I just… I feel safer with you. Especially after what happened at the jewelry store. Plus," she added, her voice dropping even lower, "I have this… overwhelming urge to show you how grateful I am for keeping me safe. And the bathroom seems like the only place where we can have a modicum of privacy."

Riley, who had been pretending to examine a wall of manga, perked up her ears at Olivia's words. She shot a quick, envious glance at Olivia before returning to her feigned interest in the comics. Damn Olivia for being so forward. She wanted to be the one dragging Junior into a secluded space for a quickie.

Junior considered her request for a moment, his eyes scanning the surrounding area. Darrel and Andrew were outside, guarding the Behemoth, and Noah and Caleb were too engrossed in their anime haul to notice anything. "Alright," he said. "But we make it quick. We still have a few more stops to make, and I don't want to leave Darrel and Andrew out there for too long."

He turned to Noah and Caleb, who were now arguing over which Attack on Titan season was the best. "We'll be back in a few minutes," he said, his tone leaving no room for argument. "Don't get into too much trouble." Noah, still clutching a stack of Blu-rays, gave a distracted wave. "Yeah, yeah, whatever. Just hurry back when you're done."

Junior allowed Olivia to pull him along, a smirk playing on his lips. He could practically feel Riley's burning gaze on his back, and the knowledge that he was inciting a little jealousy only added to his amusement. In the back of the store, Olivia opened the door that led to the employee corridor. The hallway was dark and deserted. The air smelled faintly of stale popcorn and disinfectant, not exactly the most romantic ambiance, but she didn't care.

As soon as they were inside the hallway, Olivia didn't hesitate. Her hands went straight to his belt buckle, fumbling with the leather strap in her eagerness. "Easy there," Junior chuckled softly, placing his hands over hers to guide her. "No need to rip my pants off." Her eyes, usually bright and playful, were now clouded with a potent mix of desire and urgency. "I can't help it," she breathed, her voice trembling slightly. "I'm turned on more than I can say." She finally undid the buckle and quickly unfastened the button of his jeans.

He watched her, his expression a curious blend of amusement and arousal. The raw, unfiltered desire in her eyes was a powerful aphrodisiac. He lowered his voice even further, barely a whisper against her ear. "And what exactly did you have in mind to show your gratitude?" Before he could finish the question, Olivia had dropped to her knees in the hallway, her hands tugging his jeans and boxers down. The cold air of the mall sent a shiver down his spine, but the chill was quickly replaced by a surge of heat as Olivia's lips closed around him.

Junior leaned against the hallway wall, a low groan escaping his lips. Olivia's ministrations were nothing short of expert, each movement precise and deliberate. He closed his eyes, surrendering to the moment, the sounds of the deserted mall fading into a background hum. He ran his fingers through her hair, the silkiness a stark contrast to the rough concrete against his back. "God, Olivia," he rasped, his voice thick with pleasure. "You are going to be the death of me." He briefly wondered what Riley was doing and instantly turned his thoughts away from her. One thing at a time, he thought. Don't be greedy.

He glanced down at Olivia, her face flushed, her eyes half-closed in concentration. He had to admit, her possessiveness was definitely a turn-on. "Almost there," Olivia murmured against him, her voice muffled but no less insistent. Her hands tightened their grip, and Junior knew he was on the verge. "Olivia…" he groaned, his body tensing. He couldn't hold back any longer. A wave of release washed over him as he filled her mouth with cum. He tightened his hold on Olivia's hair, her name a ragged whisper on his lips.

A moment later, he sagged against the wall, breathing heavily as Olivia swallowed every drop. She looked up at him, her eyes shining with a mixture of triumph and adoration as she nursed out every drop. Then licked her lips, a slow, deliberate gesture that sent another shiver down Junior's spine. "Happy now?" he asked, a faint smile playing on his lips. He felt incredibly drained, but also strangely exhilarated.

Olivia nodded, nuzzling against him. "More than you know," she whispered. He chuckled, a low rumble in his chest. "Yeah, well, I'll try not to let it go to my head." He gently pulled her up, brushing a stray strand of hair from her face. "We should probably get back to Riley and the others before they think we've been eaten by rogue mannequins."

The chill of the deserted mall clung to Junior's skin, a stark contrast to the heat that had just pulsed through him. He adjusted his clothing, a slight smirk tugging at the corner of his mouth. Olivia's little display had certainly been... effective. He still felt the remnants of it thrumming beneath his skin, a potent reminder of her dedication. "Alright, lover boy," Riley's voice cut through his thoughts, laced with a playful, yet undeniably sexual, edge. She stood near a display of anime figurines, arms crossed, a knowing glint in her eyes. "Took you two long enough. Find any good hiding spots to make out in?"

Junior chuckled, raising his hands in mock surrender. "Hey, blame Olivia, not me. Besides, you know I'm always professional." He smiled. "And I do get a platinum star for productivity. So, what's the damage? Find anything good?" "Damage is minimal, supplies are high," Riley drawled, tilting her head towards a pile of anime box sets Caleb and Noah had assembled nearby. "The boys were on a mission. Brian's going to be one happy camper. But, uh, speaking of missions…" She paused, her eyes narrowing, a possessive fire igniting within them. "When we get back, you're mine. First. No arguments."

Junior's eyebrows shot up, a grin spreading across his face. "Well, aren't you just full of surprises? I had no idea you felt this way." He leaned in, his voice dropping to a whisper. "You always could have just asked, you know." Riley scoffed, though a blush crept up her neck. "Please. It's too damn cold here to get into anything serious. Besides, a girl's gotta have some standards. But don't think this means you're off the hook. I'm calling dibs.

First shower when we get back, then I'm dragging you to bed. And you better fuck me like you've never fucked me before, end of discussion." She punctuated her point with a playful shove to his shoulder. "So, yeah, get your head out of the gutter and let's finish this mission. Jennifer's sex swing isn't going to find itself."

Junior's grin widened, practically splitting his face. "Promises, promises," he purred, enjoying Riley's uncharacteristic assertiveness. The cold air seemed to be doing more than just nipping at her cheeks; it was igniting a whole other kind of fire. He loved it. "As you wish." He turned to Olivia, catching her eye. He saw that same possessive glint, only amplified, and a healthy dose of arousal. He winked. "Don't worry, my darling, you're getting yours too. After all, sharing is caring."

Olivia's eyes narrowed, and she pursed her lips into a smirk, "Damn right it is baby. We'll see how well you listen." She states. "Alright you two lovebirds, let's get moving and grab the last of this stuff, now, before anyone else does." Caleb and Noah, oblivious to the simmering desires swirling around them, began pushing the overflowing cart towards the mall concourse. "Alright, team," Junior announced. "Gifts for Jennifer and Jessica, then we head back. Adult boutique, here we come!" He punctuated the statement with a playful salute, adding a little skip to his step. Riley's explicit intentions had put a definite spring in his gait.

The adult boutique wasn't exactly what they'd hoped. It was a smaller portion of a larger store, and smelled faintly of cheap latex and desperation. Still, Riley, with her laser focus on the mission, quickly located a treasure trove of pasties in various shapes, sizes, and…levels of detail. She practically squealed with delight, grabbing handfuls and tossing them into a shopping basket.

Olivia, meanwhile, was busy examining a selection of vibrators, her expression a mix of amusement and scientific curiosity. "These things look…interesting," she mused, turning one over in her hand. "I wonder if they still work." Junior nodded. "Probably, if you can find batteries for them."

Junior wandered towards the back of the store, hoping to find the elusive sex swing. He poked around in the dimly lit corners, rummaging through boxes of questionable lingerie and inflatable…things, then sighed in frustration. "Anything?" Riley asked, joining him with a basket overflowing with pasties and other assorted novelties. Junior shook his head. "Nothing. Not a single sex swing in sight. Just…a lot of…other…stuff." He gestured vaguely at the array of toys that surrounded them. "Well, damn," Riley said, her face falling. "Jennifer's going to be disappointed."

"Hold on a minute," Junior said, a thoughtful expression crossing his face. "I know another place. It's really close to here, and I'm pretty sure they'll have what we're looking for." He glanced at the overflowing baskets in Riley and Olivia's hands. "We can swing by there on the way back. Let's just get all this back to the truck."

As they pushed the carts laden with their…erm…acquisitions through the deserted mall concourse, Olivia and Noah scanned the surroundings. The silence of the mall was eerie, broken only by the squeak of the cart wheels and the distant echo of their footsteps. "Think Darrel and Andrew are still awake?" Noah muttered, his breath misting in the cold air. Olivia snorted softly. "Knowing those two? Probably playing 'I Spy' in the truck."

Finally, they reached the main entrance, the behemoth parked outside. Darrel and Andrew were indeed cozy inside the cab and the music was booming. Andrew, curled up in the passenger seat was playing "Mario cart" on a recently acquired DS, while Darrel was in the back sorting out their loot. "Whoa, you guys got a haul!" Darrel exclaimed as the group approached, his eyes widening at the sight of the overflowing baskets. "Let's just say, Christmas is going to be…interesting this year," Riley said with a mischievous grin.

Junior effortlessly lifted the heavier of the two baskets and rolled it into the back of the Behemoth. "Alright, let's load up and hit the road. Next stop, sex toys. Hopefully, they'll have what we're looking for."

Chapter 49:

Infected with Brainworms

The Behemoth lumbered down the road, its massive tires crunching over debris scattered across the asphalt. The strip mall was eerily silent, the closed sandwich shop and vape store flanking the adult boutique adding to the desolate atmosphere. "Alright, everyone out. Let's be quick about this," Junior instructed, hopping out of the driver's seat.

As they approached the boutique, Caleb glanced nervously around. "You sure this is a good idea, Junior? This place looks…dead." "Relax, Caleb," Riley said, giving him a playful shove. "We're just grabbing a few items." Junior kicked at the front door, the lock snapping with a satisfying crack. He pulled the door open, revealing the dark interior, illuminated by the collective head lamps. "Alright, party time!" he announced, stepping inside.

The air inside was thick with the scent of cheap wax and plastic. Shelves lined the walls, displaying an assortment of…adult novelties. "Wow," Noah breathed, his eyes wide "They've got everything here." Darrel, ever the comedian, picked up a rubber chicken wearing a tiny leather harness. "I think I found dinner," he quipped, winking at Olivia.

Olivia rolled her eyes, unimpressed. "Put that down, you perv. We're here for one thing: Jennifer's surprise." She gestured impatiently towards the back of the store. Junior, meanwhile, was rummaging behind the counter, tossing aside dusty boxes and faded promotional posters. "Bingo!" he exclaimed triumphantly, emerging with a large, velvet-lined box. "Feast your eyes on this, people."

He opened the box with a flourish, revealing its contents: a gleaming chrome sex swing, complete with plush, blood-red cushions and an array of adjustable straps that looked capable of supporting a rhinoceros. The chrome glinted in the moving light, an unsettling juxtaposition against the dingy surroundings. "Perfect!" Riley declared, clapping her hands together in delight. "Jennifer's gonna love this! Finally, something to spice things up around the plantation."

As Junior and Riley admired their prize, Noah, Andrew, and Caleb were enthusiastically loading small baskets with an eclectic assortment of…adult merchandise. High-end vibrators alongside leather restraints, feather boas, and mountains of assorted pasties that Jessica would undoubtedly find amusing.

Darrel, still clutching the chicken, sauntered over to Junior, a curious look in his eye. "Hey, Junior," he said, adopting a mock-serious tone. "You do realize your dad is going to… you know… bang your mom in that swing, right?" Junior paused, considering the image for a moment. He shrugged, a nonchalant expression on his face. "Yeah, so? Dad banging Mom isn't exactly breaking news, Darrel." He paused. "Besides, Mom likes to have sex." He thought for a minute and grabbed a second swing, as well as some spreaders and strap cuffs. "Now this is a Christmas surprise."

Caleb, who had been carefully examining a selection of... novelty gag balls, glanced over, brow furrowed. "What are those... spreader things for?" Junior grinned, that familiar devilish spark igniting in his eyes. He held up a spreader bar, a length of polished steel with adjustable wrist and ankle cuffs attached. "Let's just say they add a certain... flavor to the experience. Think of it as maximizing available real estate." He waggled his eyebrows suggestively. "They spread the legs."

Noah choked on his own saliva, his cheeks flushing scarlet. "Dude! Seriously? Isn't that a bit... excessive?" Darrel burst out laughing, the sound echoing in the otherwise silent adult boutique. "Maximize available real estate! Dude, you're a poet! A depraved, kinky poet, but a poet nonetheless!" He clapped Junior on the back, nearly sending the chicken flying.

Noah, still recovering from his near-choking experience, spluttered, "But... but your mom? With... with those things?" Junior smirked, unfazed by their reactions. "Look, guys, my dad isn't exactly known for his vanilla approach to, well, anything. Especially not in the bedroom. Besides, Mom loves Dad. She trusts him implicitly. And yes, Noah, especially with those things."

He placed the spreader bar and cuffs carefully into the boxes they came in. "Besides, it's not just for Mom. Don't forget about Tiffany, Summer, Elena, Jessica, and

Kayla! They all like his control. Plus, haven't you noticed the collars?" Olivia, who had been quietly observing the exchange, spoke up, her eyes widening slightly, "That's right... the collars! They all wear... collars!" She snapped her fingers, a realization dawning on her face.

Riley, who had been sifting through a pile of vibrators with the detached air of a seasoned shopper, finally piped up, "Took you long enough, Liv. It's kinda obvious. Jennifer's got that permanent metal ring, Summer's always rocking the silver chain, Tiffany's got the decorative choker, Jessica practically sleeps in hers, and Kayla? Always some kind of choker. The rest usually sport them when they're around David..." She shrugged. "It's their thing."

Andrew, who had been quietly observing the whole exchange, his face a mask of polite confusion, finally found his voice. "Wait, hold on. 'Permanent'? You mean, your mom can't take it off?" He looked at Junior with a mixture of disbelief and morbid curiosity. "Like, ever?" Junior chuckled. "Nope. Been on her since before I was born. She cleans it, obviously, but she never takes it off. It's a symbol of her commitment to my dad, and him to her. She loves it. Don't worry, it's not like it's strangling her."

Andrew pondered this for a moment, brow furrowed in thought. "So...David was always...this way? Or is this something he and his wives explored together? Like, did he suddenly wake up one day and be like, 'Honey, I'm thinking about investing in some chrome and leather'?" "Chrome and leather," Junior repeated, a slow grin spreading across his face. "That's... actually a pretty good way to put it, Andrew. But no, Dad didn't just wake up one day thinking about it. It was more...intrinsic. Part of who he is." He paused, considering how to explain it to someone who clearly hadn't grown up in the delightfully unconventional environment he had.

He glanced at the bagged sex swing components, then back at Andrew. "Look, Dad's always been...dominant. He has this natural authority, a presence. And some women are just drawn to that. Especially Tiffany and my mom. They practically tripped over each other to get his attention." Olivia chuckled, remembering stories Tiffany had told. "Tripped is an understatement, Andrew. She practically seduced him at every turn. It's a little embarrassing, honestly."

Riley snorted, adding, "And Jennifer? She was like a puppy following him around. Couldn't get enough of him. She literally became his shadow, anticipating his every need." Junior nodded, confirming, "Yeah, Mom was…persistent. She followed him everywhere. She basically built her entire life around being his sex slave."

Junior grinned, clapping his hands together. "Alright, enough philosophical debate in the porn shop. Let's get this show on the road! Olivia, can you start the truck? Riley, you take point on the spreaders. Andrew, you're on swing duty. Darrel and Caleb, help Noah pack the rest into the Behemoth. Let's move, people!"

As they began loading the "gifts" into the Behemoth, Andrew still couldn't shake his fascination. He carefully lifted the box containing the sex swing, picturing Jennifer, this seemingly sweet, playful woman, enjoying such…extreme activities. It was a jarring contrast to the image he had of her gardening, tending to her herbs, and doting on David. He caught Junior's eye. "Hey, Junior, no offense, but don't you find it a little…weird…thinking about your parents like…that?" Junior shrugged, unfazed. "Nah, not really. I grew up with it. It's just…normal for me. Honestly, I'd be more weirded out if they weren't into that stuff."

Andrew continued to stare at the swing box, a maze of confusion etched on his face. "But...don't they ever…compete? I mean, with so many wives, and…the uh…power dynamic you mentioned…doesn't that create tension? Jealousy?" Junior slammed the back door of the Behemoth shut, securing their illicit Christmas haul. He leaned against the vehicle, crossing his arms. "Man, you're really stuck on the jealousy thing, huh? Look, it's not like some messed up reality show where they're constantly fighting over Dad. They all love him, sure, but they also respect each other. It's more of a…team effort."

He paused, watching Andrew's still unconvinced expression. "Okay, look, it's complicated. It's not like they didn't know what they were getting into. They all chose this. Hell, some of them practically recruited each other!" Junior chuckled, pushing himself off the truck. "Come on, let's get back to the house. I'll give you the abridged version on the way."

He hopped into the driver's seat, Olivia already sitting behind the driver's seat. Andrew climbed into the back seat, with Darrel, Caleb, and Noah in the back of the truck. As they rumbled down the desolate highway, Junior continued his explanation, raising his voice over the engine. "Alright, so, Mom and Summer have, more or less, been friends since high school. Can you believe it? Mom was always the wild child, Summer was the smart one, and they were both crushing hard on Dad even back then."

"Wait, so they…shared him?" Andrew balked, picturing high school sweethearts willingly dating the same guy. "Not exactly shared," Junior clarified. "They were just…aware of each other's feelings. Things got serious later. They even went to senior prom together. All four of them. Dad, Mom, Tiffany and Summer." "Then there's Tiffany, she was older, but she got close with both Summer and Mom. Elena came into the picture next. She befriended Tiffany, Summer and Mom, and the relationships just kept building from there."

"Then came Taylor and Nicole. They were assigned to the same company after Basic Training and were even roommates. Dad was their senior instructor and even helped them out with some personal issues. After a while, they both came back and basically joined the family." "How did Jessica join?" Caleb questioned.

Junior considered how best to answer "Jessica is different. She was in love with dad before she even knew him, it's difficult to explain. The short version is, she was drawn to him very early on and was really close to Summer too." He paused, wondering if he should say more. "Kayla was our neighbor, and she just kinda got sucked in to his gravitational pull. Then Tanya. She was someone David wanted to find. Someone he had hurt before."

Andrew leaned forward, his eyebrows practically touching. "Hurt? What do you mean he hurt her? This is getting even weirder!" Darrel chuckled from the back of the truck. "Welcome to the David-verse, noob. Prepare for your mind to be thoroughly scrambled." Junior sighed, gripping the steering wheel tighter. "Look, Dad… knows… things. Tanya was someone he met in a previous life, more or less. He felt obligated to…well, not make amends exactly, more like…give her the opportunity to choose a different path this time around, knowing who he is."

Andrew slumped back in his seat, his mind reeling. The information overload was hitting him hard. Previous lives? Choosing paths? This wasn't just polyamory; this was some next-level, multi-dimensional, cosmic relationship arrangement. He looked back at Noah and Caleb, who seemed unfazed, almost bored. Darrel, on the other hand, was grinning like a Cheshire cat, clearly enjoying his befuddlement.

"So," Andrew stammered, trying to piece things together. "They all…know about the previous lives thing? And they're okay with it?" "Yes, It's kind of a required learning." Junior replied, glancing in the rearview mirror. "Mom, Summer, Tiffany… they're his team, been with him since the beginning. The rest, well, their connection is more supernatural." "And the…gravitational pull thing? That's real?" Andrew asked, gesturing vaguely.

Junior snorted. "Dude, I've seen it happen. It's like watching someone walk into a black hole made of charisma and wisdom. Resistance is futile." "So, gravitational pull, huh?" Andrew finally repeated, his voice laced with disbelief. "That's…that's a thing?" Junior chuckled. "Look, I know it sounds crazy. Hell, it is crazy. But let me put it this way: when Kayla was just our neighbor, before she moved in. There was a period, maybe a few months, where she was practically a different person. She started hanging around the house, like… a lot. And when she wasn't around him, she was… withering. Like a plant without water."

Junior snorted, recalling the moments. "When she had to go home, she looked like she was gonna sprout roots right there on the porch. It was literally like watching someone go through withdrawal," Junior continued, his voice serious. "She was anxious, irritable, couldn't sleep. She lost her appetite, had no energy. It was… intense. Then, she would come over, and she was okay again. For a while, anyway. Until the pull got too strong."

"So," Andrew started again, his voice wavering slightly, "This gravitational pull… Are we talking magnets here? Like, stick-to-the-fridge magnets?" Darrel burst out laughing. "Dude, you're killing me. It's not like a literal magnet! More like… a cosmic homing beacon. A really, really strong one." Junior sighed from the driver's seat.

"Every one's different, Andrew. Each relationship has something I can't quite understand myself."

He paused, glancing in the rearview mirror. "Look at Jessica, for example. Before she came to her senses, she had an existential crisis when her pull became too strong. She started questioning everything. Her life, her choices, whether any of it meant anything without David around. It was intense, man. Intense even for Jessica." "So," Andrew began again, fidgeting in his seat, "he...he has that effect on all of them?"

Junior sighed. "Pretty much. Look, I'm not a scientist. I'm a gunsmith who can also whip your ass six ways to Sunday. All I know is what I've seen. They're all drawn to him. Different ways, different reasons, but the draw is… real. Like, a physical thing that can actually be observed." He paused, choosing his words carefully. "And honestly, if you want real answers, ask them. Ask the wives. They're not gonna lie about it, and it's not like knowing the truth will change anything at this point."

Olivia, who had been quietly observing the conversation, piped up from the back. "It's hard to explain, Andrew. It's not like a spell or some mind control thing. It's more... a deep-seated understanding. A feeling that you're exactly where you're supposed to be." Caleb added, "It's like meeting the person you were always meant to meet but multiplied by ten. And amplified by a hundred."

Junior expertly maneuvered the Behemoth into the work shed, the mammoth vehicle barely squeezing through the doorway. The engine, a roaring beast moments ago, sputtered and died, leaving a ringing silence in its wake. He cut the ignition and turned to face Andrew, who looked like a deer caught in the headlights. The cavernous work shed, usually filled with the clatter of tools and the hum of generators, was now dominated by the sheer presence of the Behemoth. Junior clapped Andrew on the shoulder, a gesture that felt more like a friendly punch.

"Alright, gents, ladies," Junior announced, his voice still rough from the long drive. "Unloading can wait. Let's grab something to eat and get some sleep for now. Wedgwood was… fruitful, but I'm beat." Susan, practically buzzing with relief, clung to Andrew's arm as he stepped out of the cab, her gaze fixed on him like he was the only person in the world. "I'm so glad you're back," she whispered, squeezing him tighter. "I missed you so much."

Parker, leaning against a workbench, raised an eyebrow at Junior. "Trip went well then, huh? Find anything interesting?" Junior winked. "Trip was productive, Parker. Don't let anyone in this thing until it gets unloaded," he said, pointedly. "Sophia has breakfast waiting for y'all," Susan said, tugging Andrew's arm. "C'mon, let's get you something to eat."

Junior grinned at Susan, giving her a playful salute. "Thanks, Suze! You're a lifesaver, as always. C'mon, you lot," he said, gesturing towards the main house. "Sophia's holding down the fort with breakfast. Sounds like a feast after that drive." He squeezed Olivia and Riley's hands. Darrel, Noah, and Caleb, a trio of weary travelers, perked up at the mention of food. They shuffled after Junior, their steps a little lighter now.

As they entered the main house, the aroma of bacon and eggs wafted through the air, a beacon calling them to the kitchen. Sophia stood guard by the kitchen island. "Took you long enough," she said, a hint of a smile playing on her lips as she gestured to the spread of food. "I was starting to think I'd have to fight off the vultures myself." "Sophia, you're a saint," Junior said, grabbing a plate and loading it with food. He caught David's eye and offered a respectful nod. "Morning, Dad. Trip went well."

Junior inhaled deeply, the scent of Susan and Sophia's cooking momentarily distracting him from the post-mission weariness. He noticed Darrel, Noah, and Caleb's rapt attention wasn't solely focused on the breakfast buffet. They were practically craning their necks, observing David and his wives like they were characters in a particularly strange nature documentary. He suppressed a chuckle. It seems their earlier conversation sparked a renewed interest in their dynamic.

Jessica, perched on a stool at the island, nursing a now-content Poppy, noticed the rather blatant ogling. Her brow arched, a playful smirk tugging at her lips. "Alright, boys, what's with the staring? Is there an inside joke I'm unaware of? Or is my nursing distracting you?" she asked, her voice laced with amusement. Junior swallowed a mouthful of scrambled eggs, then gestured with his fork. "Sorry, Jessica. We, uh… we had a conversation on the way back. About… relationship dynamics." He answered. "Apparently, it's become a topic of interest."

Just then, Jennifer breezed into the kitchen, her smile bright and her eyes sparkling. As she crossed the room to plant a kiss on David's cheek, Andrew couldn't help but fixate on the solid metal ring around her neck, her eternity collar. He had never seen anything like it before, and up till now, hardly noticed it. Driven by a curiosity he couldn't suppress, he blurted out, "Jennifer, is that... is that comfortable? Do you even like wearing that?"

Jennifer paused, her smile widening even further. She reached up, grabbing the collar. "Like it? Andrew, darling, I love it. It's a constant reminder." "Of what?" Andrew pressed, emboldened by her openness. "Of who I belong to," Jennifer said, tilting her head in David's direction. "Think of it as a very stylish leash. Daddy likes to keep his pets close," Jennifer purred, the words hanging in the air like a provocative challenge. Andrew, emboldened by her playful nature, pushed further, completely oblivious to the bomb he was about to drop. "So, you can't take it off? Ever?"

Jennifer trailed her fingers along the cold steel of the collar, a thoughtful expression on her face. "Well, technically, I could. It requires a special tool, a little hex wrench. But... I haven't taken it off since Master gifted it to me. Why would I want to?" Darrel, who had been silently observing the interaction with a mixture of fascination and apprehension, decided to step in. "So, um, Jennifer," Darrel began, carefully choosing his words, "hypothetically speaking, would you... maybe be willing to take it off, just for a second, so we can see how it works? No pressure, of course! Just... you know, for educational purposes."

Jennifer's smile abruptly vanished, replaced by a look of profound unease. Her eyes widened, and her hand flew to her throat, clutching the collar as if it were a lifeline. Her breathing became shallow, and her lower lip began to quiver. Before anyone could react, tears welled up in her eyes and spilled down her cheeks. "Oh, God, I... I can't," she choked out, her voice thick with emotion. "Just... just talking about it... it feels... wrong. Like... like dying."

David, who had been watching the exchange with a growing sense of concern, immediately stepped forward, wrapping his arms around her. "Easy, sweetheart. It's alright. They didn't know." Tiffany rushed over with a dishtowel and pressed it gently into Jennifer's hands. "Here, sweetie. Just breathe." Jennifer took the towel and dabbed at her eyes, her body trembling slightly. "I... I'm so sorry," she mumbled. "I just... the thought of removing it... it's like severing a part of myself. I can't do it."

Darrel, mortified by the unexpected reaction, stammered, "No, no, it's okay! We didn't realize... we wouldn't have asked if we knew." Caleb and Noah nodded in agreement, their faces etched with concern. Andrew, who had initiated the whole thing, was especially stricken with guilt. He stepped forward, his voice filled with genuine remorse. Jennifer reached out and gently pulled him into a hug. "Oh, honey, don't feel bad. You didn't know. Honestly, I'm fine. Just… sensitive, I guess. And no, I never take it off." She pulled back from the hug, her eyes locking with his. "And don't feel guilty for asking. It's a reasonable question." She gave him a warm, reassuring smile.

David, watching the exchange with a knowing look, squeezed Jennifer's hand. "Perhaps," he suggested gently, "we could explain things a little better. It's not always easy to understand from the outside." "Yeah," Jennifer agreed, taking a deep breath and managing a watery smile. "I want to help you understand. Ask away."

Andrew, Darrel, Caleb, and Noah exchanged bewildered glances. The depth of Jennifer's reaction, the palpable distress at the mere thought of removing the collar, was far beyond anything they had imagined. They were used to the casual, often raunchy banter of the night shift, but this… this was something else entirely. "It's… it's more than just a piece of jewelry, isn't it?" Caleb ventured cautiously, his eyes fixed on the simple titanium ring around her neck.

Jennifer nodded, her voice still a little shaky. "It is. It's a symbol, yes. But it's far more than that. It's… well, you saw a little bit what it does." She gave a small, self-deprecating laugh. "It's a connection, a bond. Taking it off would be like… like willingly losing a vital part of myself." "So… it's about control?" Noah asked quietly, his gaze drawn to David. Jennifer shook her head, still gripping the collar. "No, It's about strength. Master is my strength."

Jennifer took a deep breath. "Some of us feel it stronger than others, it's true," she said, her voice regaining some of its strength. "It's... it's hard to explain. It's a deeply personal thing." She paused, choosing her words carefully. "For a few of us... David is like oxygen. We simply cease to exist without him." She looked pointedly at Jessica.

Everyone knew who she meant. Jessica, usually a vibrant, sparkling presence, didn't even hide it. "I… I can understand loyalty. Devotion, even," Darrel spoke up. "But… dying? That seems like a massive overstatement." Jessica flinched, a look of mild offense on her face. Before she could respond, Jennifer jumped in. "It's not an overstatement, Darrel. It's the truth. If you knew Jessica as well as we do, you'd understand. All of us are completely certain she would die. She simply refuses to live without him."

Jessica rolled her eyes, a faint blush highlighting her cheeks. "Hey, don't act like I had a choice in the matter! It's not like I signed up for this 'existential David-dependency' program. I was screwed from the start!" She waved a pancake around for emphasis. "I was a goner before I even finished puberty!"

David chuckled, a warm, rumbling sound that seemed to smooth the air. "My dear, you exaggerate. You've always had a fiery spirit." "Fiery spirit that's completely consumed by you," Jessica retorted playfully, with a grin. "I didn't exactly stand a chance, did I? Before I even met you, it was game over. It's like I was inflicted with Daddy loving brainworms from the start."

Noah, who had been quietly observing the exchange with a bewildered expression, spoke. "Brainworms? What are you talking about?" Jessica sighed dramatically, setting down her pancake. "Okay, picture this. Before I even knew David existed, I was having these... dreams. Vivid, intense dreams. Always him." She shivered slightly. "He was... everywhere. In my thoughts, my hopes, my... well, you get the picture."

Tiffany smiled knowingly. "It's happened to others, darling," she said gently. "It's part of the... connection." "Connection?" Noah repeated, his eyes widening with confusion. Jessica continued, ignoring Noah's increasingly bewildered gaze. "So, fast forward to actually meeting David. It was like... all the air rushed out of my lungs. Resisting him, ignoring that pull... it felt like suffocating. Like a part of me was dying. And honestly," she added with a wry grin, "It feels like a small part did die. The part that thought I had any control over my life."

Andrew leaned forward, curiously. "So, wait, are you saying all the wives get these... brainworms? Before they even meet David?" He glanced around the table, a flicker of apprehension crossing his face. "Is it, like, a prerequisite for being a wife?" Jennifer snorted, spewing her coffee back into her cup. "It's not really brainworms, sweetie. Some of us are just naturally drawn to him, like moths to a very bright, very powerful, very sexy flame. But yeah, there are a few of us that seemed destined to be here, like a calling." She paused, thoughtfully tapping her chin. "Nicole, Taylor, Kayla, and Tanya definitely have that connection, a sense of familiarity."

"But," Jennifer continued, her voice taking on a more serious tone, "Kayla and Jessica… their experiences are different. They've talked about terrifying withdrawal symptoms, feelings that extend beyond just missing him. Like a part of them is being ripped away." "Withdrawal symptoms?" Noah asked. "Like… drug withdrawal?"

Jessica grimaced. "Worse, I think. It's not a physical thing, not exactly. It's like… a piece of your soul is missing. You feel empty, lost, like you can't breathe. The world loses its color." Kayla, who was quietly listening from the couch, finally spoke. "It's like… static. A constant, grating static in your head. The only thing that quiets it is him. Being near him."

Noah scratched his head. "So, if David goes on a long trip, do you guys need, like, a David patch? Or a David lollipop? Is there some kind of support group? 'Wives of David Anonymous'?" Jessica rolled her eyes, but a small smile played on her lips. "Don't be ridiculous, Noah. Though, I wouldn't turn down a David lollipop," she muttered under her breath. "We're not Dad-ohaulics." She looked at David, who was trying and failing at maintaining his composure.

Caleb turned his attention to Olivia and Riley, leaning closer. "So, uh, you two… do you feel that strongly about Junior? Like, brainworm level? Or are you relatively free agents?" Olivia chuckled, taking a sip of her orange juice. "I wouldn't say I have brainworms for Junior. He's amazing, don't get me wrong. He's kind, funny, ridiculously strong, and a damn good kisser. But it's not this… involuntary, existential dread kind of thing. I'm more like Tiffany, I think. A strong attraction, definitely. But I can function perfectly fine if he's not around."

Riley, who was meticulously buttering her toast, snorted. "Definitely not brainworm level. I'd probably relate more to Elena. I love Junior dearly. He's the best, truly. But I also like my relative autonomy. I like being able to go off and do my own thing without feeling like I'm being torn away from my soulmate." She paused, a thoughtful expression on her face. "Maybe it's because Junior is a new soul. You know, unlike his father."

Sophia chimed in from the kitchen. "I always thought you all were just, like, really good friends who happened to share a husband. I didn't know it was so deep." Jennifer laughed. "We are really good friends, Sophia. And yes, we do share David. But he isn't just our husband, he's our leader and Master. And before you ask, yes. Most of us do worship him, he's that important."

Caleb shifted his attention to Sophia. "Hey, Sophia," He paused, trying to sound nonchalant. "Do you…I mean, have you ever felt anything like that? You know, that pull…towards David?" He asked, cringing internally. Sophia paused, a flicker of surprise crossing her face. She turned, leaning against the counter. "Towards David? Like… romantically?" She tilted her head, her brow furrowed in genuine confusion. "No. No, not at all."

Caleb felt a wave of relief wash over him so potent it almost made him lightheaded. He tried to play it cool, nodding slowly. "Right, right. Of course not. Just…curious. You know, trying to understand the dynamics around here." Sophia laughed, a warm, genuine sound that filled the kitchen. "Oh, Caleb, you're funny. I respect David. I really do. He's an incredible man. But… I don't, like, like him like that, you know? He's like… a father figure, maybe? Or a really, really awesome older brother."

Chapter 50:

Candy in the Wrapper

"First off," Junior continued, a grin spreading across his face, "massive thanks to Susan and Sophia for holding down the fort while we were out playing Santa's reindeer. Breakfast was a hit and Dad seems pleased." Susan blushed, ducking her head shyly. Sophia offered a small, polite smile. "Seriously, you guys are lifesavers. I know it's not cool or glamorous, but we were able to bring back a massive haul. And you two helped support that mission." He paused, letting them enjoy their moment.

"Okay, business time. So, during our scavenging run," he gestured toward the guys, "some of you expressed wanting to go back to the base to check on the remaining security forces and recruits." Several heads nodded as he spoke. "Well, I've been thinking about it, and I've decided we're going to do it. Tonight." A murmur ran through the group as Riley raised an eyebrow. "Tonight? That's… ambitious, even for you, Junior."

"Decisive, Riley, not ambitious," Junior corrected. "There's a difference. This is just checking on some people we left behind. Besides," he leaned back in his chair, lacing his fingers behind his head, "what do we have to lose?" He swept his gaze across their faces. "Look," Junior continued, softening his tone slightly, "I know it's short notice. But every day that passes out there is a day they are more likely to be dead. Those guys, even though they chose to stay. Should get a chance to reconsider."

He paused, letting his words sink in. "So, here's the deal. I want two volunteers to come with me tonight. We'll make a quick run to Goodfellow, see if we can find the security forces and recruits. If they are alive, maybe we can bring them back. If they aren't… well, at least we'll know we tried. Any takers?" A beat of silence hung in the air, thick with unspoken concerns. Then, predictably, Darrel's hand shot up.

"I'm in," he declared, his bouncing knee replaced with a sudden surge of energy. "I mean, I wanna see what happened after we left." Junior chuckled. "Fair enough. One down. Anyone else?" He looked around the table again, his gaze stopping on Noah, who looked like he almost wanted to go. Before Noah could muster a response, however, Susan spoke up. "I'll go," she offered, her voice surprisingly firm. Andrew immediately turned to her, concern etched on his face. "Susan, are you sure? It's going to be dangerous," Andrew said.

Susan turned to him and nodded her head. "Yeah, I'm sure. You guys aren't gonna keep be in the kitchen every time something has to get done. Besides," she added, "I'm just as capable as the rest of you guys." Junior grinned at her. "Alright then. Darrel and Susan, you're with me. We leave at 1900 hours. The rest of you, will start sorting and wrapping gifts while we're out."

A collective groan rippled through the room. Caleb, already yawning, whined. "Wrapping? Can't we just wait and hand everything out?" Junior shook his head. "No. I want everything offloaded, sorted, inventoried and stored in the storage bunker tonight." He turned to Riley. "I want a coded inventory of all the gifts, then we'll wrap everything in craft paper. Presents for years," he said with a smile. Olivia, perched on Junior's lap, spoke up. "We can use the pallet boxes again, once we have everything wrapped." Riley added, "True, we don't want to give away everything at once."

Junior stood up, stretching. "Alright, team, dismissed! Get some shut-eye. We've got a busy day ahead of us." He leaned down and planted a kiss on Olivia's forehead before playfully slapping Riley's rear. "And you, remember our appointment," he muttered with a wink. Riley grinned, a saucy glint in her eyes. "Oh, I definitely will."

As the group began to disperse, Caleb watched Junior, Riley, and Olivia with a pang of something he couldn't quite name. It wasn't jealousy, exactly. No, it was more of a yearning, a longing for a connection like that. He glanced over at Susan, who was affectionately reassuring Andrew, whispering something in his ear that made him blush.

Caleb sighed inwardly. He liked Sophia, really liked her, but the thought of actually telling her how he felt? That was a whole other level of terrifying. Darrel, ever observant, bumped Caleb's shoulder with his own. "Penny for your thoughts, bro?" Caleb jumped, startled. "Uh, nothing, man. Just...tired."

Darrel raised an eyebrow, unconvinced. "Sure, pal. Whatever you say. But if I had a dollar for every time you looked at Sophia, I could buy David's entire stock of ammo." He grinned, then clapped Caleb on the back. "Seriously though, you gonna burn a hole through her if you keep staring. You know we got your back, that's why the rest of us leave her alone." He leaned closer. "You know, bros before hoes."

Darrel's last comment earned him a playful shove from Caleb. "Shut up, man! It's not like that." But even as he said it, Caleb knew Darrel was right, at least partially. He just didn't know how to navigate the post-apocalyptic world of romance. Especially when Sophia always seemed so… composed. "Whatever, dude," Darrel chuckled, holding his hands up in mock surrender. "Just saying, don't let her slip through your fingers. Especially since we all know how scarce the ladies are around here."

Caleb chewed on his lip, watching Sophia carefully collect the empty coffee cups from their morning meeting. She always seemed almost sadly content. Her soft smile accompanied by weary eyes. Taking a deep breath, he walked over to her, trying to project an air of casualness he definitely didn't feel. "Hey, Sophia," he said, his voice coming out a little higher than he intended.

Sophia looked up, her dark eyes meeting his. "Hey, Caleb. Need something?" "Uh, no, not really. Just…thinking." He mentally cursed himself for sounding so awkward. "About what?" she asked, tilting her head slightly. He found the gesture endearing, which only made him more flustered. "Just...relationships, I guess?" He winced internally. Way to be subtle, dude.

Sophia's expression didn't change, but he could sense a subtle shift in her demeanor, a slight tightening of her shoulders. "Relationships," she repeated, her voice flat. "Yeah. Like, after that conversation with David's wives this morning, I was just wondering what you thought about them. You know, in general." He rambled, desperate to fill the silence. "I mean, it's kind of crazy, right? That they're all so drawn to him?"

Sophia sighed, leaning against the counter. "It's definitely... intense. I guess it comes down to what people value in a relationship." Caleb seized on the opening. "Yeah, exactly! So, what...what do you value?" He held his breath, waiting for her answer. Sophia looked away, her gaze fixed on the doorway. "I don't know," she said softly. "I haven't really thought about it much, to be honest. I've been too busy trying to survive."

Caleb's heart sank a little. He should have known. Romance was probably the last thing on her mind. "I guess," he said, trying to sound nonchalant. "But, you know, even in the apocalypse, people still need...connection. Right?" Sophia finally looked back at him, a hint of amusement in her eyes. "You're really digging for something here, aren't you, Caleb?"

He felt his cheeks flush. "Maybe," he admitted, running a hand through his hair. "I just...I was curious." "Connection is important," Sophia admitted, her voice barely a whisper, "But I don't want to settle." Caleb's eyebrows shot up. "Settle? What do you mean?" Sophia pushed herself off the counter, pacing the small dining room. "I mean, just because the world went to hell doesn't mean I have to grab the first… adequate partner that comes along. You know? Like, 'Oh, look, he can shoot a gun and knows how to ration water. Husband material!' That's not how it works."

He chuckled nervously. "Yeah, I get it. You're not desperate." "Exactly! I value… intention. I value effort. I value someone who knows what they want and aren't just looking for a warm body to survive with." She stopped pacing and turned to face him. "Look around, Caleb. Look at the relationships here. They're not just… happening. People here work really hard at them."

Caleb frowned, considering her words. "You mean David and his wives?" Sophia sighed dramatically. "Okay, obviously, that's the most… unique example. But yeah, even them! You don't think Tiffany, Jessica, Summer, all of them, just fell into that situation and shrugged? They're actively choosing it, every day. They have to be, to make it work." "So," Caleb began, the word feeling heavier than it should, "Would you… would you consider me a partner, or at least… potentially?" He asked as he held his breath.

Sophia blinked, tilting her head slightly. The amusement from earlier had faded, replaced by a thoughtful expression. "Caleb, wow. That's… direct." She chuckled softly. "Okay, let's unpack that for a second. You're funny, I'll give you that. Not afraid to be yourself, even when yourself is being a total dork. And at your core, you're actually thoughtful. But… why all of a sudden are you interested in me?"

He shifted uncomfortably. "What do you mean, all of a sudden? I… I don't know." He stammered, mentally kicking himself. "We've known each other since Basic Training, kinda, almost fourteen months now. We survived Goodfellow and now we're here. And yet, you've never exactly, let's say… expressed an interest. Until, apparently, roughly an hour ago, when we were all dissecting Jessica's brainworms. So, yeah, color me curious as to what sparked this sudden revelation."

Caleb groaned inwardly. So much for subtly. He ran a hand through his perpetually messy hair. "Okay, okay, you're right. It's not like I've been serenading you with rock anthems. But the truth is…" He hesitated, suddenly feeling incredibly vulnerable. "The truth is, I've always been attracted to you, Sophia." Sophia's eyebrows rose again, this time with genuine surprise. "You have?"

He nodded, unable to meet her gaze. "Yeah. I was just… afraid. Afraid of scaring you off, sounding like an idiot, ruining what we already have, assuming you feel the same way." He finally looked up at her, his expression pleading. "You know? All the usual stupid reasons. Plus, there was always something more important going on, and I didn't want to seem like those other guys, trying to hook up during training."

Sophia considered his confession. "That's… both thoughtful and incredibly counterproductive, Caleb. You waited until after we've survived the end of the world to tell me you were attracted to me? What were you waiting for, the apocalypse 2.0?" He winced. "Okay, yeah, I know. Bad timing. But what was I supposed to do? Confess my undying love while we were in training, or starving to death? It just didn't seem appropriate."

Sophia leaned back in her chair. "There's no right answer, I suppose. You could have confessed immediately and completely grossed me out. You could have waited until we were both old and gray and wondering what could have been. I guess you went for the slightly-less-awful middle ground." Caleb felt a flicker of hope. "So... are you saying I haven't completely blown it?"

"Not completely," she conceded. "You get points for honesty, and for not being a complete jerk about it. And I appreciate that you were trying to be respectful. But you have to understand, Caleb, this is a lot to take in. I always considered you a friend, someone I could rely on. Now you're telling me you've been harboring secret desires this whole time?"

He nodded miserably. "I know, I know. It sounds creepy when you put it like that." He cleared his throat. "Look, I wasn't trying to pressure you or anything. I just... I didn't want to keep it bottled up anymore. Especially after that conversation with Jennifer, Tiffany, and Jessica. They were so open about their attraction to David, and it made me realize I was being a coward."

Sophia sighed, running a hand through her own hair. "So, to clarify," she said slowly, "you're telling me that a philosophical discussion about polyamory and brainworms inspired you to confess your undying love for me?" Caleb chuckled sheepishly. "When you frame it like that, it sounds even dumber." "A little," she agreed, but her eyes softened. "But I can see the logic. You're surrounded by relationships that are built on honesty and mutual respect. And you want that too, right?"

He nodded eagerly. "Yeah, exactly! I mean, I'm not saying I expect to be David, with a harem of beautiful wives. I just… I want to be honest about how I feel. And I want to know where I stand with you." Sophia smiled mischievously. "Okay Caleb. Since we're being completely honest, since you want to clear the air. Do you want to go to bed with me?" Caleb swallowed hard, unsure of what the correct answer was. "C'mon Caleb. The raw unfiltered truth," she smirked.

Caleb instantly thought of Andrew and Susan. The apocalypse certainly does have a way of cutting through the bullshit alright. "What do you mean, 'go to bed with you'?" he hesitated. Sophia's smile widened. "Do you want to have sex with me, today, right now?" she asked, leaning closer. Sophia's blatant question hit Caleb like a rogue wave. His face flushed, and he stammered, "Uh… well… I mean…" He was caught between the thrill of the possibility and the fear of ruining everything.

He took a deep breath, trying to collect his scattered thoughts. "Okay, Sophia, since we're being completely honest, yeah. I do. Badly. But…" He paused, trying to put distance between his desires and morality. "I want you to want to as well. I don't just want to have sex, I want that trust and that closeness that leads to it."

He looked down at his hands, feeling incredibly vulnerable. "I know I probably screwed everything up already by dumping all this on you. But I promise, I'm not trying to pressure you. If you're not interested, or if you just want to be friends, I can accept that. But I needed to be honest, you know? And I needed to know if there was even a chance of something more."

Sophia observed him carefully, her smirk fading into a gentler expression. She seemed genuinely surprised by his answer, as if she hadn't expected him to prioritize her feelings. "Okay," she said softly, "That's… actually really sweet, Caleb. And it makes me feel a lot better about all of this." Caleb's heart did a little tap dance. He hadn't completely blown it. "Really? That's… good. Really good." He let out a nervous chuckle.

Sophia tilted her head, her eyes still locked on his. "So, Mr. Honesty Pants, have you ever, like… fantasized about me being your girlfriend? Or, dare I say, your wife?" she asked as she raised an eyebrow. Caleb's brain short-circuited for a moment. Girlfriend? Wife? Those were big words. He'd definitely thought about them, but he'd never actually visualized it.

He swallowed, trying to find the right words. "Okay, so… I haven't exactly, like, pictured you in a wedding dress, if that's what you mean," he admitted, shuffling his feet. "And I haven't, like, imagined us arguing about whose turn it is to do the dishes or anything." He paused, trying to articulate the fuzzy feeling in his head.

"But… I do think about you. A lot. And when I do, it's usually… I don't know… just you being there. Next to me. Or me next to you. Doing stuff." He gestured vaguely with his hands. "Like… if I'm patrolling the perimeter, I might think, 'Man, it would be a lot less boring if Sophia was here.' Or if I'm trying to fix a generator, I'll think, 'Sophia would probably know how to do this way faster than me.' Or if we're just sitting around, like now, I'm just… glad you're here."

He took a deep breath, feeling a bit ridiculous. He was making a mess of this. "It's not about the… the labels, I guess. It's just… you. And wanting you to be around." Sophia was silent for a moment, her expression unreadable. Then, she smiled. A genuine, warm smile that reached her eyes. "That's… actually really nice, Caleb," she said softly. "I think I get what you mean."

Caleb, still reeling from his verbal stumble, watched Sophia's smile deepen, her eyes crinkling at the corners. He felt a wave of relief wash over him. He hadn't completely botched it. He wasn't entirely sure he'd even explained himself, but somehow, she got it. Sophia leaned forward, resting her elbows on the table. "See, that's what I mean. You haven't created some idealized 'girlfriend' or 'wife' version of me in your head. You just… like the actual me." She emphasized the "actual," as if she was as surprised by it as he was. "Exactly!" Caleb exclaimed, snapping his fingers. "It's like… I don't want to force you into a role. It's more like... seeing what roles we could play together. Organically." He cringed internally. "Did that sound as cheesy as I think it did?"

Sophia glanced at the digital clock on the wall, her eyes widened slightly. "Oh, shoot! It's almost ten. We should probably get to bed." Caleb's heart sank a little. He'd been enjoying their conversation, lost in the surprisingly comfortable space they'd created. "Right, right. Sleep. Vampire hours." He stood up, pushing his chair in awkwardly.

Sophia stood up too, that warm smile still playing on her lips. She reached out, her fingers brushing his hand. "See you later, Caleb," she said softly, her eyes holding his for a moment longer than necessary. Then, with a quick squeeze of his hand, she turned and headed towards the hallway that led to the girl's rooms.

"Yeah, see ya, Sophia," Caleb mumbled, feeling a sudden, overwhelming urge to tell her to wait, to ask her to stay for just a few more minutes. But the words caught in his throat, replaced by a wave of self-consciousness. He watched her go, acutely aware of the way the worn fabric of her jeans hugged her hips. He was a goner.

Caleb stared at the empty hallway, a goofy grin plastered on his face. He was a mess, a total disaster of a human being, but... maybe, just maybe, Sophia didn't hate him. Progress! He practically bounced on the balls of his feet as he turned and practically skipped across the garage to his room. The familiar, comforting neutrality of the space washing over him. His window displayed a quiet strawberry field lit by the moon. Caleb kicked off his boots, the soft carpet a welcome change from the tile floors of the communal areas.

He began to strip off his clothes, tossing them haphazardly onto the chair in the corner. He pulled a clean t-shirt and a pair of well-worn sweatpants from one of the drawers. As he pulled the t-shirt over his head, he replayed the conversation in his mind, each word, each gesture. He focused on the moment Sophia's fingers had grazed his hand. A jolt of electricity had shot through him, making his heart pound like a bass drum.

He flopped onto the bed, staring up at the ceiling. Organically. Ugh. He'd actually said that. He squeezed his eyes shut, willing the memory to disappear. He could practically hear Darrel and Noah mercilessly roasting him for weeks. But then, he thought about Sophia's smile, the genuine warmth in her eyes. Maybe, just maybe, she hadn't been completely repulsed. Maybe she even… liked him a little? He dared to hope.

He rolled over, reaching for the small, worn copy of "The Hitchhiker's Guide to the Galaxy" that he kept on the nightstand. Douglas Adams was his go-to guy for situations like this. Absurdity, aliens, and existential crises always seemed to put things into perspective. He opened the book, flipping to a random page. "The ships hung in the sky in much the same way that bricks don't." He smiled. Yep, that was exactly what he needed to hear.

Caleb jerked awake, a strangled gasp escaping his lips. The book tumbled from his hands and landed with a soft thud on the carpet. He blinked, disoriented, trying to focus in the dim light filtering through the window. He'd been dead asleep just a moment ago... or at least, he thought he had.

Then he felt it. The subtle shift in the mattress, the almost imperceptible dip beside him. Someone was in his bed. His heart hammered against his ribs, a frantic drumbeat against the sudden quiet. He stiffened, every muscle in his body coiled tight. Was it Darrel and Noah pulling a prank? Had Junior finally decided to initiate him into some bizarre night-shift hazing ritual?

He slowly, cautiously, turned his head. And there she was, Sophia. Wearing a t-shirt and shorts, her dark hair slightly mussed, she was curled up beside him, her breathing soft and even. She looked... peaceful. Adorable. Caleb's brain short-circuited. The blood drained from his face, leaving him clammy and lightheaded. He stared at her, utterly speechless. This couldn't be real. This had to be some incredibly vivid, incredibly cruel dream.

He cautiously reached out a hand, his fingers trembling, and hovered it just above her arm. He had to confirm this wasn't an illusion. He grazed her softly, her skin surprisingly warm against his frigid hand. Nope. Not a dream. Caleb swallowed hard, his mouth suddenly dry. Okay, new plan. Don't panic. Don't scream. Just... breathe.

He took a deep, shaky breath and tried to piece together what was happening. Had she sleepwalked? Was she sick? Maybe she was just incredibly lost and confused?

His gaze swept around the room as if the answer was etched into the drywall, only to find nothing but his usual disarray. Books haphazardly stacked on the nightstand, clothes strewn across the chair. Definitely his room.

He glanced back at Sophia, who remained blissfully unaware of the internal crisis raging within him. He considered gently nudging her awake, but the thought of facing her, of having to explain this bizarre situation, filled him with an overwhelming sense of dread. What would he even say? "Hey, Sophia, just wanted to let you know you're currently sleeping in my bed. No reason. Just thought you should know." Yeah, that would go over great.

Suddenly, without opening her eyes, Sophia reached over and pulled his hand over her waist. Then, she instinctively backed into him, snuggling closer. Caleb froze. His hand, now resting tentatively on her side, felt like it had suddenly gained about a thousand pounds. His heart threatened to burst out of his chest. He was paralyzed. He couldn't move. He couldn't breathe. He was pretty sure he was going to faint. This was it. This was how he died. Not from starvation, not from bandits, but from sheer, unadulterated awkwardness.

Just when he thought he could hear distant angel songs of heaven, Sophia spoke, her voice still thick with sleep. "Caleb... you're so tense. Relax." Her words were a bucket of ice water to his face. Relax? RELAX?! He was fairly certain his soul was trying to escape his body. "I... I... uh..." he stammered, eloquently. Sophia sighed. "You can be yourself around me, you know? No need to be all...

stiff." She shifted slightly, her back pressing more firmly against him.

And with that, she was silent, leaving Caleb to stew in his internal turmoil. He lay there, wide awake. Was this a test? Was she trying to gauge his true feelings? Or was she just half-asleep and completely oblivious to the significance of her actions? He desperately wanted to crawl out of bed, flee the room, and never face Sophia again. But he also couldn't bring himself to move, afraid of waking her or making things even more awkward. He was trapped, a prisoner of his own overthinking brain.

Eventually, exhaustion won out. The sheer mental effort of trying to decipher Sophia's intentions had drained him, and he drifted back to sleep, his body still tense, his mind still racing. Time blurred. Then, something changed. Without fully waking, Sophia rolled over in her sleep, her face now inches from his.

Instinct took over. Before he could consciously process what he was doing, Caleb's arm wrapped around her, pulling her close. He pressed a gentle kiss to her forehead, a silent expression of the emotions he usually kept hidden. "I love you so much," he murmured, the words falling out of his mouth. The moment the words were out, icy dread washed over him. He was instantly wide awake. Why the hell did he just say that? She had given him an inch, and he took the whole damn mile.

His eyes snapped open, darting around the room, searching for any sign of Sophia's reaction. She was still asleep, her face buried in his chest, her breathing slow and even. But she had to have heard him, right? There was no way she could sleep through that. He lay there, paralyzed once again, waiting for the inevitable explosion. Would she be angry? Disgusted? Amused? All three were equally terrifying possibilities.

He carefully eased his arm from around her, inching away, trying to create some distance between them. He needed to get out of here, to formulate a plan, to come up with some kind of plausible explanation for his sleep-deprived confession. As he pulled away, Sophia stirred slightly, her eyes fluttering open. She looked up at him, her expression soft and unfocused.

Caleb's heart hammered against his ribs. He was trapped, cornered, and unarmed, except for the verbal grenade he'd just lobbed in his sleep. He stammered, "I... I didn't mean to wake you." Sophia blinked, her dark eyes slowly focusing on him. "Are you usually this restless when you sleep?" she mumbled. "No! No, definitely not," Caleb squeaked, his voice cracking. He tried to force a laugh, but it came out as a strangled cough. "I guess... I guess I'm just a little... nervous." He cursed himself internally. "Nervous? That's the best you could come up with, you idiot?"

She tilted her head, a strand of dark hair falling across her face. "Nervous?" she repeated softly. "About what?" He swallowed hard. The truth hung heavy in the air, a declaration he'd mumbled in his sleep, a secret now demanding to be acknowledged. He opened his mouth to say something, anything, to deflect, to change the subject, but no words came out. Then, a slow smile spread across Sophia's face, chasing away the sleepiness. "If you love me so much," she whispered, "why are you trying to leave?"

Caleb's jaw tightened. He hadn't processed that she wasn't offended, just... curious. "I-I... don't want to leave," he stammered, the words tumbling out in a rush. "I just... I didn't mean to... it just kind of... slipped out." He cringed. "Slipped out? Seriously, Caleb? You sound like a cartoon character who accidentally dropped a banana peel."

Sophia chuckled. "It's okay, Caleb," she said, reaching out to gently touch his arm. "I'm not mad. If I was bothered by the possibility of you declaring your love to me, I wouldn't have come into your room in the first place, right?" Caleb's eyes widened. "So... you're not going to run screaming and demand I be banished to the barn?" He asked, a flicker of hope igniting within him.

Sophia laughed. "No, Caleb. I'm not going to do that. Though, the image of that is admittedly amusing." He lowered his head slightly. "So... what is your plan then? Why did you... uh... get into my bed?" Sophia shrugged. "I wanted to see how you'd treat me," she admitted nonchalantly. "You confessed your feelings. I wanted to experience those feelings firsthand, and gauge how you behave around the object of your affection."

Caleb felt his cheeks flush again. "Experience... firsthand? But... you could have just asked if I wanted to get to know you better. I would have said yes. Definitely would have said yes." "Where's the fun in that?" Sophia teased, her fingers tracing circles on his arm. "Besides, actions speak louder than words, Caleb. Especially mumbled, half-conscious words." She paused, her expression turning serious. "However," she added, her voice firm but gentle, "there are boundaries. My limit is no tongue and no sex, until I say so. Understand?"

Caleb's head swam. "So… the candy stays in the wrapper for now?" he managed, the analogy feeling incredibly apt. He felt like he was holding the most delicious, tempting treat, and he was being told he could look, but definitely couldn't touch… not yet. Sophia's lips curved into a knowing smile. "Exactly. The candy stays firmly in the wrapper. For now." She emphasized the last two words, letting them hang in the air like a promise, or perhaps a playfully delivered threat.

He swallowed hard, trying to process the rules of this new game. "Okay… okay, I understand. Candy… wrapper… got it. But… but how will I know? When… when the wrapper comes off, I mean." Sophia leaned closer, her breath warm against his ear. "You'll know, Caleb," she whispered, her voice laced with a hint of mischief. "Trust me, you'll know. I'll be the one to initiate it."

Caleb carefully adjusted his position, easing back onto the mattress. He was hyper-aware of every inch of Sophia's body, pressed against his back. Her warmth radiated through his thin shirt, a comforting heat that battled with the nervous chill prickling his skin. He could feel the gentle rise and fall of her chest as she breathed, a rhythm that he tried to match his own to, hoping to calm the frantic drumming in his ears, and the frantic thumping of his heart. It was so loud he was sure it would wake her up.

"Don't wake me up again," she'd said. The words echoed in his mind, a direct order that he intended to follow to the letter. It didn't mean he wasn't acutely aware of her presence, of the soft weight of her arm draped across his waist, of the faint floral scent that clung to her hair. It was a sensory overload of the most delightful, terrifying kind.

He closed his eyes, trying to focus on anything but the girl molded against his spine. He tried counting sheep, but they kept morphing into Sophia, each one wearing a different outfit, each one offering him a tantalizing glimpse of that metaphorical candy. He even tried mentally reciting the alphabet backwards, but he got stuck on "S," his mind stubbornly filling in the blank with "Sophia." He groaned inwardly. This was going to be a very long night.

Chapter 51:

A Proposal for Junior

The artificial sunrise painted Junior's bedroom wall with a hopeful glow, but any thoughts of a peaceful awakening were quickly dispelled. A symphony of groans emanated from the bed. "Ten more minutes," Riley mumbled, while Olivia remained a muffled lump beneath the covers, staging a silent protest. Junior, suppressing a chuckle, gently disentangled himself from the pair, his movements careful not to further disturb their slumber. He stretched, grabbed a pair of boxers from the floor, and headed for the bathroom.

His reflection confirmed his suspicions. The previous night's activities had left their mark. Scratch marks and love bites adorned his skin. Back in the bedroom, Riley was stirring, her stretches punctuated by winces. "Ow," she groaned, "I think I fractured something." Olivia, still buried in her pillow, offered a muffled, "Probably your pelvis."

Riley shot a glare in Olivia's general direction. "Thanks for the sympathy, Liv." Turning to Junior, she adopted a pained expression. "Junior, honey, I'm serious. I think... I think you fertilized every single egg in my ovaries last night." Junior choked back a laugh. "You think?" "I know," she insisted, dramatically clutching her stomach. "I'm pretty sure I'm going to die from egg-xhaustion."

Olivia finally emerged from her cocoon, looking equally disheveled. "Egg-xhaustion? Really, Riley? That's the best you could come up with?" Junior fought back another chuckle as he observed the unfolding morning chaos. Riley's over-the-top pronouncements never failed to amuse him. "Alright, ladies, let's get you both up and moving," he said, clapping his hands together. "I gotta get ready to head back to San Angelo. And Riley, maybe try stretching next time, huh?"

Riley attempted to stand but crumpled back to the floor with a soft thud. "Oh, sweet Jesus," she groaned, her face contorted. "I'm not kidding, Junior. I can't even feel my feet. And… oh god," she paused, her eyes widening. "Is that…?" She looked down at her legs, a horrified expression spreading across her face. "Cum? Are you kidding me? I'm still leaking!"

Olivia snorted from the bed. "Serves you right for demanding a rematch. I told you we should have stopped after the second round." "Hey!" Riley protested, still sprawled on the floor, a picture of wounded pride. "It was a tie! A best-of-three is only fair!" She looked towards Junior. "Baby, please, could you carry me to the bathroom?" Junior stared at Riley, a mixture of amusement and exasperation painted on his face. "Carry you? Riley, you weigh like, a hundred pounds. You're not exactly a sack of potatoes."

Riley's pout deepened. "But I'm broken! You broke me! It's your responsibility to fix me, even if that means carrying my egg-xhausted butt to the bathtub." Her eyes widened, "And speaking of fixing... Can you make sure the water is hot? I need a scalding bath to soothe my wounds." He sighed dramatically, rolling his eyes at Olivia, who was now preparing coffee. "Fine, fine. But you owe me big time."

"Deal!" Riley chirped instantly, her spirits lifting with the promise of a princess carry. She held out her arms, already anticipating the lift. "Come on, my valiant knight! Rescue your damsel in distress!" With a final, long-suffering sigh, Junior carefully scooped Riley up, making a show of grunting despite her light weight. "You're lucky I love you, you ridiculous woman," he muttered, carrying her towards the bathroom.

As he closed the bathroom door behind him, a thoughtful expression settled on his face. A moment later, Riley's voice, slightly muffled by the running water, drifted out. "Hey, Junior?" He pushed himself off the doorframe. "Yeah, babe?" "Can you come here for a sec? I need to tell you something, and it's kinda...private."

Intrigued, he opened the door to find Riley already submerged in the steaming water, her red hair plastered to her forehead. "What's up?" he asked, perching on the toilet. Riley nervously fiddled with the tap, her gaze averted. "It's just... I wanted to say thank you. For, you know...everything." Junior frowned. "Everything? What do you mean?"

She finally met his eyes, her expression uncharacteristically serious. "Before... before the EMP, before all this," she gestured vaguely around the room, "I wasn't exactly popular. I was… different. People made fun of my hair, said I was too dramatic. I always felt like I was on the outside, looking in."

He knew fragments of this story from Olivia. "I always felt like I was trying too hard, but never quite measuring up," she continued, her voice barely above a whisper. "I know it sounds stupid, especially now, with everything that's happened. But those old insecurities, they don't just disappear, you know?" Junior nodded, understanding dawning on him. "So, what does this have to do with… us?"

Riley took a deep breath. "It's just… you make me feel… seen. Like, you actually see me, the real me, not just the ginger weirdo everyone else saw. And… desired. Before, I always felt like I had to tone myself down, be someone else to be liked. But with you, I can be loud, and dramatic, and… myself. And you don't just tolerate it, you seem to… like it." She blushed, ducking her head again. "I know I tease you a lot, and act all confident, but honestly, I'm still kinda surprised you're with me. You could have any girl you wanted, and you chose… me."

Junior's brow furrowed, the weight of Riley's confession settling heavily on him. "Hey," he said softly, reaching out to cup her chin, tilting her face up to meet his gaze. "Don't talk like that. You're not some charity case, Riley. I didn't 'choose' you out of pity, or because you were an outcast." He paused, searching for the right words. "I chose you because you're… real. You're funny as hell, you're smart, and yeah, you're dramatic, but that's part of what makes you… you."

He leaned in closer. "And as for the other stuff… you are beautiful, Riley. I'm actually quite fond of my ginger firecracker." He gently stroked a strand of her wet hair. A small smile played on his lips as he watched the color rise in her cheeks. "And by the way," he chuckled, "don't think I haven't noticed how you look at me. You may act tough, but you can't hide those eyes of yours. But I love it. I love seeing that softness in your eyes."

Riley's eyes searched his, a flicker of disbelief still lingering in their depths. "But Olivia… she's amazing, too. So pretty, and… and quiet. The polar opposite of me." Junior grinned. "True, but what do the two of you have in common? You're both honest about yourself." He paused, then added with a wink, "Plus, she's got curvy hips."

Junior saw a glimmer of a smile break through Riley's earlier seriousness. "It's just… it's kind of funny, isn't it?" Riley said, a slightly hysterical giggle escaping her lips. "That you, the super-soldier, the golden boy, ended up with the two outcast weirdos." Junior threw his head back and laughed, the sound echoing in the small bathroom. "Honey, my entire family is nothing but outcasts."

Sitting next to her, Junior took the soap and loofa in his hand. "Last time, my dad spent his life alone, because he tried to be what other people wanted. It was only when he embraced his uniqueness, that he flourished. Then there's his wives. Raised in single-parent homes, dysfunctional families, you name it. Why else do you think Jessica calls him Daddy?" he said, as he began to gently wash her back. "Besides, I need you to challenge me if I suddenly decide to pull a gun on someone again."

She smiled, leaning into his touch. "So, we're here to keep you in check?" "Exactly," he confirmed, his voice laced with affection. "Someone's gotta keep me from going full killer mode on the next person who can't just answer a simple question. Plus, you both add a human touch." As Junior continued to wash her, Riley couldn't help but marvel at the absurdity of it all. "You know," she said, turning to face him, "sometimes I feel like I'm dreaming. Like, any minute now, I'm going to wake up back in my barracks room, with my microwave popcorn and Tiktok."

Junior stopped washing, his brow furrowed. "And you wouldn't rather be here?" Riley laughed, shaking her head. "No! God, no. It's just… unbelievable. One minute, I'm the soulless ginger with no friends, the next minute, I'm the firecracker trophy-wife of Mr. Apocalypto himself." A flush crept up Riley's neck. She hadn't meant to say "trophy-wife." It sounded… presumptive. She still saw herself as a 'friend with benefits' or, at best, a concubine. Was she overstepping?

However, Junior's eyes lit up. He actually liked the term. "Firecracker trophy wife? I like the sound of that." He grinned, the kind of cocky grin that made Riley's stomach flip. "Though, if you're going to call yourself my wife, you need to know the family traditions." Riley's eyes widened. She hadn't considered any traditions. Or, truthfully, ever thought this thing between them would go far enough to have traditions. "Traditions?" she echoed, her voice a little higher than usual.

Junior leaned in, capturing Riley's lips in a lingering kiss. It was a kiss that spoke of comfort, amusement, and a surprising depth of affection. When he finally pulled away, he smiled. "I'll let you discover the traditions in due time. Some things are best experienced, not explained." He stood up and walked out of the bathroom, leaving Riley sputtering slightly, a mixture of nerves and anticipation bubbling inside her. What traditions could they possibly have dreamt up in this crazy new world? She scrubbed the rest of her body quickly, her mind racing. Tattoos? Matching denim vests? Ritualistic goat sacrifices?

Meanwhile, Junior sauntered into the kitchen. Olivia was perched on a stool at the island, cradling a steaming mug of coffee. He didn't say a word, just walked straight to her and initiated a deep kiss, his hands gently cupping her face. Olivia gasped softly, her eyes fluttering closed, and she leaned into the kiss. Junior deepened it, savoring the taste of her tongue before pulling back slowly, leaving her breathless. "Good morning," he said.

Olivia blinked, trying to regain her composure. "Morning? Junior, it's almost six o'clock." He shrugged, unfazed. "Morning to me. Just got done making sure Riley didn't dissolve in the bathtub." He leaned against the counter, watching her. "You know, she's calling herself the 'firecracker trophy wife', right?" Olivia took a sip of her coffee, her gaze thoughtful. "She is kind of a firecracker sometimes."

Olivia set her mug down with a quiet clink. She hesitated, then leaned closer, her voice dropping to a confidential whisper. "Speaking of Riley..." Junior raised an eyebrow, instantly intrigued. "What about her?" Olivia's eyes twinkled mischievously. "She's... smitten. Utterly, completely in love with you." Junior chuckled. "Really? Riley? She's always seemed so indifferent, perhaps amused. But not smitten." "Oh, it's true," Olivia insisted, a genuine smile gracing her lips. "Butterflies. Lip-biting fantasies. Little girl crush kind of love. She's trying to be all cool and independent, but underneath... trust me, she's head over heels."

As if summoned, Riley emerged from the hallway, wrapped only in a large towel. Ignoring the warmth creeping up her neck, she confidently wrapped her arms around Junior's neck and planted a wet, enthusiastic kiss squarely on his lips. The kiss, initially playful, quickly turned passionate. It was Junior who pulled away, his eyes twinkling with amusement. "Alright Riley, calm down, you're going to set me on fire." Riley reluctantly loosened her grip. A mischievous grin stretched across her face. She turned to Olivia, her eyes sparkling with excitement. "Olivia, guess what? Junior's family has a tradition for wives. Like, a right of passage or something." She paused, drawing a dramatic breath. "And I want to do it."

Olivia choked on her coffee. Eyes widening, she looked between Riley, who was radiating naive enthusiasm, and Junior, who was trying very, very hard not to laugh. Taking a deep breath, Olivia carefully placed her mug on the counter. "Riley," she began, her voice measured, "are you sure about this? About wanting to… become his wife?" She gestured vaguely, trying to find a tactful way to express the gravity of the situation. "I mean… this family does marriage differently."

Riley's declaration hung in the air. Olivia stared at her, a complex mix of concern and amusement warring on her face. "Riley," Olivia repeated, her voice a careful blend of gentle and serious. "This isn't some game. This is… life. Permanent life. Especially with David's family and the wives in his family." She gestured towards the hallway. "It's a… unique situation."

Riley, dripping dry on Junior's kitchen tile, shrugged, seemingly unfazed. "Yeah, so? You act like I haven't been paying attention. David's wives are always together, plus, it isn't like David doesn't do everything in the open." Her eyes were bright with genuine excitement. "There's no such thing as dates anymore. Even Alissa got married at fifteen for god's sake! And have you ever seen her unhappy?"

Riley's confidence, bordering on blissful ignorance, hung heavy in the air. She was ready to embrace the unconventional, the unknown, and the potential chaos that came with the territory. But were Riley and Olivia truly prepared for the deep dive? Only time, and perhaps a few unexpected family traditions, would tell.

Olivia pinched the bridge of her nose. "That's... not exactly the point, Riley. Alissa knew Aidan for years first. This is bigger than... than just deciding you like a guy!" "Okay, so what is the point then?" Riley countered, her excitement slightly dampened. "I love Junior, a lot. And I know he cares about us both. I mean, he actually picked us! Why is it so hard to believe I want to commit to that?"

The seed of an idea had been planted, a concept so audacious that Olivia hadn't even dared to consider it: becoming a wife in this family. Riley, ever the impulsive one, had voiced the unspoken possibility, throwing Olivia's carefully constructed world into disarray. Olivia sighed, rubbing her temples. "It's not that I don't want to, Riley. It's just... David's wives, they're not just wives. They're... a unit. They support each other, they raise the kids together, they run this whole place! It's a level of commitment that goes beyond just being married."

Riley, however, saw the potential for something truly special. "They're the best support system any family could ever ask for. And that's what I want! I want that kind of family. I want to be part of something bigger than just... me." "So," Riley continued, "haven't you thought about it, Olivia? About becoming... you know... more with Junior? We could be sisters! Even David's wives see each other as sisters, especially the first three."

The word "sister" hung in the air, a foreign concept in Olivia's mind. She had been so consumed with navigating the unusual dynamic between her, Junior, and

Riley, a subtle competition for his affection, that the idea of genuine sisterhood felt almost unattainable. "Riley," Olivia said, slowly turning to face her, "are you serious? You want... us to both be married to Junior? And be sisters on top of all of that?" Riley nodded enthusiastically. "Yeah! Why not? We already get along. We like the same guy. It's like, half the battle is already won! Plus, who else understands us better?"

Olivia paced, the conversation echoing in her head. Riley's simple logic was both appealing and terrifying. "So," Riley said, breaking the silence, "are you in or out? Are we doing this sister-wife thing or what?" Olivia stopped pacing. "Riley, it's not like ordering pizza. This is David's family, his legacy. We can't just waltz in and say, 'Hey, we want to be sister-wives!'"

"But why not?" Riley persisted. "We already share Junior. We get along. We want the same things. What's the difference?" "The difference is... commitment!" Olivia exclaimed. "These women, they've built this life together. It's not just about sharing a husband, it's about the whole legacy." Riley sighed. "I'm done being the awkward ginger. I'm done being on the outside. I want to be part of this family, this community. And I love Junior."

Olivia, recognizing the vulnerability in Riley's eyes, softened. She, too, knew the feeling of being an outsider. Perhaps this was a chance to build something lasting, to finally belong. "Okay," Olivia said hesitantly, "I'm not saying no. But... we need to think about this. Really think about it. And maybe... maybe we should talk to someone.

Someone who knows what it's like." Olivia bit her lip. "Well… Jennifer, maybe. She's been with David since the beginning, plus she'd be our mother-in-law. She also knows how the wives club works."

Riley's brow furrowed. "Jennifer? But… isn't she kinda… intense?" Olivia chuckled. "That's one word for it. But she's also very smart, honest, and…" Olivia hesitated, a blush creeping up her neck. "I think… I think she's also… been with some of the other wives, sometimes." Riley's eyes widened. She glanced at Junior, a question forming on her lips. "Wait, seriously?"

Junior simply shrugged. "Yup. Mom is bisexual, and she's probably the only other one who's had sex with all of David's wives. She's kind of the… uh… ambassador of pleasure, I guess you could say." Riley blinked. "Wow. Okay. I… I did not see that coming." Olivia, still blushing, avoided Riley's gaze. She felt a strange mix of embarrassment and… intrigue. "So… you think she'd be a good person to talk to?" Junior interrupted them with a kiss. "I have to get going. Don't worry too much you have an entire sorority of women to talk to, plus my sisters," he said, before running out the door.

Riley stared at the closed door, a whirlwind of emotions churning inside her. She glanced down at the towel barely clinging to her, a stark reminder that she probably shouldn't have this conversation naked. "Okay," Riley said. "Clothes first. Then… diplomacy with the pleasure ambassador." Olivia giggled, the tension in the air easing slightly. "Diplomacy is the right word. Just… brace yourself. Jennifer doesn't mince words."

A few minutes later, Riley, now decently clad in a pair of jeans and one of Junior's oversized hoodies, followed Olivia towards the main house. Jennifer, Kayla, and Elena, were already in the kitchen cooking. "Hey, you two," Jennifer greeted. "Come to help with dinner, or just looking for trouble?" "Just came to talk to you, about marriage." Olivia said nervously.

Jennifer nodded towards the living room, calling out to Nicole, subtly indicating that the conversation needed privacy. Olivia was impressed by their seamless teamwork. It was like a perfectly choreographed dance, a silent understanding flowing between them. Maybe this "flock" thing wasn't so crazy after all.

Jennifer, removing her apron, turned to the girls. "Okay, you two, let's find a more private space for this conversation. How about my room? Tiffany won't mind." She led the way out of the kitchen, Olivia and a hesitant Riley trailing behind. Jennifer gestured toward Tiffany's bed. "Have a seat, girls. Let's talk."

Jennifer settled into a plush armchair. "So, Olivia, Riley, you want to know what the wives do in this family? The answer, in its simplest form, is that we support David. His vision, his goals, his well-being… everything revolves around that." Olivia nodded slowly, absorbing the information. "So, we… dedicate ourselves to him." "Precisely," Jennifer confirmed. "We offer our skills, our strengths, our love, to create a stable and thriving environment where he can be the best version of himself.”

Riley, still perched on the edge of Tiffany’s bed, spoke hesitantly. “But… how does that work with Junior? If we were to… become his wives, wouldn’t our focus shift to him?” Jennifer smiled, understanding dawning in her eyes. “That’s a very insightful question, Riley. And the answer is yes. As Junior’s wives, your primary focus would become supporting him. But it’s not as simple as replacing one leader with another.”

“What do you mean?” Olivia inquired, her brow furrowed. “Think of David as the sun,” Jennifer explained, using a familiar metaphor from David’s frequent lectures. “He provides the energy, the light, the foundation for everything in this community. Junior, being David’s son, is very much aligned with David’s vision.” Jennifer sharpened her tone before continuing. “You see, Junior is his father, all the same skills, the same knowledge and strength. He just… grew up with his own experiences, so the two are basically one in the same.”

“He’s… an extension of that sun, shining his own light in a specific area. Your role as his wives will be to amplify that light, to nurture the growth around him.” “So, we’d be helping Junior fulfill David’s larger vision?” Olivia clarified. “Exactly! You’d be managing his home and his projects, ensuring he has everything he needs to excel in his role as our vanguard, combat trainer, and gunsmith. You’d be a team, working together to strengthen the community.” Jennifer paused, then added with a mischievous look in her eyes, "And, of course, ensuring he's happy and well-cared for in the bedroom."

"So," Jennifer drawled, breaking the silence, "are you two sure this is what you want? Being a wife in this family… it's not a walk in the park. It's… dedicating your whole life, completely, wholeheartedly to the family." Olivia's voice was a little shaky, but her gaze was firm. "Yes, Jennifer. We are. We love Junior, and we want to support him, to be a part of something bigger." Riley nodded vehemently, her hands clasped tightly in her lap. "We know it's not going to be easy, but we're willing to work hard, to learn, to do whatever it takes."

Jennifer's smile softened. "I believe you. I can see the sincerity in your eyes. But understand, this isn't just about loving Junior. It's about embracing a whole new way of life. You'll be learning constantly, adjusting to new roles, and working as a team with all of us." She gestured around the room, imagining the rest of the wives scattered throughout the house. "It's a sisterhood, and it's a strong one."

She paused for a moment, letting her words sink in before continuing. "There will be days when you're exhausted, when you feel like you're being pulled in a thousand different directions. There will be challenges, disagreements, and moments of doubt. But the strength of this family comes from our unwavering commitment to each other and to David."

Olivia and Riley exchanged a nervous glance, their initial enthusiasm now tempered with a healthy dose of reality. They knew, intellectually, that this wouldn't be a simple love story. But hearing it laid out so bluntly was a little daunting. "But beyond the practicalities," Jennifer continued, her tone growing more serious, "there's the emotional aspect. This is a family built on trust, respect, and open communication. Each of us has our own unique strengths and weaknesses, and we rely on each other to fill in the gaps."

She paused, her gaze sweeping over the two young women. "You'll have to learn to be vulnerable, to ask for help when you need it, and to offer support to the other wives. You'll have to learn to navigate the complexities of our relationship with David, accept his vision, and find your place within it."

Riley fidgeted, finally blurting out the question that had been gnawing at her. "What… what exactly is our relationship with David? Jennifer, we don't want to offend anyone, but… will we also be expected to…?" She trailed off, unable to voice her fear of becoming another of David's concubines. Olivia's eyes widened with a mixture of anxiety and embarrassment, but ultimately she was grateful Riley asked the question first.

Suddenly, Jennifer stood and opened the door. "David, could you come here for a sec?" she asked, her voice carrying a hint of urgency. "Olivia and Riley have some questions. I think you should answer them." David raised an eyebrow, then glanced at Jessica and Taylor, offering a reassuring smile before standing. "Be right back, ladies." He followed Jennifer out of the living room and into the bedroom, where Olivia and Riley sat looking like lambs to the slaughter.

"What's this all about?" David asked, his tone gentle but firm. Jennifer cut straight to the chase. "They're wondering about the… mechanics of joining our family, Master," she added with a playful emphasis on the title. Just as Jennifer sat back down, the bedroom door still open, and David strolled in, a calm and reassuring presence. He gave Jennifer a quick peck on the cheek before turning his attention to the two younger women. "Everything alright in here?" he asked, his voice warm and concerned. "Jennifer tells me you two are giving serious thought about joining the family… and more importantly, about marrying my son, Junior."

He walked over to the window, gazing out at the darkening valley. He turned back to face them, his expression earnest. "Riley, Olivia… I understand you might have some… reservations." He paused, choosing his words carefully. "About the… structure here." He took a deep breath. "The most important thing for me is Junior's happiness. He loves you both. And if he loves you both, then I trust his judgment implicitly."

Then, with a softer tone, he asked, "So, tell me… how committed are you two to Junior? And, perhaps more importantly, to each other?" Olivia spoke first. "David, sir, with all due respect… Junior means the world to both of us. He saved our lives. We trust him, we admire him, and… well, we love him. And we've become incredibly close as friends, as sisters, really." She glanced at Riley for confirmation, who nodded emphatically. "We'd do anything for him, and for each other. That's not the issue."

Riley jumped in, her usual sarcasm dialed back for the serious conversation. "It's just... well, it's a big adjustment, the... the whole family dynamic. We were just worried about joining your wives and becoming your concubines."

Chapter 52:

The Airbase Reckoning

David held back a chuckle, a barely perceptible twitch at the corner of his mouth. Jennifer, however, was far less restrained. She practically doubled over, clutching her stomach as peals of laughter erupted from her. "Oh, Riley," she gasped between giggles, "you have the best timing!"

Olivia, completely bewildered, turned to Jennifer with a furrowed brow. "I... I don't understand. What's so funny?" David, regaining his composure, fixed a gentle gaze on Riley. "So, Riley, out of curiosity, what exactly have you heard about my wives and... their role in the family?" Olivia, sensing an explanation was needed, spoke up again, her voice laced with concern. "It's just... we kept hearing about 'joining the wives' sisterhood,' and well, we just assumed...that you had your way with all of the wives." She blushed slightly, suddenly feeling incredibly naive. "I mean, it's a valid assumption, right? I thought that by marrying Junior, we would also become...involved with you."

David turned away, unable to contain his laughter, as Olivia and Riley watched them, a feeling of confusion washed over them. David finally managed to stifle his laughter, though his shoulders still shook slightly as he turned back to face Olivia and Riley. He cleared his throat, his eyes twinkling with amusement. "Alright, alright, I think we need to clear up a few... misconceptions." He gestured for Jennifer to continue, still finding it difficult to speak without dissolving into mirth.

Jennifer wiped a tear from her eye, still chuckling. "Okay, okay, where to begin? Look, girls, the 'sisterhood' is real. We are a tight-knit group. We support each other, we help each other, we share the load. We work together to make sure we get the most out of our time, all while supporting David's vision" She paused, choosing her words carefully. "But it doesn't involve... that."

She gestured vaguely between David and the two young women. "David has his wives, and that's his business. Junior is your man, and David would never dream of interfering with that. We are the sisterhood of wives. But it's about shared values, shared goals, and...frankly, shared childcare," she added with a wink. "It takes a village, especially when the village is rebuilding the world." Olivia and Riley exchanged relieved glances. "So," Olivia began, cautiously, "marriage to Junior doesn't... obligate us to anything else?"

David stepped forward, his expression serious now. "Absolutely not. I consider myself a traditional man in many ways. And one of those ways is respecting the sanctity of marriage. Junior is responsible for your happiness, your well-being, and your protection. He is your husband, he is your partner, and he is the only man you will be with." He locked eyes with each of them in turn, wanting to ensure they understood the gravity of his words.

"I take the vows of marriage very seriously. Loyalty, honesty, commitment… these are not just words to me. They are the foundation upon which a family is built. I would never betray that trust, nor would I ever expect someone else to betray it."

He added, with a hint of steel in his voice, "And I expect the same level of respect and commitment from everyone in this family. Relationships are hard work. They require open communication, understanding, and a willingness to compromise. But they should never involve coercion or exploitation. That is simply not who we are." Riley's shoulders relaxed slightly. "Okay," she said, the sarcasm finally banished from her voice. "Okay, that makes a lot more sense. Honestly, we were picturing some kind of… Byzantine harem situation."

"A Byzantine harem situation?" Jennifer sputtered, bursting into laughter again. "Oh, honey, you've been watching too many historical dramas!" She composed herself, taking a deep breath. "Look, the commitment ceremony is up to Junior. He's the one who gets to decide how he wants to formalize things with you both."

David nodded in agreement. "My wives each have their own unique ways of showing their commitment and love, but each process has involved tattooing my name." He looked at Olivia and Riley, a gentle smile playing on his lips "First, you and Junior need to decide what feels right for you. And then, you just… do it. There are no hard and fast rules. It's about the heart, not the ceremony."

Olivia and Riley exchanged another look. This was surprisingly... straightforward. "So, really, that's it?" Riley asked, still a little skeptical. "We can just... decide?" Before Jennifer could launch into another story, David stood up. "Alright, enough talk. Time for action. Olivia, Riley, come with me." He led them out of the bedroom, leaving Jennifer chuckling and the conversation in the living room abruptly cut short. As they walked, Olivia and Riley exchanged nervous glances. What was this about?

Back in the living room, David cleared his throat, the room instantly silencing. "I'd like to make an announcement," he began, his voice resonating with authority. He placed a hand on each of the women's shoulders, turning to them with a warm smile. "From this moment forward, Olivia and Riley are officially Junior's wives. Welcome to the family, ladies." The announcement dropped like a sonic boom. Olivia and Riley stood frozen. The silence that followed David's words was so thick, you could spread it on toast. Then, the dam broke.

Tiffany surged forward, engulfing Olivia in a hug that nearly popped a seam on her denim jacket. "Welcome, dears! We're so happy to have you! More girls mean more gossip!" she chirped, her eyes twinkling. Summer offered a gentler embrace to Riley. "Congratulations, darling. You'll find we're all very supportive."

The other wives joined in, a flurry of congratulations, pats, and offers of celebratory snacks. Alissa, waddled over, her face beaming. "Oh, this is wonderful! More hands to help with the babies!" she exclaimed, patting her belly. "And more people to discuss the joys of morning sickness with!" Josh, whistled. "Junior's a lucky man. Two wives? That's impressive, even out here." Lily gave both Olivia and Riley a shrewd once-over. "Don't worry about any drama. Everyone gets along here."

The whirlwind of congratulations and well-wishes swirled around Olivia and Riley, each hug and exclamation a little more disorienting than the last. Olivia managed a weak smile, while Riley, her normally sarcastic composure cracking, looked like she'd swallowed a live grenade. Before either of them could process the implications of David's announcement, a familiar voice cut through the din. "What in the…?"

Junior stood in the doorway, his expression a mixture of confusion and disbelief. Susan and Darrel hovered behind him, equally perplexed. Junior's gaze darted from Olivia and Riley, to David, and then to the assembled wives, his jaw slowly working its way downward. "Uh… what's going on here?" he finally managed, his voice a little higher pitched than usual.

David beamed at his new daughters in law. "Junior, my boy! Come, join the celebration! We're welcoming two new members to the family! Olivia and Riley are now officially your wives." The room fell silent again, this time the silence thick with a different kind of tension. Junior's eyes widened, his face cycling through a spectrum of emotions that would have made a chameleon jealous. He stared at Olivia and Riley, then back at David, his mouth opening and closing like a landed fish.

Darrel, always one to call it as he saw it, couldn't resist chiming in, "Wait, both of them? At the same time? Dude, you just hit the jackpot!" Susan simply whistled. Junior spluttered, "But... but... I was just going to say goodbye!" He looked desperately at Olivia and Riley, pleading with his eyes. "We didn't even talk about this! I just wanted to say goodbye before I head back to San Angelo!"

Olivia, recovering slightly from the initial shock, offered a nervous smile. "Well, surprise?" she squeaked, her voice betraying her own uncertainty. Riley, on the other hand, seemed to have entered a state of frozen shock. She simply stared at Junior, her mind clearly struggling to process the information.

"Didn't... didn't you want to marry us, Junior?" Olivia asked, her voice small and laced with a worry that mirrored Riley's frozen face. All eyes in the room were glued to Junior, waiting for his answer. The pressure seemed to snap Junior out of his stunned state. His gaze softened as he looked at Olivia, then at Riley. He broke into a wide, relieved grin. "Are you kidding me?" he exclaimed, his voice finally returning to its normal pitch. "Of course, I want to marry you both! More than anything!"

The room erupted in a cacophony of cheers and whistles as Olivia and Riley, emboldened by Junior's enthusiastic agreement, practically tackled him. The kiss was passionate, a whirlwind of relief, excitement, and a dash of sheer disbelief. Junior, momentarily caught off guard, quickly succumbed to the embrace, his hands instinctively finding their way around their waists, pulling them closer.

As the kiss finally broke, leaving Junior slightly breathless and thoroughly flustered, turned to David, his expression a mix of gratitude and exasperation. "Okay, Dad, that was… unexpected, to say the least. But thanks. I think?" David simply chuckled, a twinkle in his eye. "You're welcome, son. A father always wants what's best for his children. And who am I to deny them happiness?" He spread his arms wide, as if basking in the glow of his own benevolence.

Sensing an opportunity, Junior squared his shoulders. "Alright, Dad, since you took the liberty of making this decision for me, I think it's only fair that you take on the responsibility of making their dreams come true." David raised an eyebrow, intrigued. "What are you getting at, son?" "Their wedding, Dad. You announced it. You organize it. Olivia and Riley deserve the best, and I trust you to give it to them." He paused for effect, "And I don't want them to lift a finger."

A ripple of laughter went through the room as the other wives realized what Junior was doing. Jennifer clapped. "Oh, I like this! Uno reverso, Master!" "Yeah, Daddy," Lily piped up. "You made the call, you gotta make it happen!" David, despite his initial surprise, couldn't suppress a smile. He admired his son's quick thinking.

"Alright, alright, you drive a hard bargain, Junior. But I accept your terms." He turned to Olivia and Riley, his voice softening. "Tell me, my dear daughters, what are your dreams? What does your perfect wedding look like?"

The room buzzed with anticipation. Olivia looked at Riley, a silent question passing between them. They'd thought about their dream wedding, of course, fantasized about it since they were children. Now, it was suddenly within reach, and orchestrated by none other than David himself.

Junior leaned in, his voice barely audible above the excited chatter. "Listen, you two," he whispered, his breath tickling their ears. "I have to head out soon. The airbase can't wait. I don't want you going easy on Dad. This wedding? This is for you. Make him work for it. He can handle it. Besides, you absolutely deserve the best wedding ever." He said. "Think big. And don't let him off the hook."

The air crackled with a mix of amusement and genuine excitement. Junior, having successfully shifted the wedding planning burden onto his father, flashed Olivia and Riley a mischievous grin before excusing himself to prepare for his trip to the airbase. Susan and Darrel, already geared up, followed him out. Jennifer, gushing with excitement, ran to her room to retrieve their own wedding photos.

Nearly an hour later, miles away in the rumbling Ford Transit, Darrel couldn't contain his curiosity any longer. He turned to Susan, who was staring out the window. "Yo, Susan, no offense, but why did you want to go back? I mean, those dudes at the airbase chose to stay. They figured they were better off." Susan sighed. "I know, Darrel. It's just… I can't shake the feeling that we left them to die. I mean, I know we're talking about Airmen and soldiers. Maybe they stayed because their resources would last longer, or maybe some just wanted to stay. However, we know what we have and what they don't."

Darrel nodded slowly, his brow furrowed in thought. "Yeah, I guess. But still, it's risky. We're wasting gas, risking our necks. For guys who might not even want to be rescued." Junior chuckled, his eyes fixed on the desolate highway stretching before them. "Darrel, you're overthinking it. Think of it as a training exercise. Besides, if they're still alive, they'll be grateful as hell to see us. If not…" He shrugged, his expression grim. "Well, at least we tried. And we loot whatever is there."

"Yo, Junior," Darrel started. "You think Davis is still being a… you know?" He trailed off, searching for a polite term for the aggressive, loud-mouthed Senior Airman. Junior's lips twitched in a slight smile. "Davis? Probably. That guy was a walking, talking testosterone factory. Doubt time has changed that. He probably saw the blackout as an opportunity to be even more in charge." Susan, finally tearing her gaze from the grim landscape, shuddered. "God, I hated him. So full of himself. Always strutting around like he was Rambo in a training video." "He gave me gladiator vibes, man," Darrel chimed in.

"Like, he was just waiting for the apocalypse to unleash his inner warlord."

Junior chuckled humorlessly. "Well, if he's still alive, he's had plenty of time to practice his warlord impressions. Hopefully, Miller kept him in check." He paused, a flicker of doubt crossing his face. "Though… Miller wasn't exactly the most assertive guy." "Assertive?" Susan scoffed. "He was practically invisible! Davis ran that whole show. He just let him do whatever he wanted."

Darrel snorted. "Speaking of running shows, you think Caleb will ever get his act together and tell Sophia how he feels? The dude's been crushing on her since day one!" Susan shook her head, a smile playing on her lips. "Caleb? He's too caught up in his video games. He probably thinks confessing his feelings is some kind of complex strategy level."

Junior cut in. "Hey, give him a break. It's tough to put yourself out there, especially in… well, this." He gestured around at the desolate highway. "He'll get there. Besides, what's the rush? They've got plenty of time now. Maybe a little too much time."

A long silence stretched between them, then Darrel, ever the comedian, broke the silence. "This drive is longer than a Tolkien novel, man. My butt's starting to resemble a pancake." He shifted uncomfortably in his seat. "And I swear, I just saw a coyote flipping me off." Susan burst out laughing. "A coyote flipping you off? Darrel, you're losing it!" "I'm serious!" Darrel insisted, feigning offense. "It gave me the stink eye, then just... bam! Middle finger, right in my face. Rude."

Junior chuckled, shaking his head. "Maybe it was just trying to scratch itself, Darrel. You know, coyote-style." "Nah, man, this was intentional. It was a statement. Maybe they're forming a rebel alliance out here. 'Coyotes Against Humanity' or something."

The Ford Transit rumbled down the debris-strewn streets of San Angelo, a metal behemoth cutting through the eerie silence. "Well, this is... cheerful," Susan quipped, her voice tight with a nervous energy. She gripped the armrest, her knuckles white. "Reminds me of a zombie movie, only without the fun parts." Darrel piped up. "Hey, maybe they just had a really good Thanksgiving and everyone's in a food coma. A city-wide food coma! That's gotta be a record."

Junior, his face grim, ignored them. He scanned the surroundings, his eyes narrowed. He had a bad feeling creeping up his spine. The air felt stagnant, heavy with a sense of abandonment that went beyond the physical desolation. No one had been here in a while. "Alright," Junior said, his voice low and serious. "We're approaching the base. Stay sharp." He slowed the Ford Transit to a crawl, the engine a low growl in the oppressive silence. "Davis and his cronies are probably holed up somewhere, assuming they're still... functional." "Functional? You mean, assuming they haven't devolved into cavemen and started worshiping the microwave?" Susan muttered under her breath.

"Alright, lights out," Junior commanded, his voice barely a whisper. "Switch to night vision and thermal. Let's not announce our arrival with a light show." Susan fumbled with her gear, adjusting the settings on her goggles. "Ugh, this is so disorienting," she complained. "Night vision in one eye and thermal in the other? My brain is protesting."

"Yeah, feels like my eyes are having a rave and I wasn't invited," Darrel added, grinning despite the tension. He adjusted his own goggles, his eyes widening as he took in the transformed world. "Dude, this is like Predator vision! So cool!" He paused, then added, with genuine sincerity, "Seriously though, this is the best family ever!"

Junior shook his head, a ghost of a smile growing on his lips. "Less family bonding, more focusing," he said sternly, despite the underlying warmth in his tone. He carefully maneuvered the Ford Transit, its massive frame surprisingly silent as it rolled down the deserted street. He rounded the corner of the barracks building, killing the engine. The silence that followed was absolute, broken only by the wind.

"Alright, before we go any further," Junior said, cutting the tension with his calm, steady voice. He turned to face Darrel and Susan, his gaze sweeping between them, "I need to know. Out of everyone we left behind, the recruits and the security forces, who do you trust the most?" Susan chewed on her lip, her brow furrowed in thought. "Honestly?" she started, "Ryan seemed alright. Quiet, but… decent. Maybe Marshall too, he was always trying to keep the peace." She shuddered, "But Davis… that guy gave me the creeps. And Jacobs was always up his ass, agreeing with everything he said."

Darrel nodded in agreement. "Ryan's good people. Kept to himself mostly, but he's got a good heart. Marshall's the same. As for trust… I wouldn't trust Davis to water my houseplants if he was holding a fire hose. Jacobs is just Davis's shadow." Darrel grinned, though it didn't quite reach his eyes. "The only Airman I ever trusted was Turner, He was alright."

Junior nodded, absorbing their answers. "Alright, Darrel," he said, turning his attention to him. "I need you to lead us to where they were all sleeping. But be careful. Anything seems off, you say so." He patted the sidearm strapped to his thigh. "I've got your back. But your eyes are on point, alright?"

Darrel straightened up, a determined glint in his eyes. "Got it, Junior. I'm on it." He took the lead, his footsteps light and cautious as they approached the barracks entrance. As they reached the double doors of the barracks lobby, Susan paused at the threshold, a strange look on her face. "Something's wrong," she whispered, her voice barely audible. "It's… quieter than it normally is. Even with the power out, there was always some kind of noise. The wind, the animals… this is… too quiet."

Darrel stepped into the lobby. The interior was trashed. Furniture overturned, papers scattered across the floor, and a thick layer of dust coating everything. It looked like a tornado had ripped through the place. "Damn,"

Darrel breathed, his eyes scanning the wreckage. "What the hell happened here?"

Junior's hand tightened on his weapon. "Stay close," he instructed, his voice low. "Something definitely isn't right." "Whatever happened here, it wasn't peaceful," Susan said, her voice trembling slightly. "Look at this place... It's a mess. And that smell. What is that?" She pinched her nose, disgust evident in her voice. A faint, acrid odor hung in the air, something vaguely chemical, mixed with a hint of decay.

The acrid smell intensified as they moved further into the lobby, the air thick with a sense of unease. "Spread out, but stay within sight," Junior commanded, his voice low. "Susan, stay behind me. Darrel, keep point; you know this place better than I do." Darrel, his face grim, nodded and cautiously moved forward, his eyes darting from one overturned piece of furniture to another. Susan, her face pale, kept close behind Junior, her hand hovering near her mouth as the stench threatened to overwhelm her.

As they neared the front desk, Susan suddenly stopped, her eyes widening in horror. She pointed a trembling finger towards the counter. "There... there's someone there!" Junior moved quickly, his weapon raised, and peered over the top of the destroyed front desk. Lying sprawled on the floor was a figure, unmoving and still. He cautiously approached, his heart pounding in his chest. "It's... it's Kurt," Darrel said, his voice tight with shock. He moved closer, kneeling beside the body. "Damn it, Kurt!"

Junior knelt beside Darrel, assessing the situation. Kurt's face was pale and waxy, his eyes staring blankly at the ceiling. It was clear he was long gone. But what caught Junior's attention were the bullet holes riddling Kurt's chest. "Shit," Junior muttered, his gaze hardening. "This was an execution. And look…" He pointed to a distinct pattern in the dust around the body. "He was dragged here."

Darrel swore under his breath. "But… none of the recruits had guns. Only Miller and his security forces had weapons." He looked up at Junior, his eyes filled with confusion and dread. "What the hell happened here, man?" As they examined the body, Junior's ears perked up. "You guys hear that?" Junior asked, standing. Darrel looked confused. "Hear what? I can't hear anything over Susan trying to keep the contents of her stomach inside her stomach." Susan waved a hand dismissively, her face still green. "I'm fine! Mostly. But no, I don't hear anything."

Junior frowned, adjusting his grip on his rifle. "I swear I hear voices upstairs. Faint, but definitely there." He quickly slung his rifle and pulled out a tomahawk, the polished steel gleaming in the dim light. Darrel raised an eyebrow, giving Junior a double take. "Bad ass," he muttered under his breath. Darrel, unsure of what spooked Junior, nodded at Susan before slinging his own rifle and pulling out his Kamas. "Fuck it, when in doubt, follow suit, am I right?" Darrel said, his voice low. He twirled the Kamas once, a silent promise of violence. "Let's go get some Christmas chopping done."

Junior, tomahawk in hand, moved swiftly and silently down the hallway. Darrel followed close behind, his eyes constantly scanning the shadows. Susan, paler than a ghost, brought up the rear, clutching her stomach and trying to keep her breathing steady. When they reached the door from where the whimpering emanated, Darrel stopped Junior with a hand on his shoulder. "Hold up a sec," he whispered, his voice barely audible. "There's no way you heard that from downstairs. This place is practically soundproofed.

Junior stilled, his brow furrowed in concentration. He pressed his ear against the door, trying to glean any information before barging in. The voices were definitely female, laced with a palpable terror. He could make out snippets of sentences, "...he'll be back...", "...can't trust anyone...", "...gotta stay quiet..." With a nod to Darrel, signaling him to be ready, Junior shouldered the blocked door with a burst of strength. The barricade several wall lockers and a small dresser flew against the opposite wall, crashing into the cinderblock.

The reaction was immediate and chaotic. Reagan, adrenaline spiking, swung a metal pipe with all her might, aiming for the first visible target, Junior's head. But Junior caught the pipe mid-swing with a resounding clang. The force of the blow still reverberated through his arm. Inside the room, Callie scrambled back against the wall, her eyes wide with terror. Emma, huddled beside her, let out a choked sob, burying her face in her knees. The room itself was a mess, the window blacked out with blankets, clothes scattered everywhere, and a pervading smell of fear and stale sweat hung in the air.

Junior, his hand still gripping the metal pipe, lowered it slowly, his gaze shifting between Reagan, Callie, and the trembling Emma. The stark terror in their eyes was a punch to the gut. Susan's words cut through the tension. "Reagan! Stop! It's okay! It's… it's us! We're here to help!" Reagan's face crumpled. The fight drained out of her, replaced by a rush of overwhelming relief and then, a tidal wave of bitter regret. Tears streamed down her face, blurring her vision. "Susan? Is that really you? Oh, sweet Jesus… you came back." She let go of the pipe, then slid down the wall, sobbing uncontrollably. "We were so wrong… so, so wrong to stay."

"Reagan, it's alright. We're here now. You're safe." Susan looked up at Junior, her eyes pleading, "Junior, these are some of the women who stayed behind." Junior knelt near Reagan. "What happened here?" he asked, his voice low and measured. He saw it all now: the fear etched on their faces, the barricaded door, the sheer desperation that permeated the air. This wasn't just a group of soldiers who had chosen to stay behind; this was a group of prisoners.

Susan hesitated, glancing at Reagan and then at Emma, who still hadn't moved from her huddled position. "It's… it's a long story, Junior. A lot has changed since you were here last time." Reagan took a shuddering breath, wiping her eyes with the back of her hand. "After you left, Sergeant Miller was still in charge. He was… okay. He kept things as by the book as he could. But then in September, he left with Turner, Bishop, Vasquez and Cook to try and find water in the city. They never came back." Her voice cracked. "After that… Davis took over."

Callie, who had remained silent until now, shifted nervously. "Davis… he changed everything. He said Miller ran off and left him in charge. He started hoarding the food, making us work harder. We were already rationing water, but he barely gave us any, even when we were working. He kept us up all saying we needed to be prepared." We were exhausted all the time, it was unbearable…"

Reagan continued. "It was just… cruelty. It was like he enjoyed seeing us suffer. Then he started with the… the punishments." "Punishments?" Junior's voice was dangerously low.

Reagan swallowed hard, her eyes darting towards Emma, then back to Junior. "If you didn't do exactly what he said, no matter how tired you were… if you questioned him… you paid the price." She paused, the silence pregnant with unspoken horrors. "Kurt… Kurt argued with him about the water rations. Davis… he just shot him… repeatedly… like it was nothing." "And Emma?" he asked, his voice barely a whisper.

Reagan's gaze flickered back to Emma, then to the floor. "Emma… she tried to help Kurt. She fought back. Davis… he… he…" Reagan swallowed, trying to say the words. Callie finished the sentence, her voice trembling. "He… he raped her. In front of everyone. To show us what happens when we disobey him. Marshall tried to help, but Jacobs killed him. That was the last straw. We locked ourselves in here, but it's so cold."

Darrel, who had been quietly observing the scene, finally spoke up. "What about Ryan and Daniels? Are they...?" He trailed off, the implication hanging heavy in the air. Reagan averted her gaze. "They... they just went along with it. Did whatever Davis told them to. They didn't try to help anyone. They were too scared." A flicker of disgust flashed across her face. "They're still out there, somewhere."

Junior stood up, his jaw tight. He looked at Susan, then at Darrel. "Alright. Susan, stay here with them. Make sure they're comfortable. Darrel, let's go find Ryan and Daniels. And then... we find Davis." Darrel nodded, his eyes narrowed. "Let's do it." As they were about to leave, a raspy voice cut through the silence. It was Emma, barely audible. "What... what are you going to do to them?"

Junior stopped, turning back to face her. His gaze was unwavering, his expression resolute. "What do you want me to do?" Emma's eyes remained fixed on the floor, her voice barely a whisper. "What... what are you going to do to Davis? And Jacobs?" Junior's voice was low, filled with a cold promise. "I'm going to kill them."

Susan gasped softly, while Reagan and Callie exchanged nervous glances. Darrel, however, simply nodded in grim agreement. Callie, her voice trembling, spoke up. "What about Ryan and Daniels? What's going to happen to them?" Junior's face remained impassive, a mask of cold determination. He didn't flinch, didn't soften.

"Nothing," he stated flatly. "They can stay here. Rot, for all I care."

A wave of shocked silence washed over the room. Susan, her brow furrowed, looked from Junior to the terrified faces of Reagan and Callie. She understood. This wasn't about blind rage. This was about justice, a brutal, unforgiving justice. "But… what's going to happen to us?" Reagan asked, gesturing to herself, Callie, and Emma. Junior's gaze softened, as he looked at the three women. "I'm taking you home," he said, his voice now carrying a weight of finality.

Andrew   Caleb

Darrel   Kathy

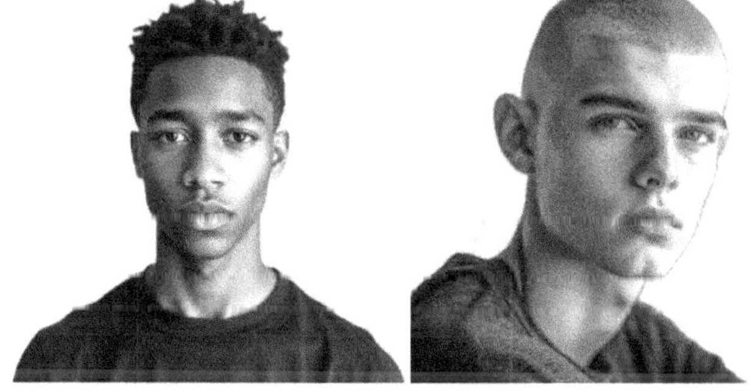

Marvin   Noah

Olivia

Riley

Sara

Sophia

Susan

9 781968 027391